A Rose in Plotlands

Dawn Knox

© Copyright 2025 Dawn Knox

The right of Dawn Knox to be identified as the author of this work is asserted by her in accordance with the Copyright, Designs and Patents Act 1988

All rights reserved. No parts of this publication may be reproduced, stored in a retrieval system, or transmitted in any form or by any means, electronic, mechanical, photocopying, recording or otherwise without prior permission of the copyright owner.

A Record of this Publication is available from the British Library.

ISBN: 9798307573433

This edition is published by Affairs of the Heart

Cover © Fully Booked

Editing – Wendy Ogilvie Editorial Services

To Mum and Dad.
Thank you for believing in me.

Also by Dawn Knox

The Great War – 100 Stories of 100 Words Honouring Those Who Lived and Died 100 Years Ago

Historical Romance: 18th and 19th Century

The Duchess of Sydney

The Finding of Eden

The Other Place

The Dolphin's Kiss

The Pearl of Aphrodite

The Wooden Tokens

Historical Romance: 20th Century

A Plotland Cottage

A Folly in Plotlands

A Canary Girl in Plotlands

A Reunion in Plotlands

Humorous Quirky Stories:

The Basilwade Chronicles

The Macaroon Chronicles

The Crispin Chronicles

The Post Box Topper Chronicles

Chapter One

♥

1 1931

Rae poked out her tongue at the boy, and in case he was in any doubt about how upset she was, screwed up her face to show how much she meant it.

She'd instantly known it had been the wrong thing to do, but by then it was too late. Sucking her tongue back in, she clamped her lips tightly together as if she might undo her rudeness. How many times had Mama told her to think before she acted?

So, why didn't she?

Why did she find it so hard?

At nine years of age, she ought to have known better.

But she'd always hated being stared at, as if the grown-ups didn't think she had any feelings at all. They looked right through her, like she wasn't even real and talk over her head as if she couldn't hear. They'd laugh at her for what appeared to be no reason. And that was the hardest to bear – when people treated her like she was a joke, especially when she was being serious. It felt as if they'd all ganged up on her. Them – peering down at Rae with their clever words. Rae – looking up at her 'betters', tongue-tied and red-faced. All thoughts pushed out of the way, except that somehow, she was a fool. She'd failed, although exactly what she'd failed at, she had no idea.

And it wasn't as if Mama ever stood up for her. In the past, if Rae had cried, Mama had told her not to be so silly. "The trouble with you, Hannah-Rae, is you've got an inflated sense of your own pride."

Rae still didn't understand. Apparently, she should take pride in her schoolwork, her appearance, her family and lots of other things, but when she felt people were poking fun at her and she got upset, her pride had taken over and that, apparently, was a fault.

Mama made up rules as if they changed with the wind, never explaining why they mattered. And Papa? He didn't help at all – just laughed and patted her head, like she was still five years old. Why didn't anyone take her seriously? As for her brother, Joe, he was a boy… He thought it was his job to make her life uncomfortable.

And now, this boy, Jamie MacKenzie, had stared at her so hard, she'd flushed scarlet, and, in her embarrassment, she'd tried to stop him and had acted without thinking.

She was so stupid.

But then, it hadn't been her fault alone.

The boy was to blame, too. After all, wasn't it rude to stare?

Mama had told her off for looking at the man in the village who only had one leg. He'd fought in the Great War and Mama said Rae should show some respect. Or Miss Tomkins who lived in the tumbledown cottage and walked up and down the High Road, talking to herself. Mama said her mind was wandering, and that Rae wasn't to gawk. The rule appeared to be that if someone had something wrong with their body or their mind, you couldn't stare.

Other than her ridiculous curly hair, and her silly snub nose, there wasn't much wrong with Rae's body – at least she had all the bits she was supposed to have. And as far as she knew, her mind didn't wander like Miss Tomkins'. Sadly, it often didn't do as she wanted either, but that was a different matter. Rae appeared to be normal, and that meant people could prod and poke her with their eyes as much as they wanted. She didn't have to like it, she just had to put up with it.

But the boy hadn't simply stared. He'd smiled too. A stupid smirk that showed he'd found her idiotic. The corners of his lips had twitched – only a tiny movement. She didn't think anyone else would've seen it except her.

Unfortunately, everyone had seen her poke her tongue out.

The boy's brow had furrowed. He'd even looked hurt.

Hurt? He was *hurt*?

Well, what about her feelings?

Then, as Papa and her brother, Joe, gasped at her naughtiness, the boy half-stepped towards her. It took her completely by surprise and as she moved backward, she caught her heel and stumbled, throwing both arms out sideways, trying to remain upright.

In her imagination, she could see how ridiculous she looked. Arms whirling like windmill sails. Falling onto her bottom like a clown. Face as red as the stupid coat she was wearing.

It wasn't surprising the boy had found her so amusing. She knew how ridiculous she looked. That morning, Mama had insisted she wear the hideous coat Auntie Sadie had made for her. Rae's cheeks always matched its ghastly shade of red when she thought of it – let alone wore it.

It had been kind of Auntie Sadie, but really, Rae wished she hadn't. The coat had a black velvet collar that reminded Rae of a dead rat. But the hat – oh, the red, Robin Hood-style hat! With its ridiculous black feather pinned to her head like a flag announcing to the world: look at me, the girl in the stupid outfit. If it hadn't been so securely attached, she'd have pulled the ridiculous hat off.

On the drive to Chichester Harbour, Papa had said she looked beautiful – although she hadn't believed he'd meant it.

Her brother, Joe, hadn't been interested. He simply wouldn't have noticed if she'd been wearing a coal sack. But at least he hadn't made up silly jokes about her like he usually did.

During the journey, she'd hoped Papa would park the car in the boatyard. Not that there'd been room the last time they'd visited. He'd had to leave the car further along the road. But perhaps this time? And if they could drive straight into the yard, it was unlikely they'd bump into anyone – well, not anyone they knew, anyway. Just Mr MacKenzie, the boatyard owner, and his men.

That morning, when Mama had fetched the coat for Rae to put on, her jaw was set and her eyes hard. She definitely wasn't in the mood for an argument. Hot tears had stung the inside of Rae's eyelids as she'd known she had no choice. Usually, she'd have refused, but not that morning. Any other day, she'd have willingly taken whatever punishment Mama thought fit for defying her. It would probably have meant being sent to her room. Rae didn't mind that. At least she wouldn't have felt so foolish. She'd have read a book. It wasn't like she didn't already spend a lot of time on her own.

Hours and hours.

But that morning, Rae had been desperate to go with Papa. If she gave in without a fuss, she'd take the hat and coat off when she got home and bury them at the back of her wardrobe. Mama was so busy she'd soon forget about them and in a few months, Rae would most likely have outgrown them, and the problem would have gone away.

Luckily, she was the only girl in the family, so her baby brother, Jack, wouldn't have to worry about the red outfit being handed down. Although why she was worried about Jack's feelings, she didn't know.

If it hadn't been for him crying most of the night, Mama might've been in a better temper and then Rae might have dared to defy her. But seeing Papa's face and his silent plea as they put their coats on, had settled it. Rae had allowed herself to be buttoned into the dreadful red coat, then she'd stood patiently while the hat was carefully positioned and pinned on her blonde curls. Finally, she'd nodded obediently when Mama had warned her to make sure she kept clean.

"No climbing trees or... or... whatever it is you usually do to get dirty, Hannah-Rae." Mama had said.

Rae had squeezed her fists tightly and clenched her teeth to stop her shouting, "Please call me Rae."

One-year-old Jack had just started to speak, but 'Hannah-Rae' was too hard for him to say and he'd begun to call her 'Hammeray' which the grown-ups thought was 'charming'. Joe, however, teased Rae with the stupid name. It had been quite funny at first, but typical Joe – he kept going on and on.

Why did people like to embarrass others? Rae often wondered. Why was it so funny to see someone squirm?

But whereas, in the end, Mama always told Joe he should be quiet and stop teasing Rae because he was giving her a headache, no one had stopped the boy in the boatyard from staring and smirking.

And now, she'd fallen backward into a puddle on the muddy ground. Everyone stared. Eyes boring into her. Even a man who was out walking his dog craned his neck to get a better look.

She wanted to disappear. Sitting in a puddle was a thousand times worse than simply wearing the stupid coat. The boy put his hand out to help her up but, with her nose in the air, she ignored it, and struggled to her feet.

It was his fault. If only he hadn't been so mean, she wouldn't have mud all over her hands and water trickling down her legs. If she'd looked silly before, now she looked completely ridiculous.

He was staring at her again. A rush of anger bubbled up. Then, in another thoughtless moment which she later knew she'd regret for the rest of her life, her fist curled into a ball and she punched him on the nose.

To his credit, the boy hadn't tried to hit her back. He'd just stood there with pain in his eyes and blood dripping from his nose. For a second, no one had moved. Then Joe broke the spell by bursting into laughter – and Rae had burst into tears. What had she done? She'd never hit anyone before.

"Enough!" shouted Papa. "Rae, apologise immediately. And Joe, be quiet. I'm ashamed of you both. You obviously can't behave like civilised children, so the pair of you can sit in the car while I look at the boat. You've been so ill-mannered today, I've a good mind to cancel the order. Neither of you deserves it."

Joe gasped at the thought of losing out on the yacht he'd been longing for and looked at Rae as if it was her fault it was in danger of being cancelled.

"Please, Papa, I'm really sorry," Joe said.

"It's not me to whom you owe an apology, son."

"I'm sorry, Mr MacKenzie."

The owner of the boat builders took the pipe from his mouth and nodded. His face was blank. It was hard to know what he was thinking.

Papa nodded at Joe. "Get in the car. I don't want to hear another sound from you until we get home."

He turned to Rae. "Well, Missy, what have you got to say for yourself?" Despite what sounded like an invitation to speak, she knew he didn't want to hear an explanation about how awkward she'd felt.

Nobody would care. She shouldn't have let her anger get the better of her, and now Papa was telling her to apologise.

This was it – her worst moment ever. She couldn't sink any lower if she tried. Mr MacKenzie, Papa, the boy – and even the man who was walking the dog were all staring at her, waiting for her to utter the words *I'm sorry*. She looked down at her coat – it was muddy and bloody. When she got home, Mama would be furious. And although Joe wouldn't dare say anything in the car, he wouldn't forget this, and he'd make sure all his school friends heard about it, too. A world of shame awaited her.

There was only one thing she could do to stop everyone from fixing her with their stares.

"I'm sorry," she whispered.

"That was a poor excuse for an apology, Hannah-Rae," Papa said sternly.

A tear slipped down her cheek. "I'm very sorry," she said loudly. "I hope I didn't hurt you."

The boy smiled at her.

"Shake the lass's hand, Jamie," Mr MacKenzie said in his sing-song Scottish accent.

The boy held out his hand.

Oh, how she longed to ignore it. To turn and walk away. To keep whatever pride she had. But who was she trying to fool? She had no pride left. And if Papa cancelled the order for the boat, Joe would never let her forget it.

There was nothing for it. She shook Jamie's hand. Then, without looking him in the eye, she turned and raced back to the car, her head bowed to hide her scarlet cheeks.

"Are you all right, Jamie?" She heard Papa ask the boy.

"Yes, thank you, sir."

"Good lad, Jamie," Mr MacKenzie said proudly. "That lass of yours can certainly pack a punch, Dr Kingsley," he added to Papa.

She could tell from his voice it wasn't a compliment.

Chapter Two

♥

"I hope you're satisfied," Joe muttered as Rae slid back to the car, mud still caking her hands. His arms were crossed tightly, his glare making her squirm. "Sometimes I don't know what gets into you."

How many times had her parents said that to her? Too many to count, and each time it cut deeper. Now, even Joe was using it against her – it stung in a way she hadn't expected. Rae swallowed hard, her voice barely a whisper. "D'you think Papa really will cancel the boat?"

Joe shrugged. "Well, if he does, it'll be your fault, and I'll never forgive you."

As he turned his back towards her, tears pricked her eyes again.

No one spoke on the journey home to the small village of Barlstead. It lay about five miles from MacKenzie & Sons Ltd. Boat Builders, near Dell Quay on the Fishbourne Channel. The mud had dried on Rae's hands like a tight pair of gloves, and the water had soaked through to her knickers, but she wanted the ride to last longer, not flash by faster than ever. What would her mother say? Rae had a good idea.

When Papa pulled into the drive of their house, Mama was waiting at the front door, holding Jack.

She shrieked when Rae got out of the car. "What on earth happened to you? I thought I told you not to get dirty. You're filthy." She gasped as Rae drew closer. "Is that blood? Good heavens, Hannah-Rae, what have you done to yourself?"

Rae looked down at her filthy hands and shoes and shook her head. She couldn't push words past the lump in her throat.

"She punched someone," Joe said. He snorted scornfully as he walked past his mother into the house.

"You punched someone? Hannah-Rae, is that true?" Rae flinched at the high-pitched accusation. Her mother's voice always pierced through her defences like nails scraping a blackboard.

There was no point denying it. Rae tried to swallow down the bulge in her throat, but if anything, the lump was growing. Words came out as a whisper. "Yes, Mama, I'm afraid I did."

"Hannah-Rae, sometimes, I simply don't know what gets into you."

Rae washed her hands and then trudged upstairs. Why wait for her mother to tell her? She knew exactly where she was going – the bedroom, her usual refuge. She might as well save Mama the trouble of sending her there.

The weeks dragged before Papa finally let Joe and Rae join him at MacKenzie's boatyard again. It was as if time moved slower without the promise of their new boat on the horizon. The fact that Papa had continued to drive to the yard each weekend reassured Rae he hadn't cancelled the order, but what would be the point of having a splendid sailboat if she wasn't allowed to use it?

However, on Saturday morning, Papa suggested a trip to Chichester Harbour to see how the boat was getting on, and Rae gasped with surprise and pleasure. Joe's eyes flicked toward her, narrowing slightly, a silent warning that hung in the air between them. Rae felt the weight of his gaze, a reminder of the trouble last time, but she straightened her shoulders and looked away, pretending she hadn't noticed – she didn't need to be told to behave.

Over the last few weeks, she'd bitten her tongue when Joe had teased her about her haircut, and she'd smiled politely at the next-door neighbour when she'd called her Harriet. With great effort, she'd kept her temper under control and had tried to have pride in the right things – or whatever Mama thought were the right things, anyway. She'd played with Jack when he'd been fretful, and had tidied her bedroom, although Mama didn't appear to notice her efforts.

That morning, Mama had been too busy with Jack to be interested in what Rae wore. There'd been oil in the puddle she'd fallen into and the various stains on Auntie Sadie's red coat had never come out. Rae hadn't been able to wear it again – even if she'd wanted to.

"Such wanton negligence, Hannah-Rae," her mother had said. "A poor child would have loved that coat and hat."

Rae had neither pointed out she wanted to be called Rae nor added she'd happily have given the outfit away to anyone who'd asked, and why hadn't Mama suggested that before? It had been difficult, but she'd kept silent. Not that her mother had noticed.

Why didn't Mama ever see how much effort Rae made to do as she was told? Why did she always catch Rae out on the odd occasion when she slipped up?

Thankfully, on the day of the proposed trip to the boatyard, it was sunny, and Rae chose a blue skirt and white blouse – the right sort of clothes to wear to a boatyard. She wouldn't stand out, so no one would have any reason to notice her. If that dreadful boy, Jamie MacKenzie, was there, she'd simply ignore him. She'd been practising in the mirror to make sure she looked believable. With her chin up, she'd be able to look right over the top of his head as if she'd seen something interesting in the distance. Her only worry was that she'd blush and spoil the whole effect.

Mama didn't like sailing, so she stayed home with Jack, and it was just Papa, Rae and Joe who set out to check the boat.

"D'you think it'll be ready for us to use during the summer holidays, Papa?" Rae asked as he pulled out of the drive into the lane.

"Yes, it's almost finished now. That's why I brought you both. I'm assuming you've both learned some manners since the last time you came. Especially you, Rae. Honestly, I don't know what got into you."

"Yes, Papa. I'm really sorry," Rae said. Didn't Mama always say that if you did something wrong, you must apologise and that would be the end of the matter? Why didn't that apply to Rae?

She glanced about as they entered the yard, looking for the ghastly boy, Jamie, but thankfully, he wasn't there.

Mr MacKenzie came out of his office and wiped his huge hands on his apron.

"It's good to see you again, Dr Kingsley... and you two," he said, smiling at Joe and Rae. He shook Papa's hand. "I think you're going to be pleased," he said and led them to the boat.

Rae was thrilled. It was nearly finished. They'd be able to sail in the summer.

Papa suggested Joe and Rae go for a walk around the harbour and look at the other boats while he sorted out the finances for the yacht in Mr MacKenzie's office. She hesitated, unsure if Papa was giving her a moment of trust or just a distraction while the adults talked. Either way, it was a relief to slip out into the sun, away from any more disapproving looks.

Rae allowed herself a sigh of relief as they left the yard. That awful Jamie hadn't appeared, and it was pleasant walking along the waterfront, listening to the slap of water against the hulls and the clink of the rigging. Imagining what fun they'd have when they finally had their own boat.

"Look, there's that chap you thumped," Joe said, pointing ahead to a boy who was fishing off the harbour wall.

Rae stopped sharply and turned to walk in the opposite direction. She'd expected Joe to go with her, but he continued towards Jamie MacKenzie.

"Where are you going?" she called as loudly as she dared, hoping the boy wouldn't hear her.

"Where does it look like I'm going?" Joe shouted over his shoulder, not keeping his voice down. "I want to see if he's caught anything."

After a few moments' hesitation, Rae walked towards a bench and sat down, pretending to be interested in a man hauling a bucket of water onto his deck. Without turning her head, she watched the two boys out of the corner of her eye. Jamie was showing Joe his fishing rod and allowing him to have a go.

Would Papa be much longer? It already felt as though he'd been with Mr MacKenzie for hours. How long did it take to pay for something?

"Rae!" Joe called. "Come over here."

She turned her head away and stared at the gulls wheeling over the harbour as if they were the most absorbing things she'd ever seen.

Out of the corner of her eye, she saw Jamie packing up his fishing things. Good. Perhaps they'd go off on their own for a walk. But no, they were now heading for her. She clenched her teeth and groaned quietly, continuing to watch the birds circling above.

Heat crept up Rae's neck, spreading to her cheeks, a blush that refused to die down. She could feel their eyes on her, making her squirm in her seat. Maybe if she stood and casually wandered off... but that would just make it worse. She was stuck. If she walked away, Joe would guess what she was doing, and he'd probably shout at her to stop.

There was nothing for it. She'd have to pretend to catch sight of the boys for the first time and appear surprised. The only problem was her cheeks. They were still burning. Would they give her away? No one in their right mind would blush just because they'd been watching birds fly.

She swung around, her mouth a small 'O' of surprise, and flapped her hand to show she'd seen them. The instant she'd done it, she wanted to groan, fearing she'd looked more like a seal waving its flipper than a young girl greeting anyone.

Luckily, the boys were deep in conversation and neither of them noticed.

Joe was a year and a half older than Rae and she guessed Jamie was of a similar age. They were as tall as each other but, where Joe was blond like her, Jamie was dark. He was explaining something to her brother, holding his hands apart as if showing how large something was and then, as both boys began to laugh, she saw how handsome Jamie was. He had a friendly, open face with dark eyes. Not that she cared how good-looking he was, of course.

Joe stopped when they reached the bench and Rae stood up to say 'hello', but Jamie kept walking.

"See you, Joe," he said, and with a slight nod in Rae's direction to let her know he'd seen her. He rearranged his fishing gear and walked back to his father's yard.

"How rude," said Rae, watching Jamie saunter away. She was half-pleased he'd gone and half-annoyed he hadn't bothered to speak to her.

"Yes, you are rude. Utterly rude," Joe snapped, turning on his heel to follow Jamie without another glance at her.

Rae stood there, speechless. Joe teased and played jokes on her, but he was usually on her side. Rude? He'd said she'd been rude. Had she? Well, yes, possibly. But so had Jamie MacKenzie.

Rae hung her head. She was usually very polite. It was that boy. She'd only met him twice, and both times had been a disaster.

Chapter Three

♥

On the Saturdays when Papa wasn't on duty at the London Hospital in Whitechapel, the Kingsley family sat down to breakfast together. Most mornings he left home early to catch the London-bound train and often returned late, so Rae didn't see much of him during the week.

Years ago, he'd met Mama when she was a nurse, but she'd stopped working when they'd got married. However, she often talked about going back to work when Jack started school. For the last few years, she'd tried to 'keep her medical knowledge current,' as she put it. So, in the evenings, Rae often found her in Papa's study going over her nursing books.

Rae woke early on Saturday and got ready quickly. Not only was today one of Papa's Saturdays at home, but it was the day she and Joe would be allowed to sail their new boat for the first time.

A glance out of the window showed her the weather was fine for sailing – as had been forecast. The sun was still low, but there were no clouds, and the wind barely moved the leaves in the trees at the bottom of the garden. There'd be more of a breeze down by the coast, she was sure, and the sailing would be perfect.

And first, there'd be breakfast together. Mrs Bolton, who came in to help Mama cook and clean the house, was in the kitchen humming a tune Rae didn't recognise. It wasn't surprising because Mrs Bolton's version of any tune was nothing like the original, but at least she sounded happy and she smiled at Rae when she offered to help. Mama, Papa and Jack arrived shortly after and then a sleepy, tousle-haired Joe.

Everyone was in a good mood, and it was hardly surprising, thought Rae. She and Joe were looking forward to sailing the new boat, Mama and Papa were enjoying the family time and the prospect of a picnic and day out together. And who knew why Jack was happy? Perhaps he just enjoyed dipping bread 'soldiers' in his boiled egg. But everything was perfect until Mama said she had an announcement.

Rae had never seen her mother look so excited. She was smiling and even after taking a letter from her pocket, her mouth turned up at the corners as if it had a life of its own. Finally, Mama read the contents out loud.

Apparently, she'd gained a place to study medicine at the Royal Free Hospital in London.

"Isn't your mama clever?" Papa said. He looked proudly at her with shining eyes.

"So, you're going back to school?" Rae stared at her mother. Why would anyone choose to go back to school? Rae would far rather be outside doing something thrilling than sitting in a stuffy classroom or even upstairs in her own bedroom reading. Pretty much anything rather than being at school.

"I'm going to be a doctor like your papa." Mama was so excited she was almost giggling.

Rae stared at her. She'd only ever seen Mama like that one Christmas after she'd had too much sherry. But this was breakfast time.

"I've always longed to study medicine. My mother forbade me, so I went into nursing."

Papa grinned. "She didn't really want you to do that either, did she?"

"But in the end, I did it anyway," Mama said, her voice strong and determined. She and Papa exchanged glances and laughed.

Rae was amazed. Mama had defied her mother? That was hard to imagine. But worse – she was laughing about it? It was unbelievable.

"So," added Papa, trying to look more serious. "There will be a few changes... Mama will spend much of her time in London and when she's at home, she'll have a lot of studying to do."

More chores, thought Rae. She wanted to roll her eyes to the ceiling, but didn't dare. That was always certain to make Mama cross. It was easy to anger her without meaning to, so anything Rae knew was certain to irritate her was definitely worth avoiding.

She's going to say I need to do more in the house. Or perhaps she's going to ask Mrs Bolton to come in more often. Well, that wouldn't be bad.

Rae liked Mrs Bolton. She never got cross, and she never shouted.

"So, we thought it would be best if we had a live-in nanny to look after Jack," said Papa.

"Someone living in? Oh, no!" Rae's mouth opened in surprise. That would surely mean more rules.

"But it won't bother you, dear," said Mama with unexpected gentleness. "Well, only at the weekends, anyway. You and Joe will board at your schools during the week."

"Board?" Rae's chest tightened until she couldn't breathe. "But I don't want to board." She stared at her mother with wide eyes. Her parents were sending her away? How could they do that?

Please, please let it be a joke.

"You don't want to board? Why ever not?" asked Joe. "I want to. I think it'll be rather a lark."

"It's only from Monday to Friday, Rae," said Papa, placing his hand over hers and giving it a squeeze. "You'll come home at the weekend if you want to."

"If I want to?" Rae stared at her parents in horror. Had the world gone mad? "Of course, I'd want to. I don't want to go away at all." The words 'boarding school' clanged in her ears, growing louder with each repetition.

She put the piece of toast she'd been eating back on the plate. Her appetite had gone. Her stomach felt as though it were full of rocks.

"Well, it's all been decided," said Mama, her mouth setting into a hard line. "I thought you'd be pleased for me, Hannah-Rae."

"My name is Rae!" she shrieked, her face growing hot. The words hung in the air, heavy and sharp. Would Mama finally listen?

But Mama hadn't even looked at her. "Stop shouting. You'll upset Jack."

The shouting, however, continued for some time.

Mrs Bolton quickly washed up and left.

"Got enough problems of me own. I don't need to listen to all that racket," she muttered as she tied her scarf under her chin and with her basket over her arm, told Papa she was leaving early.

Jack cried, not understanding why suddenly everyone was shouting. Mama took him to the bathroom to quieten him down and to clean the egg off his face.

Joe went back to his bedroom with a smile on his face. He'd begged to be allowed to board at Bishop's Hall Boys School for some time. All his friends were boarders, but until that morning, he hadn't been allowed to even think about it.

Only Rae and Papa were still at the breakfast table.

"No, Rae, of course, we don't want to get rid of you. You're being melodramatic. That's not it at all. This isn't about you. It's about Mama. It's going to be hard for all of us, but she's waited a long time for this. Surely you can see it's going to be impossible for her to do all the things she does now and study at the same time?"

Rae wasn't sure what 'melodramatic' meant, but she knew her claim that she wasn't wanted had upset Papa. "I'd do more in the house," she pleaded. "And Mrs Bolton might come in for longer if you ask her."

"We've already asked her, and she said she can't do any more hours. And after this morning, I'm not sure she'll come back at all. You know how she hates it when... when things get heated."

"Heated? You mean when Mama shouts." Rae had clenched her fists so tightly, her fingernails bit into her palms.

"Rae! You've done your fair share of shouting this morning, too. You're more like your mother than you know."

Papa's words stung, but Rae couldn't help feeling he didn't understand. She had reason to shout – didn't she? She was nothing like her fiery, unreasonable mother... Nothing at all.

Before she could tell him how untrue and unfair that was, Papa reached out and, taking hold of one fist, he uncurled it and smiled at her. "Perhaps this will please you. I was saving the best piece of news till last... I've named the new yacht in honour of you and Mama."

"What've you called her?" Rae hated fighting with Papa and reluctantly pretended to be distracted from the thought of boarding school.

"You'll have to wait and see." Papa's face lit up with mischief.

Rae thought it might be *Ray of Sunshine*, which was what Papa often called her.

That would be a perfect name for a boat, but he'd said she'd been named after Mama too.

"You haven't called her *Hannah-Rae*, have you?" She held her breath. What was the point of trying to stop people from calling her by that name if the boat was a reminder?

Papa shook his head and smiled mysteriously. "You're just going to have to wait, I'm afraid, my little ray of sunshine."

Ray of Sunshine. That must be it.

Although what that had to do with Mama, Rae didn't know.

However, later when Rae was hunting for her shoes, she overheard Papa and Mama talking in the living room, "... she'll see sense eventually, Amelia, I'm sure of it, just leave it to me," Papa said.

Who were they talking about, and what was Papa going to do to make her see sense?

Of course, he could have been referring to someone Rae didn't know. Perhaps Mrs Bolton, who regularly handed in her notice? She often did that, usually after Mama had upset her, which happened quite often. However, Rae suspected he'd been talking about her. But how could Papa be certain she would be so quick to see sense? Rae didn't hear any more because the sound of Joe galloping down the stairs two at a time stopped the conversation in the living room.

The picnic basket Mrs Bolton had been going to pack for them before she'd walked out, was only half-prepared and it was decided that since the quarrel at breakfast had unsettled Jack who now refused to let Mama out of his sight, they would both remain at home. Papa would take Joe and Rae, and instead of a picnic, he'd buy lunch for them in the harbour café.

To prevent squabbling about who was to sit in the front when Mama wasn't in the car, Papa always insisted they both sat in the back and now, while Joe whistled a tune, Rae stared out of the window at the blur of hedgerows and the occasional glimpse of cows in a field. From time to time, Joe asked a question about boarding in September, and he and Papa chatted. Rae, however, was silent. If Papa thought she was so easily won over, well, he'd have to think again.

"You've been very quiet, poppet. Is there anything you'd like to ask me about school?" Papa asked her, his voice gentle.

Before she'd really thought about it, she'd replied, "No." Her fingers curled tightly into her palms, leaving small crescents in her skin. She bit her lip, staring out the window at the passing trees, willing herself not to cry, but she knew Papa would be able to see her brimming eyes in the rearview mirror if he looked.

Why had she been so stubborn? There were a lot of things she wanted to know.

Papa pulled into a lay-by and stopped the car, then turning towards her, he said, "I have a feeling there are things you'd like to ask me, Rae."

"Why've we stopped?" asked Joe. "We're in the middle of nowhere. Oh, we haven't broken down, have we? That would be such rotten luck."

"No, son, I just need to have a word with your sister, and it's hard to do that without looking at her."

Joe grunted, crossed his arms and sank back into the seat. "Typical Rae. She always has to spoil things."

Normally, such unfairness would have caused an angry comment from Rae, but her throat had closed up, and she wasn't sure the words would come out.

"I can see you're not happy, poppet, so it's probably best we sort this out now. Then you can enjoy the rest of the day."

Rae shrugged as if she wasn't happy about discussing it, but she'd do it for her father's sake.

"I need you to understand Mama has done something remarkable."

"Remarkable?" Well, that was true. She was remarkably irritable. Remarkably cross and unreasonable.

"Yes, poppet. It wasn't many years ago that women weren't allowed to study medicine and now your mother has won a place at Medical School. You should be extremely proud."

"Women weren't allowed? Why ever not?"

"Because men were in charge of the selection process and, for a variety of reasons, they decided women weren't capable of becoming doctors."

Despite herself, Rae was now interested. "But that's awful, Papa."

"I know. And that's why we need to do all we can to encourage Mama. When you've finished school, Mama and I will help you do whatever you want... and hopefully, by then, there'll be even more opportunities for girls than there are now. But until then, Mama needs your support."

Rae sighed. Why was he always so reasonable?

"But Papa, why can't I stay home and support her? Why do I have to board?"

"Because in order to study, Mama needs to be assured you're all safe. And you know how reckless you can be, poppet. Joe's bad enough, but sometimes, you're worse than him. If you two are looked after at school, then she'll be able to concentrate on her studies. Why can't you be pleased like Joe?"

"Because he's got lots of friends at school who're already boarders. I haven't."

"Well, I'm sure you'll soon make some. And you can come home each weekend."

"But we'll have a stranger living with us."

"Jack needs someone to care for him. And I'm sure in time, we'll all get used to having a nanny in the house. You might even like her."

"Can we go now?" Joe asked, scowling at his sister.

"Can we, poppet?" Papa asked. He wasn't asking for her permission to move. She knew he wanted to find out if she was going to continue to sulk and make their lives difficult.

"I s'pose so," she said.

Papa drove the rest of the way to MacKenzie & Sons and while Joe resumed his shrill whistling, Rae tried to imagine what sort of changes lay ahead.

Perhaps she would like the new nanny. And if not, she could always ignore her. And if school got too bad, she'd simply run away. She'd done it before, although admittedly, she'd always returned home before nightfall, but this time, she was older, and she was sure she'd make a better job of it.

Papa took her hand when she got out of the car and she walked along beside him, enjoying the feeling of togetherness. This was the sort of thing she'd miss when she was boarding, but it wasn't like Papa was there to hold her hand during the week – she rarely saw him. And at the weekend, she had to compete for his attention with Jack and Joe. So, perhaps it was sensible not to fight while she had him to herself.

And to think he'd named the boat after her. Well, not exactly after her because he'd said it was for Mama too, but it made her feel special. She wondered if it involved the name Poppet because he sometimes called Mama that, too. Yes. That was it. It would be something like *The Sea Poppet* or *Jolly Poppet* or even *Sunshine Poppet,* which would include his special name for his ray of sunshine.

She wanted to skip beside him to the boat, which was now moored in the harbour, but she was too old for such silliness. Joe had run ahead and had obviously found the new yacht as he waved madly and climbed onto it. Rae walked with Papa. She was enjoying the comfort of his hand around hers – it made her feel safe and protected.

Finally, they were close enough to see the name of the boat.

There must be some mistake. Rae narrowed her eyes and looked at the other boats, searching for the right one. Joe must be on the wrong boat because the one he'd boarded was called *Wild Spirit.* So why hadn't Papa called him back?

Instead, Papa shouted to Joe, asking him how he liked it.

Rae stopped and stared. "I thought you said you'd named it after Mama and me," she whispered.

"I did," said Papa. He smiled at her.

She stared at him. How had he not realised the catch in her throat was the result of shock – not happiness?

"I think it captures you and your mama exactly," he said.

Wild Spirit? Is that what he thought of her? Something savage and vicious, like an animal?

Even the thought of sailing the new boat couldn't make up for the hurt.

Chapter Four

♥

Mama's father arrived the following day for afternoon tea.

Pop, as the children called him, dropped in periodically, but that afternoon, he'd come especially to congratulate his daughter on her acceptance into Medical School.

Since Mrs Bolton had failed to appear that morning, Papa had helped Mama clear the plates and cups from the table. They were accompanied by Jack, who was still unwilling to let his mother out of his sight, holding up his arms and pleading, "Carry hold, Mama, carry hold," in a wavering voice. He kept that up all morning.

Rae had gone for a walk and kept out of everyone's way until Pop had arrived.

Joe had disappeared upstairs to his room to add the stamps Pop had given him to his collection, and only Rae remained with her grandfather at the table.

"So, my darling, you must be very proud of your mama." Pop reached over and patted her hand.

"Yes," said Rae without much conviction, then realising how

half-hearted she'd sounded, she added, "I am…"

"But?"

"Well, I *am* proud. It's just that I don't know why I can't stay home. I wouldn't be any trouble."

Pop smiled. "Trouble is your middle name, my darling. Remember last summer when you fell out of that tree? I don't know how you didn't break anything, neither can I work out how you got up there. And your mama's best dinner service, how could you have broken so many pieces at once? And what about that horse? What were you thinking?"

"But Pop! I'm older now. I don't do silly things like I did when I was young and if it meant I didn't have to board, I'd be really, really good."

"Hmm. I know you mean to be good, Rae, but sometimes you act without thinking and that's when the problems arise. Your parents have to make sure you're safe at all times – well, as safe as anyone can keep you – and that's why they need to send you to school."

"Couldn't I come and live with you, Pop." Rae squeezed her eyes tightly shut, waiting for the reason why she couldn't.

He sighed sadly. "If only that could be, my darling, but my life's a bit disorganised at the moment, and I'm often away on business. You know, throughout my life, I've discovered that things are rarely as dreadful as you expect them to be. You might find you enjoy boarding. And if not, well, you'll be home at the weekend. I know at your age even a day seems like a long time, but trust me, the older you get, the faster time flies."

Her shoulders slumped. Living with Pop had been her last hope, even though she'd suspected he'd say no. Now it looked as though she'd have to do as everyone wanted.

Pop tapped his chin. "What is it you're afraid of, darling?"

"Afraid? I'm not afraid." Rae sat up straight and pushed out her lower jaw.

"Good gracious, you look like a bulldog," Pop said with a laugh. "There's nothing wrong with being afraid, you know. Everyone's scared of something. So, let me rephrase my question. What is it you're not looking forward to?"

Rae lowered her head. "I don't like any of the girls who board, so I'm going to be on my own a lot of the time. And I don't like the thought of a stranger in our house. Suppose I don't like her? Suppose she doesn't like me?"

"As you go through life, Rae, there will be plenty of people you don't like – trust me, I know – but part of growing up is learning to live and respect people you don't actually want as your friends. It's an important lesson."

"I s'pose…" This wasn't what Rae had hoped to hear. Why wasn't anyone on her side?

"I suspect, darling, it's the idea of change that's bothering you, rather than who you might or might not be friendly with."

"I s'pose…"

"There's no getting away from change. Life's all about changing and growing."

"That's what my teacher says."

"A wise woman."

"She says if life doesn't change, it's called death."

"Ah, well, that's a bit more brutal than I had in mind, but I suppose there's truth in that." Pop looked uncomfortable.

"Oh, I'm sorry Pop, did that remind you of Gran?"

"Gran?" Pop's eyebrows shot up.

Rae was sorry she'd mentioned Pop's wife – her grandmother. There was always an awkward silence whenever Gran came up and

Rae didn't usually mention her, although she would have loved to have known more about her. Even Mama was strangely quiet when her mother came up in conversation.

"Another cuppa, Pop?" Mama called from the kitchen.

He sighed. "Perhaps later, thanks, love. Rae and I are just going to admire the garden."

Pop rose and Rae took the hand he held out to her. "It's about time you knew about your gran. It might help you deal with your current situation, too."

Rae sat on the wooden swing and Pop pushed her as he'd done when she was much younger. Although she now prided herself on being able to fling her legs forward and then backward to swing higher and higher on her own, she knew Pop enjoyed treating her like a little girl.

He cleared his throat, struggling to find words. Finally, he began. "What do you know about your gran, darling?"

That was a surprise. She'd assumed Pop would concentrate on boarding school and why she should go, rather than bring up the subject of her grandmother. "Nothing really. I know her name was Ivy, and she had two children – Mama and Uncle David. And that she died a while ago."

Pop fiddled with his sleeve button. "Hmm. Well, your gran and I definitely had two wonderful children. But... the fact is, she's still alive. It's just that we don't live together anymore."

"My gran's still alive?" Rae twisted around to look at Pop. Was he joking? No, that wasn't the sort of thing anyone joked about, and she could tell from his expression he was serious. And very sad. "Then why don't we ever see her, Pop?"

"Because your mama fell out with her mother and wants nothing to do with her."

Rae dragged her feet on the ground and stopped the swing. She leapt off and, with hands on her hips, she stared at Pop between the ropes in disbelief. Somewhere, there was a poor old lady living alone whose family were ignoring her. "B...but that's... dreadful. How could Mama be so mean? And what about Joe, Jack and me? We haven't been allowed to meet our own gran?"

"Whoa!" Pop held up his hands, fingers outspread to stop her. "Hold your horses there, Rae. If you'd ever met your gran, you'd have some idea why she and your mama quarrelled. I'm sorry to say this, but it's the truth. Your gran's a bitter, cold-hearted woman, and it was her fault entirely that her daughter walked out."

"My mother walked out on her mama?" Rae couldn't believe it. Mama, who always told her she must do as she was told? So that comment at the breakfast table about Mama defying her mother had been true. Rae had half-dismissed it as a made-up story.

"You have to understand, darling, Ivy was a harsh and critical mother. Nothing David or your mother did was ever good enough. Davy ran away and joined the Army as soon as he could. Your mother desperately wanted to study medicine. Not the easiest of careers to follow for a woman, but she was extremely bright at school, and I have no doubt if Ivy and I had backed her, she'd have got into Medical School and would now be as successful as your father. But Ivy didn't want her daughter to study or to work. She believed well-brought-up girls should marry, and she made things so difficult for your mother that one day she packed her things and left."

"Didn't you try to stop her?" Rae was so surprised she could barely form the words.

Pop took hold of the swing's rope and looked down as if he couldn't meet her angry gaze. "Unfortunately, I was often away travelling on business and, to my shame, I tried to avoid all the arguments. I wish I'd been firmer... but it's too late now. It's all water under the bridge. Anyway, I have a feeling it wouldn't have made much difference to the outcome. Once Ivy made up her mind about something, there was no changing it. Davy fell in love with a wonderful girl from around the corner but according to Ivy, her family wasn't good enough for our son, and, in the end, she made Davy's life so miserable, he left and joined up. I haven't seen him since he went to India. Now he has a wife and two children who I've never met. And Ivy doesn't even know about them."

Rae stared at him in silence. If it had been anyone other than Pop, she'd have thought the stories were enormous lies. So, her gran, who she'd assumed had died, was still alive, unaware she had grandchildren in India. And she wasn't a poor, lonely old lady but someone people remembered her with dislike. How could that be possible? She struggled to imagine a young Pop, Mama at the same age as Rae and the uncle she'd never met who might look like Joe, all living with a faceless woman who'd treated them all badly. They were as real as characters in a dark fairytale.

She gasped. "Wait, does she know about Joe, Jack and me?"

Pop shook his head sadly. "No, I'm afraid not. Your mama cut all ties when she walked out. And I have to respect her decision."

This was unbelievable. Somewhere, her grandmother was getting up in the morning and going to bed at night not knowing anything about Joe, Rae or Jack? And she had no idea she had a daughter-in-law and two grandchildren halfway across the world?

"Where is Gran now?" Rae whispered, unable to shake the dreadful image of a fairytale witch.

"Much to her annoyance, she's still living in the East End of London, in our family home." Pop shook his head sadly.

"London?" That wasn't very far away. Rae shook her head in disbelief. "You said, 'much to her annoyance,' why does it annoy her?"

Pop took a deep breath and looked down at the swing again. "Because she thinks it's beneath her. I've always been a big disappointment to her because I never earned enough to give her all the things she wanted. Her parents were wealthy, and they were against her marrying me because they said I wasn't good enough for her. And they were probably right…"

"Oh, Pop! Who could ever think you weren't good enough?" Rae stepped to the other side of the swing and wrapped her arms around his waist.

He stroked her hair. "Ivy thought her father would get used to the idea of us marrying and eventually forgive her and perhaps buy us a house somewhere. But he didn't. He cut her off without a penny, and when she realised how hard life really was, she started to resent me. I worked hard to give her everything she wanted, but I could never provide all she thought she deserved. I spent longer and longer working to make extra money and after a while, I realised how much I enjoyed being away and how I dreaded going home, knowing the minute I walked through the door, I'd face complaints and criticism. If it hadn't been for your mama and Davy, I think I'd simply have walked away."

With her ear against his chest, she heard him swallow.

He cleared his throat. "But looking back on it, I should have spent more time at home with my children… I should have done lots of things I didn't do. Now, I have so many regrets…"

His voice broke, and he fumbled with his free hand in his pocket for his handkerchief, then blew his nose.

Finally, he spoke, his voice heavy with sorrow. "Your grandmother... she was a hard woman, always finding fault in the smallest things. It left its mark on all of us, but children – well, they respond differently. Davy found a way to laugh through it, never let her get under his skin." He paused, a faint smile crossing his face at the memory of his son's carefree nature, before his expression darkened. "But your mama... she wasn't like Davy. She needed warmth, encouragement. And when she didn't get it, she didn't wither – she built walls. She learned early that tenderness was a weakness, something she couldn't afford. I can still see it in her eyes sometimes, that guarded look, like she's bracing herself for the next sharp word that never comes."

Rae's thoughts swirled in her mind like stirred soup. Had her mama once felt like Rae? Always in the wrong. Always a disappointment.

"Why didn't I know any of this before, Pop?"

"Because it's a tale of failure and disappointment. I'm not proud of how my life turned out. It's not something I'd normally speak about – especially to someone so young. I'm only telling you now, darling, because I want you to understand how stubbornness and pride can tear families apart. You've inherited your strong character from your mother and your grandmother. But you have a choice. Either you use your strength to bully and hurt those who are closest to you, like your grandmother, or you put your energy into something meaningful, like your mother. Only you can decide."

Rae silently stared at Pop, trying to imagine the bullying gran she'd never met and thinking about her mother who got cross at the slightest thing. So, she'd inherited her personality from them? Both Pop and Papa thought she was like Mama. But even worse, she'd now discovered she resembled her gran – a woman who'd made not only her mother's life miserable but her gentle grandad's too.

I'm not like them, she thought, *I'm not, I'm not.* Although deep down, she wasn't sure.

"Pop?" she said finally.

"Hmm?"

"Would you say I'm wild?"

"Wild? In what sense?"

"Like a wild spirit."

"Hmm, let me see. Well, yes, in that you're untamed, independent and free-thinking. Why?"

"Papa said he named the boat *Wild Spirit* after Mama and me. And at first, I was upset because I thought he meant we were beastly like wild animals."

"Oh, I see. No, darling, your papa adores you and your mama. I don't believe he meant wild as in savage. He wouldn't risk upsetting either of you. I imagine he was simply praising your energy and your passion and sometimes, your unpredictability."

"What does that mean, Pop?"

"Unpredictability?"

Rae nodded.

"When you're unpredictable, it means no one else can tell with any certainty what you're about to do next."

Unpredictable? That's me all right, thought Rae, and sometimes I even take myself by surprise.

"Are you ready to go inside, darling?" Pop asked.

Rae nodded, then remembered the reason she thought they'd come into the garden. "So, Pop, are you telling me I have to be happy about boarding school and having a nanny?" she asked, wondering what her gran had to do with boarding school.

"Good gracious, no, darling. After what I've told you about the mess I made of my life, it would be a bit much for me to tell you how to live yours. I just wanted you to know how your mama missed out when she was young. It's up to you to decide how to behave."

Later that night, Rae recalled everything Pop had told her. All that had once been so familiar now had a dark shadow hanging over it. And worse, the darkness hung over her. A tiny part of her grandmother and mother lived inside her? Was she strong enough to be herself? Who was she, anyway? Now more than ever, she needed something certain and steady. She needed an anchor to hold her in place while she came to terms with everything she'd learned. But time was running out. Soon, she'd be on her own at boarding school.

Chapter Five

The following day, when Rae arrived home from school, Mrs Bolton opened the door.

"Yer mam's gone to London for the afternoon," she said over her shoulder as she hurried back to the kitchen.

Rae followed, wondering why the usually slow-moving Mrs Bolton was rushing – her slippers slapping on the carpet. Perhaps she had something in the oven that was burning? Rae soon realised why she wanted to get back to the kitchen.

"That's enough of the flour, young Master Kingsley. That pastry'll be as hard as a rock," said Mrs Bolton as she took the dredger from the chubby fist. "Now, let's get that rolling pin working, shall we?"

For all her grumbling and complaining, she adored Jack and judging by the mess over the table, she'd been entertaining him all afternoon.

Mrs Bolton poured Rae a glass of milk and gave her a warm jam tart.

"Young Jack didn't get his hands on that one, so don't you worry," she said with a wink.

"What's Mama gone to London for?" Rae asked.

Mrs Bolton shrugged and sniffed. Her usual way of conveying displeasure or disapproval. "She's gone to one of them fancy agencies to find a you-know-what..." she paused and gave a theatrical nod towards Jack.

"Oh, you mean a nanny," Rae said.

"Shh! Don't upset the little man." Mrs Bolton frowned and looked at Jack anxiously. "Poor little mite. Fancy getting some stranger in to look after 'im. It don't seem right. What he needs is his mother."

"Mama!" said Jack. As if magically summoned, Mama returned with the scrape of the key in the front door lock.

"Did you find a nanny?" Rae asked as her mother came into the kitchen.

Mrs Bolton sniffed loudly, but Rae took no notice. It was unlikely Jack understood what a nanny was.

"Did you?" Rae asked again, holding her breath and hoping the answer would be 'no'.

"I've narrowed it down to two women and they're coming here tomorrow for an interview and to meet Jack. Hopefully, I'll have someone by the end of the day." Mama took Jack by the wrist to the sink and wiped the jam off his hands and face.

Mrs Bolton shrugged and sniffed again; her eyes narrowed, and her jaw clenched. She set about cleaning the table with more energy than usual.

When Rae returned home from school the following day, she was in time to see a woman come out of the drive, tuck her umbrella under her arm and pull on a pair of gloves.

This was a woman who meant business. With a glance up at the clouds, she adjusted her hat and then marched on sensible flat, lace-up shoes towards Rae; her thin lips clamped tightly together.

"Good afternoon," she said in a stern voice, such as a teacher might use to a class of misbehaving children.

Rae greeted the severe woman politely and turned to watch as she strode towards the bus stop, desperately hoping Mama hadn't employed her to be Jack's new nanny.

"Please, please," she muttered to herself. "Not that woman."

Her mother had seen Rae and was waiting at the door.

"Is she Jack's new nanny?" The words tumbled out and Rae bit her lower lip, holding her breath.

Mama frowned and sighed, for once not noticing Rae's rudeness. "I'm not sure. She's got some excellent references, although she seemed a bit rigid in her outlook. But there's still someone else to interview."

Rae decided it was a good sign if Mama was uncertain. Perhaps she wouldn't like the other lady either. That wouldn't put Mama off continuing her search, but at least it would delay things.

The next candidate arrived half an hour later. Rae watched from an upstairs window as an elderly, gaunt woman walked up the drive, her shapeless brown coat flapping around skinny legs. She rang the doorbell three times, and Rae smiled, knowing it would annoy Mama.

Not a promising start.

Good.

Rae crept onto the landing and listened to her mother greet the lady whose name was Miss Prescott, and invite her into Papa's study. The door was ajar, and Rae crept halfway down the stairs to listen to the interview. She expected Mama to ask lots of things, but Miss Prescott was keen to get her questions in first.

Good.

That would annoy Mama, too.

"Is there a Methodist church in the vicinity, Mrs Kingsley? I simply couldn't consider a post that didn't have one within easy travelling distance," she said.

"A...a church? Well, there's St Luke's in the vill—"

"No, it must be a Methodist church. I'm afraid I don't hold with the Church of England, nor the Roman Catholic church."

"I see. Well, now I think about it, I believe there's one in Ribbenthorpe. That's only a few miles away."

Miss Prescott cleared her throat. "I can see from your reply, Mrs Kingsley, that you are not of the Methodist persuasion."

"Err, no, I'm afraid not."

"I see. Well, I assume you will be happy for me to carry out Bible instruction with young Master Kingsley."

"Err, well, I believe he's a little young at the moment—"

"If you don't mind me saying so, Mrs Kingsley, children are never too young to learn about the Good Lord and the Good Book."

"No, indeed not. Well, perhaps we could discuss your previous employers..."

The key turned in the lock, and Joe opened the front door.

"What're you doing sitting there?" he asked Rae loudly when he saw her on the stairs, despite her waving her hands to silence him.

Why was Joe so stupid?

Mama shut the study door, and the interview carried on in private.

When Rae joined Joe upstairs, she told him what she'd heard.

He shrugged. "I hope she doesn't get the job. But even if she does, I won't see her. I'm going to stay at school over the weekend. Lots of the chaps do. I'm really looking forward to it. I don't know why you're making such a fuss about boarding, Rae. If you stayed at school, you wouldn't see her or whoever gets the job. It's Jack I feel sorry for."

Rae's chest tightened. How could he say it so easily, like it didn't matter at all? She lowered her gaze, her voice barely above a whisper.

"But you've got lots of friends at school, Joe. I haven't got anyone. Not really."

"Well, make new ones." Then, in a rare moment of brotherly affection, he put his arm around her shoulder. "Look, Rae, we break up on Thursday and we've got weeks to do exactly what we like. Don't spoil it by worrying about next term."

She smiled. "Yes, I suppose you're right."

"Atta girl. We've got lots of serious sailing to do in *Wild Spirit* before we go back for the autumn term. And I'm going to prove to the world I'm a better sailor than you."

Rae punched him playfully on the arm. "You don't stand a chance, brother dear."

After Miss Prescott had left, Rae asked her mother whether she'd chosen a nanny.

"Well, I want to discuss it with Papa first," she said. "Miss Prescott had impeccable references, but I didn't take to her at all. I think I prefer the first one."

Rae wasn't sure whether to be relieved or not. The woman she'd passed in the lane outside their house had looked and sounded rather severe. Even Mama had said she was rigid, although Rae wasn't sure exactly what that meant. But when Rae had eavesdropped on the first part of the interview with Miss Prescott, it had sounded as though even Mama was wary of the woman. Of the two possible nannies, Rae agreed. The first one appeared to be better. By the tiniest margin. But it looked as though it would be up to Papa to choose.

The next morning, Rae got up early, hoping to catch Papa before he left for work. Could she persuade him not to choose either of them? He hadn't met them, but if she told him what she knew...

Unfortunately, he'd already left.

"What did Papa say about the nanny, Mama?" Rae crossed her

fingers, hoping he'd decided against them both.

"Hmm? Oh, he said it was up to me."

Rae casually buttered a slice of toast. "And what've you decided?" She held her breath.

"The first one, Mademoiselle Thérèse Jacquet. I'll see if she can come back today so you and Joe can meet her after school."

Mademoiselle Thérèse Jacquet. Such a pretty name for such a miserable-looking woman.

Rae described the new nanny to Joe as they walked together to the bus stop.

"She's probably much nicer when you get to know her," said Joe. "But I suppose we'll find out later."

After school that afternoon, they got off the bus together at the stop near their house.

"Race you home," said Joe, setting off before he'd spoken to get a head start, but for once, Rae didn't take up the challenge. She was in no rush to see the new nanny. When she let herself in the front door, Joe was coming out of the living room, his eyes wide in astonishment, and he closed the doors carefully behind him.

"Wait till I tell the chaps at school about this," he whispered, his face alight with glee, as he tousled Rae's hair.

"Stop it!" she squealed, which made him rub harder.

"Rae? Is that you?" Mama called from the living room. "Come and meet Mademoiselle Jacquet."

As Rae opened the door, she caught sight of herself in the mirror above the fireplace and was horrified at her reflection which showed her blonde curls were in even more of a mess than usual.

"Rae! What have you been up to?" Mama asked crossly. "Really, you could have tidied yourself up before you came to meet Mademoiselle Jacquet."

Rae looked around for the barrel-shaped lady with the severe face she'd seen yesterday but the other person in the room was an elegantly dressed young woman in her twenties who was holding out a beautifully manicured hand, "Good afternoon, Miss Kingsley, I am very pleased to meet you," she said in a soft, French accent.

"Honestly, Rae, you might have been a bit more welcoming to the new nanny. I know you're not happy about me engaging one, but that's no reason to be rude. Fancy staring at her like that. I was so embarrassed. Sometimes I just don't know what gets into you."

"I'm sorry, Mama, but I thought you said you'd decided to accept the first woman who came for an interview. When I got home from school yesterday, I saw a large woman come out of our house and I thought it was her. She looked rather scary."

"Ah, I see. That must have been Mrs Oliver. Oh, yes, I did say I was going to interview two ladies, didn't I? But the agency called early and said they had another excellent candidate, and would I like to see her? Mademoiselle Jacquet came about midday. I wasn't terribly keen on the other two ladies – although they were extremely well-qualified. But Jack seemed to take to Mademoiselle Jacquet immediately. I just hope Papa's happy. He only saw the details about the other two ladies."

"I'm sure he'd prefer her to Mrs Oliver and Miss Prescott," said Rae. She frowned. Joe had spoken about nothing other than their beautiful new nanny since he'd met her. Stupid boy.

Chapter Six

♥

Finally, it was Friday and the first day of the summer holidays. As soon as Rae awoke, she jumped out of bed and after briefly wondering if Mama would notice if she didn't wash; she decided not to risk it. It would be dreadful to be sent back upstairs and waste good sailing time. How marvellous to exchange her gymslip and blazer for shorts, blouse and pullover on top of her bathing suit.

Usually slow to wake, Joe was also up early, keen to make the most of the first day of freedom and after a rushed breakfast, they put a few apples and some of Mrs Bolton's sausage rolls in Rae's bicycle basket and set off down the drive.

The sun was still low and the breeze cool, but Rae soon warmed up as they cycled through the lanes towards the harbour.

This was going to be a perfect day.

Joe dismounted when they arrived at the waterfront and pushed his bicycle towards MacKenzie & Sons.

"What're you doing?" Rae called in alarm. The last place Rae wanted to go was the boatyard.

"Papa arranged for us to leave our bicycles in Jamie's papa's place to keep them safe," he yelled over his shoulder. "You can do what you like with your bicycle. But if anything happens to it while we're sailing, you're on your own. Don't think I'm going to give you a lift on my crossbar. You can walk."

As Rae reluctantly wheeled her bicycle towards the boatyard, Jamie MacKenzie came out of the gate with his fishing gear. She stopped, and pretending she had a stone in her plimsol, she took it off and shook it.

That boy was the last person she wanted to see. Joe hadn't let her forget the day they'd first encountered each other, and the memory still made her burn with shame. If she delayed, it would give him time to go off with his fishing rod, and then she and Joe could go sailing as planned.

But Joe obviously had other ideas. "Rae, come on, hurry up. I've asked Jamie to come with us."

She'd recently learned what she understood was a very rude word, and she said it under her breath. But there was nothing for it. Now Joe had asked the boy to go with them, she'd have to put up with it – or not go sailing at all. And that was not going to happen.

"Come on, Rae. Stop dawdling," Joe yelled, as he and Jamie reached the *Wild Spirit*. "Anyone'd think you didn't want to go sailing."

"I don't with him," she muttered under her breath, but she hurried anyway. Papa had forbidden either of them to sail alone, but Joe could conceivably cast off with Jamie and leave her behind.

Jamie climbed aboard first and helped Joe, then held out his hand for Rae, but ignoring it, she scrambled onto the boat herself.

"You take the tiller, Jamie," Joe said. "I bet you know some spiffing places to go around here."

Jamie looked at Rae as if to judge her reaction to him being handed the tiller, but she pretended not to care and busied herself with the jib sail, while the boys chatted as they rigged the boat, completely ignoring her.

Joe untied the painter and they moved from their mooring into the open water. Jamie pointed in the direction of the creek towards which the boys had decided they would head. The sails flapped lazily, then filled with wind; Jamie turned the tiller, heading away from the harbour. Zigzagging in a series of tacks, they made good progress and despite feeling left out, Rae thrilled as the salt-kissed breeze whipped past, blowing her hair about her face in damp tendrils.

Finally, they turned into Jamie's inlet and the wind dropped, letting the sails slacken and flap.

"Shall we make for that beach?" Jamie asked.

"Do as you like," muttered Rae beneath her breath, upset she hadn't been consulted about anything.

She crossed her arms and looked in the opposite direction.

"For goodness' sake, Rae, stop sulking," Joe said. "You're getting on my nerves."

The boat rocked as he lunged, seizing her arm and throwing her off balance. For a second, it looked as though they'd both topple overboard, but Joe managed to grab one of the stays. Rae, however, somersaulted into the water with a splash. She surfaced, spluttering with indignation.

"What did you do that for?" she demanded. "I'm going to tell Papa what you did."

"Oh, shut up, Rae. When I tell Papa what a spoilt brat you've been, he'll say I should have done it sooner."

Jamie reached over the gunwale and offered her his hand to pull her out. For a second, she was tempted to refuse, but Joe was glaring at her, and she wondered if he might make her swim to the beach. If she'd only been wearing a bathing suit, she wouldn't have minded, but her blouse and shorts were flapping around her arms and legs, hampering her movements.

She took Jamie's hand but before she could think her actions through, she placed her feet against the hull and as he leaned out to get a firmer grip, she pushed against the wooden planking as hard as she could, resulting in Jamie tumbling out of the boat into the water.

If she'd paused to think, she might have stopped herself. But she didn't, and the consequences were immediate and painful. Jamie crashed on top of her, his cheekbone colliding sharply with the top of her head. The jarring impact sent a burst of pain through her skull, and the weight of him drove her down, plunging her back beneath the water.

Panic clawed at her, and as she gulped in shock, she swallowed a large mouthful of water. Her throat burned as she fought the urge to breathe in again. When she finally broke the surface, gasping and coughing, the air felt sharp and raw in her lungs. She blinked furiously, trying to clear her vision as the salty sting in her eyes blurred everything into a watery haze.

Finally, when she'd stopped coughing and wiped her eyes, she reached to grab the gunwale of the boat and looked up at Joe, who she expected to be furious. However, he had a strange, anxious expression on his face, which she couldn't read, and he appeared to be scanning the water behind her. She looked around, expecting Jamie to be bobbing on the surface, but he was nowhere to be seen.

Turning back to Joe, she looked at him and he shrugged. Had he knocked himself out? Was he still beneath the surface?

"Joe! Oh, Joe! Where is he? Has he drowned?" Icy coldness spread through her, freezing her muscles. Nevertheless, she turned and ducked under the water to look for Jamie, arms and legs flailing in clumsy panic. She expected to hear a splash as Joe joined her in a frantic search, but as she bobbed up for air, he was still on deck.

Screaming at him to help, she was astounded when he merely grinned at her. Then, she saw a dripping Jamie on deck with him.

The two boys slapped each other on the back, almost hysterical with laughter – their shouts and hoots echoing around the inlet, mocking her.

Rae later learned that while she was choking, Jamie had surfaced and after taking a deep breath, he'd dived and swum away from her to the other side of the boat. He'd hauled himself out of the water and Joe had realised he was paying Rae back for her bad behaviour by allowing her to believe he'd gone missing. Joe had been more than happy to play along.

Rae was glad to get back to harbour after the dreadful outing. It had looked so promising that morning when they'd set off from home and now the day was ruined. Why was it always that horrible boy who spoilt things for her?

And now, he and Joe were becoming great friends. It appeared the sailing trips she'd been longing for throughout the summer would now always be shared with Jamie MacKenzie. Well, not if she could help it. She'd rather stay at home than spend any more time with him.

But something else was bothering her. She and Joe would have to go into the boatyard to retrieve their bicycles before they rode home, and she dreaded seeing Mr MacKenzie. He would immediately notice his son's black eye. What would he do when he found out she'd dragged Jamie into the water, and they'd clashed heads? Perhaps Mr MacKenzie wouldn't be in the yard, and she'd be able to take her bicycle before he noticed them. Of course, in the end, he'd find out, but at least she wouldn't have to face him.

However, as soon as they entered the yard, Mr MacKenzie came out of the office to greet them.

"Ouch, laddie," he said to Jamie, tilting his chin up so he could get a better look at the swollen black eye. "That's a nasty shiner you've got there."

"I slipped, Dad," said Jamie. "Honestly, you should have seen me. I went down like a sack of potatoes."

Mr MacKenzie grunted and looked over his son's shoulder towards Rae. "Well, I expect you'll be more careful next time, eh, lad?"

Rae hung her head to hide her scarlet cheeks. She muttered, "Sorry." Picking up her bicycle, she quickly wheeled it towards the gate, holding her breath in case Mr MacKenzie called her back.

"See you tomorrow, Jamie?" Joe picked up his bike and yelled over his shoulder.

"No, sorry, Joe. Dad and I are off to Scotland early tomorrow. See you in August."

August? He wouldn't be back until August? Excitement bubbled up in Rae's chest. Finally, something was going her way.

Everything else in her life was going wrong, but at least the boy who was always around when everything fell to pieces wouldn't be there.

Chapter Seven

"Jamie's back tomorrow," said Joe one evening at the end of August.

"How d'you know?" Rae asked, her heart sinking at the thought of sharing Joe and the *Wild Spirit* with Jamie MacKenzie. Not only that, but his return reminded her of the end of the summer holidays and the start of boarding school.

"He said he'll be back at the end of the month on his postcard, you dolt. Don't you remember? It only came last week."

The postcard still stood on the mantelpiece in the living room, showing a handsome stag on a heather-clad moor with mountains in the background.

"Oh, yes," said Rae. She hadn't bothered to read the postcard from Scotland. If it had been up to her, she'd have put it in the dustbin. Thoughts of that boy always brought back memories she'd rather have forgotten. She'd had time over the summer to think about her behaviour after what Pop had told her about Gran, and she didn't want to be reminded of slices of the past when she should have behaved better. Not that she wanted to think of the future, either. The present was bearable, but not if Jamie MacKenzie pushed his way back into it.

Rae had sailed with Joe during the week and then Papa had joined them on the weekends. The sunny days had appeared to last for months. But now, even though there were still a few days left of the summer holidays, it felt as though they were over.

Rae was tempted to stay home and let Joe and Jamie sail on their own, but Mama was in a dreadful mood. Rae and Joe's trunks had been packed for school, and that had meant trying on uniforms and buying items to replace whatever was too small. Neither Rae nor Joe had been interested in trying on clothes and Mama had been cross with them both.

Now, the decorators had been brought in to prepare one of the spare bedrooms for Mademoiselle Jacquet, but they were noisy, messy and slow.

Papa had made Mama a cup of tea and asked her to remember that if anything should upset the men and they walked out, he wouldn't be able to find other decorators in time to finish the room. And that risked upsetting the nanny when she arrived.

So, Mama kept out of the decorators' way. Unfortunately, she was still angry about the dust, their banging, whistling and constant stops for mugs of tea. Apparently, she found it distracting, and it also upset Jack, who grizzled much of the time.

It wouldn't matter how hard Rae tried to be good, she knew she'd get in the way. In the end, Mama would be cross with her, and she didn't want her last memories of home to be unpleasant.

It wasn't that Mama was always shouting, but those angry moments lingered in Rae's memory the longest, like shadows that never fully disappeared. These days, Mama was often lost in her books, busy with her studies. And Jack, well, he needed all the attention, didn't he? Rae had come to accept that Joe was the favourite – she'd always know that. So that left her to fend for herself. Ever since Pop had confided in her about the strained relationship between Mama and Gran, Rae couldn't lose the idea that maybe she reminded Mama too much of her own childhood. Perhaps Rae's presence stirred up those old, unpleasant memories, making Mama withdraw, though Rae wished she could understand why.

She tried to be patient, really, she did. If Mama had hated how critical Gran had been when she was a girl, why couldn't she see how much Rae hated it too? Why did Mama, who wasn't unkind, repeat the same cycle? It didn't make sense. Rae often found herself thinking over Mama's words, hearing them replay in her head: "You don't think. You don't try." But Rae *did* think. She *did* try. Yet, somehow, nothing ever felt like enough.

Maybe it was easier to believe Mama's harsh words than to face the confusion of trying to understand. If only she could get inside Mama's head – see what she saw when she looked at her. But Rae would never dare ask. Asking would mean revealing just how much it hurt, and that wasn't something Rae was ready to do.

Unwelcome hints of autumn reminded Rae of how fast time was passing. Shortly after the nanny arrived, she'd be on her way back to school – the summer holidays would be over.

It felt as if her life would be over.

The next morning, she still hadn't made up her mind whether she'd go sailing with Joe. She decided to wait and see how she felt. But when she went into the kitchen for breakfast, Mrs Bolton, who was frying bacon, looked up warily. "Oh, it's you, lovey," she said with relief. "I thought it were your Mam. What with Joe throwin' up all night and young Jack playing up, she's a bit steamed up this morning. She hasn't had much sleep. If I were you, I'd keep out o' her way."

Rae took a glass of water up to her brother's room when she went to see how he was. A white-faced Joe lay in bed, looking sorry for himself. "Are you going to the harbour today?" he asked her.

"I don't suppose so. I can't sail on my own. You know Papa's rules."

"Jamie'd go with you."

"I don't like Jamie. Why would I want to spend the day with him?"

"Oh, Rae, don't be such a clot. There's nothing wrong with him. He's a lot of fun. And he'll be waiting for us. I've asked Mama to phone and tell his father I'm not well and she said she'd do it later when she had time, but I know she'll forget. And I don't want to remind her. She'll only shout at me. Please? Jamie'll be waiting. If you don't want to go, could you telephone his father and let him know?"

Telephone Mr MacKenzie? Most certainly not. Jamie might not have blamed her for his black eye while she was there, but he'd undoubtedly have told his father, eventually. It was puzzling why he hadn't simply told tales about her at the time. She'd certainly deserved it. But who knew with boys like that who appeared to enjoy causing problems for others?

Downstairs, Jack began to wail. That wouldn't help Mama's mood. A crash echoed through the house and Mama shrieked.

Rae sighed. A day at home was going to be difficult. "Oh, all right, I'll ride down to the harbour and tell Jamie. I'll check the *Wild Spirit* as well, but I refuse to go out sailing with that ghastly boy." She tossed her head as if she was doing Joe a big favour.

"Tell him I'll get down there as soon as I'm better," Joe said. He groaned, "You'd better go!" His eyes opened wide, and his face flushed as he grabbed the bowl beside his bed.

She rushed out of his room and slammed the door.

As soon as Rae rounded the bend, she saw Jamie waiting outside the boat builders.

Thank goodness for that. A promise was a promise, but even for Joe, she didn't intend to go into the yard and risk bumping into Mr MacKenzie.

Now, she'd be able to deliver the message and be on her way. Although, where that would be, she didn't know.

First things first, she'd check over *Wild Spirit*, and then…?

The beach?

Perhaps – although she'd never been on her own before.

A wave of loneliness washed over her. She could return home and try to keep out of Mama's way, but sooner or later, she'd do something wrong or be dragged into preparing the new nanny's bedroom. And at the thought of Mademoiselle Jacquet arriving, her heart sank further.

There'd be no sailing until Joe was better and, anyway, in a few days, she'd be packed off to school.

A lump formed in her throat. She didn't belong anywhere.

It was a strange feeling. She lived in a large house with her family. She was about to be sent to school, where she'd be forced to stay. But although she had places to be and people around her, she didn't feel as though anyone truly wanted her there.

"You're looking a bit cross," Jamie said as she stopped her bicycle. "Has Joe upset you?" He looked over her shoulder towards the bend. "Where is he?"

Rae gave him her brother's message about coming when he was better.

"Och, that's a shame." Jamie frowned.

She stared at him. He sounded so different, and she realised his Scottish accent, which had been barely noticeable before, was now stronger. It was… what? She couldn't think of a word to describe it, but the sound was unexpectedly pleasing. So pleasing, she wanted to hear him say something else. She blushed.

"So, where are you off to now?" he asked.

"The beach," she said decisively. She wouldn't let him know she didn't have anywhere to go.

"On your own?" He raised his eyebrows in surprise.

"Yes," she said, as if she went to the beach on her own all the time.

He stared at his feet. "D'you mind if I come?"

She hadn't expected that. Words tripped over themselves in her throat. Go to the beach with Jamie MacKenzie? He was the last person she wanted to spend time with.

"Only I've got a wee something for you," he added. "I brought it home from Scotland." He patted his pocket. "Dinnae move. I'll fetch my bike. I'll be back in a jiffy."

Before she could reply, he'd rushed into the boatyard.

Rae was tempted to ride off. If she was quick, she could be around the bend and out of sight before he returned. But that wouldn't be a very kind thing to do. Would that be something her grandmother might have done when she was young? Probably. Well, it wasn't going to be something Rae would do. And anyway, when she looked into his face, she remembered how badly she'd behaved towards him. A bloodied nose and a black eye. Why had he appeared so pleased to see her? Something in his gaze had made her feel wanted.

And anyway, Jamie appeared to be different – more grown up than he had the last time she'd seen him. He'd spoken to her in that gentle accent as if he wanted to be friends. And she needed a friend.

There was also the question of the thing he had in his pocket for her. It was probably a half-chewed toffee or a dried-up frog or something gruesome like that, but she was now curious about what it could be. And anyway, she didn't want to go to the beach alone.

Jamie cycled out of the boatyard followed by Mr MacKenzie, who told his son to be careful, then took his cap off and scratched his head as he watched them both ride off.

"Have you ever been to Cranston's Point?" Jamie called over his shoulder at Rae.

"No," she yelled back.

"Okay, follow me."

Chapter Eight

♥

They propped their bicycles against the ancient stones of the ruined watchtower.

"Is this Cranston's Point? It's very small," she said doubtfully, looking at the sandy strip at the edge of the water. It was hardly a beach at all.

He followed her gaze and frowned, as if seeing it through fresh eyes. "I haven't been for a while. Alex and I always used to come here when we were younger." His voice was apologetic.

"Who's Alex?"

"My elder brother. Haven't you seen him in Dad's yard?"

She blushed, remembering those two occasions she'd been in the boatyard – the first time when she'd punched Jamie and the second after she'd caused his black eye. On her trips with Joe and Papa, she'd remained outside as much as she could, but she certainly hadn't paid any attention to the men who worked there.

Jamie didn't appear to notice and carried on. "Alex and I are the 'sons' in MacKenzie & Sons. When I leave school, I'll work alongside Alex and Dad." He looked down and prodded a pebble with the toe of his sandal.

"Isn't that what you want?" she asked. His dad wanted his sons to work with him. That sounded exciting to Rae. At least Jamie knew he was wanted.

"Aye..." he sounded doubtful. "It's good to know I've got a place in a business once I've left school... But..."

"But what?"

"Well, I enjoy helping Dad in the yard, and I like the idea of building and mending boats, but what I'd really love to do is to sail them. I'd go to other countries. Perhaps even around the world." His face lit up with enthusiasm.

"Around the world? Oh, how wonderful that would be." The thought of doing something so exciting drove the breath from her chest. Why had it never occurred to her to do anything as adventurous? She gasped, allowing his idea to take shape in her mind. Images from pirate and adventure books filled her head. Desert islands filled with treasure. People who lived in grass huts and whose children didn't have to go to school. Travelling on dog sledges, donkeys, camels, elephants... How simply marvellous to sail away and see so many wonders. To go where she wanted. Do as she wanted. Be who she wanted.

He smiled at her hesitantly, as if pleased she thought his idea was so exciting.

"Alex and I used to fight over who got the 'throne'," he said, indicating a large, smooth rock. "He usually won. But that meant he couldn't paddle because once he'd gone down to the water, I ran up and took the throne. Pointless, really..." he exhaled slowly and shook his head. "There was enough room for us both..."

He sat to one side of the rock, making way for her, and she perched next to him. There might have been room for the bottoms of two small boys, but now Rae's arm was pressed against Jamie's. He half-twisted, turning his shoulder so his arm was behind her. For a second, she held her breath, wondering if he was going to put it around her, but he didn't. Instead, he put his hand on the rock behind him and leaned his weight against it. Half-turned towards her, she could feel his breath on her cheek and although she stared ahead, she knew he was looking at her.

"One day, I'll travel around the world," he said wistfully.

Each word whispered against her neck and cheek, making them tingle. Why did her face always redden and give away her feelings? She squeezed her nails into her palms. Why wouldn't her body do as she wanted?

"I'm going to visit all the dangerous places," he said.

Forgetting her embarrassment, she twisted towards him, her nose inches from his. "Dangerous? Like where?"

He smiled mischievously. "Forests full of cannibals, bubbling volcanoes..." Shifting his weight slightly, he added, "Earthquakes." And pretending to fall sideways against her, he looped his arm through hers as she teetered on the edge of the rock. He held her arm fast and they both burst into laughter.

If Joe had nudged her like that, she'd have been cross and pulled away. But with Jamie's arm through hers, she felt safe. Included. His silliness hadn't been at her expense, but to amuse her, to entertain her. To make her feel as if, for once, she mattered.

"Earthquake!" she said and nudged him slightly.

He pretended to teeter, still holding her arm, an exaggerated expression of shock on his face, but she dragged him towards her, pulling him close. And for some reason, that was even funnier.

On the journey to Cranston's Point, Rae had wondered if she wouldn't have been better off going to a beach on her own, even if it meant not talking to anyone all day. After all, what was there to say to a boy she barely knew? And one she didn't even like. But to her surprise, they chatted and laughed easily – much like Jamie and

Joe had done when they'd cut her out of the conversation. Or, she wondered, perhaps they hadn't ignored her. Perhaps they'd simply been enjoying each other's company and hadn't noticed she'd been sulking. Had her bad temper meant she'd missed out? Had that been a bit of Gran inside her?

"I'm trying to learn French out of a book," Jamie said, as they paddled in the water. "So, when I travel, I can talk to people – well, anyone who speaks French, anyway. But it's very hard. And so far, I've learned words I don't think I'm ever going to need. I mean, how often do pirates or explorers stop someone and ask if they have a pen? Or what's the colour of their cat?"

After they'd stopped laughing, she asked, "Don't you learn French at school?"

He shook his head. "I don't go to a private school like you and Joe. We just do the ordinary subjects at my school. We don't do anything special like French."

"Oh." It hadn't occurred to her before that learning a foreign language was something special. Something people might *want* to do. But now it was so obvious. How stupid it would be to travel to other parts of the world but not understand anyone.

"We've got a French woman coming to live with us this weekend." She told him about the new nanny. And then to her surprise, she found herself suggesting he come over to their house to talk to her.

"That'd be nice," he said. "Sometimes there are French people who visit the harbour, and I listen in, but they talk too fast, and I can't understand anything. I bought a French book from the second-hand shop, but I don't know how to pronounce anything. You know, the way French people blether. Like they're singing."

"Oh, you just need to speak like *thees*." She spoke with an exaggerated French accent and a theatrical shrug, making him laugh.

"You know, you sound different since I last saw you," she said, pushing her heel into the sand and watching the wave fill in the hole.

"Aye, every time I go back to Scotland, my accent gets stronger. But as soon as I start school again, it'll wear off and go back to normal."

Before she could stop herself, she said, "That's a shame. I like it." She blushed scarlet and pretended to watch a beetle crawl over the sand.

He said nothing. Perhaps trying to decide whether she was laughing at him, but her blushes must have told him otherwise because when she finally looked at him, he'd reddened too.

Why had she said that?

Stupid, stupid.

They'd been getting on so well, and now she'd ruined it.

They walked back to the rock, sand sticking to their wet feet, and sat down in silence as they watched the wavelets roll onto the sand.

"Oh," he said. "I nearly forgot. I brought this back from Scotland for you." He pulled a small packet out of his pocket. "It's not much… but it made me think of you."

As she untied the string and opened the brown parcel paper, she hoped it wasn't a joke.

Please don't let it be something disgusting.

But why would he have bought her anything nice? The first time she'd met him, she'd punched him and the last time she'd seen him, she'd given him a black eye. She didn't deserve anything nice. It would probably be something like a spider wrapped in the white cotton material she could see inside the packet. Or something stupid, like a stone.

She held it out so that whatever dreadful thing was inside wouldn't fall in her lap, and she flapped the material open. But the fabric contained nothing – it *was* the gift. A handkerchief. In the corner was a small, embroidered thistle with two spiky leaves entwined to form a curlicue beneath.

She stared at it, still holding the corner nervously between finger and thumb, not able to believe there wasn't a nasty surprise involved.

"You dinnae like it." His face twisted with disappointment.

"Oh, I do! I do! I was just surprised, that's all."

His face lit up. "I chose it myself. It reminded me of you."

"Me?" He'd thought of her while he was away? She could imagine he might have remembered her with anger, but not with any fondness. Certainly not enough to have bought her a present.

"Aye, it was the thistle in the corner," he said. "It's just like you. All soft and fluffy underneath but outside, as prickly as... well, a thistle."

He laughed and, leaping off the rock, pretended to duck imaginary blows from her. Despite her disappointment he'd called her prickly, she couldn't help laughing too. Since he'd twice been on the receiving end of her temper, she thought, he had a point. This gift was much more than she deserved.

When Rae went to bed that night, she lay awake for some time, going over the surprising day. What had started as a disaster had actually been very... well... nice. Much nicer than she'd expected.

Although she didn't wish Joe ill, she realised with a stab of guilt, she didn't want him to go sailing tomorrow. She wanted to go back to the tiny beach at Cranston's Point with Jamie and sit on the rock, talking about sailing around the world. She wanted to swim with him and lay on the sand, drying herself with him. She wanted to watch the long lashes flutter as he pretended to sleep. She wanted to run away from him as he leapt up and chased her into the water where he swam after her, splashing wildly, pretending he couldn't catch her. She hadn't laughed so much for... well, forever.

In her bedside drawer, she'd put the handkerchief he'd given her and the empty snail shell he'd found. At first, she'd wanted to drop it and stamp on it in disgust, but he'd said it was a good omen to find such a shell.

"Snails carry everything they need on their backs and then they travel wherever they like. That'll be us one day," he'd said.

Us, she thought, pleasure rippling through her.

Jamie had said, "Us".

The next morning, Joe had recovered from his stomach bug and was already on his bicycle, keen to escape the confines of the house, before Rae had even grabbed a slice of toast.

Jamie was waiting outside the boatyard when they arrived, and was pleased to see Joe after so long and excited to share stories about his holiday in Scotland. Rae's excitement at seeing Jamie again faded, and as both boys ignored her, the cold, hard knot of disappointment in her stomach grew heavier.

They sailed in the *Wild Spirit,* and the day passed uneventfully for Rae. The boys laughed and joked, taking very little notice of her.

The togetherness she and Jamie had shared the previous day had vanished, and she began to wonder if she'd imagined it. But no. How could that be? Jamie had given her a handkerchief. A snail shell. And he'd talked about *us.*

But today, he was like a different person.

As the boys were saying their final goodbyes until the next school holidays, Joe suddenly realised he'd dropped his pullover and cycled back along the road to fetch it.

Jamie watched him ride away, then grabbed Rae's hand. "I'm sorry I ignored you. I thought Joe might tease you if he found out how much I..." He looked up in Joe's direction, his cheeks flaming. "Will you write to me?" His voice was low and urgent. "Please."

"Y...yes," she said uncertainly. Was he joking?

Seconds later, Joe screeched to a halt next to them. Jamie had already let go of her hand and moved away from her.

As Rae and Joe cycled away from the harbour, she looked over her shoulder at the shrinking figure of Jamie, the boy she'd initially loathed.

And now? She wasn't sure. He made her heart beat faster. But what did that mean?

What did it matter, anyway? She wouldn't see him for ages. Although Mama had suggested she board during the week and return at weekends, Rae had decided to remain at school until the Christmas holidays. Home wouldn't feel like home with a nanny there. Mama would be in London attending lectures or in Papa's study, needing silence while she pored over her books. No, best she stay at school.

One day, she told herself, I'll find a place where I belong and where I know I'm wanted, if I have to travel the world to find it. And perhaps she might even meet up with Jamie...

ns Bolton had once worked in service in a grand house when she'd been young, and she'd told Rae about how the staff had lined up to greet their employer and his wife when he returned to his country estate.

On the day the nanny arrived, it felt as though Rae was taking part in a similar welcome party, except everything was reversed. Mama and Papa were the employers who were acting like the servants.

"Well, don't just stand there staring, Joe, help your father carry the luggage," Mama said when Mademoiselle Jacquet arrived. Papa had driven the new nanny from the railway station and was now struggling with her trunk and cases.

Mademoiselle Jacquet carried nothing more than a tiny handbag as she glided gracefully towards the front door where Mama, Rae, Jack and Joe were waiting.

"Welcome, Mademoiselle Jacquet," said Mama, stepping forward.

"I would be most grateful if you would call me Thérèse, please, Madame Kingsley."

Thérèse? Rae held her breath, waiting for Mama to put her in her place and tell her she would be called Mademoiselle Jacquet or Nanny. However, Rae was amazed when Mama agreed her first name would be easier for Jack to pronounce. Usually, no one told Mama what to do, but she was treating the new nanny like an important guest, not an employee.

Rae had no idea what Mrs Bolton's first name was, and she'd been working for the family since before Joe was born. In fact, it had never occurred to Rae that Mrs Bolton might *have* a first name. But before she'd even set one of her elegant feet in the house, the new nanny had told Mama what she wanted to be called.

What was happening to her family? Papa and Joe were fussing over the nanny's cases like railway porters, making sure none of the matching luggage was scuffed or scraped.

Perhaps things were done differently in France? People certainly dressed with more style if Thérèse was anything to go by.

She wore a cream cape with dark blue piping that matched her dress, high-heeled shoes and gloves. Her fashionably short hairstyle was half-hidden by a cream and blue beret, set at a jaunty angle, below which peeped a kiss curl on her forehead. Each part of her outfit was simple – plain, almost – but when put together, even Rae could see Thérèse looked beautiful.

But it wasn't just the clothes. The young French woman had something extra. Exactly what it was, Rae didn't know. Perhaps it was the way she carried herself? There was nothing rigid or stiff about Thérèse – she didn't look like a soldier on parade, which is how Rae felt when she did as Mama told her and stopped slouching and stood up straight.

Whatever Thérèse was doing appeared to be effortless and the only person apart from Rae, who wasn't delighted at her arrival, was Mrs Bolton.

"So, my cooking isn't good enough for Miss La-di-Da!" she said to Rae, who'd helped her carry the plates into the kitchen after dinner that evening. She stood with hands on hips, glaring at the food Thérèse had left. "If she thinks I'm going to start cooking all that foreign muck, she's got another think coming."

There was only one good thing about Thérèse's arrival, thought Rae the following morning – it made going to school and leaving home much easier. There were going to be a lot of adjustments and Rae suspected there would be many arguments, too.

"That bacon's not burned, it's just crispy," Mrs Bolton shouted when Mama took Thérèse's breakfast plate back into the kitchen with the nanny's comment and a request for something else.

"Please be reasonable, Mrs Bolton, Thérèse is used to different food. She's just settling in. Hopefully, it won't take long."

At least Rae would be spared any more of the nanny's 'settling in'.

On the first day of the new term, Papa had the day off so he and Mama could drive Joe and Rae to their respective schools. Breakfast that morning was to be the last meal the family would share until the school holidays.

Rae looked around the table. Papa was distracted, and she thought he was probably thinking about the patients he ought to have been treating that day. Mama and Joe watched Thérèse. Rae guessed her mother was hoping she'd be able to get back to her books later. She suspected Joe wasn't thinking about his books at all as he stared open-mouthed at Thérèse.

Jack pushed away the toast his new nanny was feeding him. "No cwusts," he said crossly.

And Thérèse glanced around the table from time to time. Rae wondered if she was weighing up the family with whom she was now living and comparing them to the people she'd left behind in Paris. Rae suspected the Kingsleys would be found wanting.

Everyone around the table was lost in his or her own thoughts. With Rae's departure to school imminent, she felt like a small boat that had slipped its moorings and was slowly drifting unnoticed out of the harbour with the tide, away from everything she'd ever known.

Papa took Mama's hand as they walked away from Rae amongst the crowds of parents. Was he comforting her? Rae gritted her teeth, a stab of white-hot resentment searing her heart. Why would Mama need comforting? It was their daughter who'd been abandoned. But she suspected they were probably discussing some medical matter that had nothing to do with her.

Rae turned away. It wasn't because she didn't want them to see her cry. In fact, her eyes were dry. Crying wouldn't change their minds. She'd tried that on the journey to school, believing that even at the last minute, they'd give in, and she wouldn't have to board.

No, she hadn't turned away to hide her sadness from them. Quite the opposite. It was to protect herself in case they didn't look back. At least she wouldn't know.

She counted slowly to ten, then swung around, still unable to believe this was happening, but her parents had gone. She lowered her head to hide her quivering chin and brimming eyes.

"Hannah-Rae Kingsley? Ah, there you are…" It was Miss Frost, the headmistress.

Rae blinked back her tears and clamped her jaws together to stop her chin from wobbling. If Miss Frost noticed, she didn't remark on it.

"I have a special favour to ask you, Hannah-Rae," she said. "We have a new girl starting at St Helena's this term and as she'll be boarding, the same as you, I wondered if you'd keep an eye on her. She's been travelling the world with her parents and has just returned from Hong Kong, so she's going to need a friend to help her adjust to life at school. The two of you have been allocated one of the senior rooms rather than sleeping in the junior dormitory, so she can get used to things. Now, how do you feel about that?" Miss Frost smiled.

How did she feel about that? Happier than Miss Frost could imagine. She'd been dreading the thought of sleeping in a room with so many girls who'd never been friendly to her, but now she'd share a room with one other person.

"Oh, thank you, Miss Frost."

"Excellent. Well, I'm sure I don't need to remind you, Hannah-Rae, that having one of the senior girls' rooms is a privilege and at the first sign of either you or the new girl abusing my trust, you will be found beds in the usual dormitory. Do I make myself clear?"

"Yes, Miss Frost."

"The girl's name is Roberta Taylor-Gale. As soon as she arrives, I'll introduce you."

"Yes, Miss Frost."

With a nod of her head, the headmistress strode away to speak to the parents of a girl who was sobbing and holding on to her mother's skirt with a determined grip. At least Rae hadn't let herself down like that girl. She would put up with it all. The only possible problem would be if she and the new girl didn't get on. That would be disastrous.

However, Roberta, or Bobby, as she insisted on being called, turned out to be the ideal roommate. She knew how to have fun without drawing attention to herself and could charm her way out of any situation, carrying Rae with her.

Although Bobby was in Rae's form, she was a year older, having missed so much schooling while she'd been travelling the world. She'd been kept back a year, but to Rae's surprise, she wasn't bothered in the slightest.

"When I've had enough of school, I'll simply leave," she said, with a toss of her auburn hair.

Rae wasn't convinced, although as the term progressed and she saw how easily Bobby got her way, she wondered if she might be right.

"When you've travelled to as many places as I have, you become worldly-wise," Bobby told her.

Rae had never heard of the term 'worldly-wise', but it was obvious what it meant. And after hearing Bobby's stories, she was more determined than ever to leave England and travel the world as soon as she could.

She'd written to Jamie to tell him about Bobby and some of the exotic places she'd visited. We must go to Hong Kong, Bobby says it's marvellous, Rae told him. After checking the post each morning for a month, Rae gave up looking for a reply from Jamie. During the first fortnight, she'd written four long, newsy letters to him.

If he couldn't bother to reply, she wouldn't write again. Stupid boy.

If she didn't write, she wouldn't expect a reply, and then she would no longer need to check the post each morning. At least each day would no longer start with crushing disappointment.

Chapter Ten

♥

The final fortnight of the autumn term passed in an excited frenzy with teachers attempting to control the girls' high spirits as Christmas approached. Rae threw herself into the festivities and deliberately avoided thinking about returning home. Joe was going to stay with his friend Geoffrey for a few days, so when she got home, things would be rather flat.

Mama didn't write often, but in one of her letters, she'd said she was going to sit an exam. Rae could imagine life at home had been impossible while Mama had been studying. And, of course, Papa would have been busy at the hospital. People didn't stop being sick just because Christmas was coming.

Bobby had invited Rae to stay at her parents' house in London for a few days, but the week before the end of term, Bobby's father had been called to South Africa and her mother and Bobby were going to stay with relatives in Cornwall.

"You'll be back at school in January, though, won't you?" Rae asked anxiously.

"I'll be here if I have to walk all the way from Truro, darling."

With her bubbly personality, Bobby had become so popular since she'd started at St Helena's, she'd soon earned the nickname *Bubbles*.

And since she and Rae had been inseparable all term, Rae had become popular too.

She was disappointed to learn Bobby's mother intended to pick her daughter up two days before the end of term. But, despite missing her friend, Rae was kept fully occupied. There was plenty going on to distract her and stop her from thinking of home.

Papa wrote to tell her he couldn't get away from work, so Pop would collect her on the last day of term. Rae had learned to hate the morning's post. It only ever brought unwelcome news or no news at all. Not that she didn't want to see Pop, but... But what? She could hardly expect Papa to allow patients to die just because she was coming home from school. But everyone had a place, like chess pieces on a board, except Rae. She was a pawn and could be placed anywhere or even sacrificed for the good of the game, without anyone noticing.

After a flurry of farewells and promises to write to her new friends during the holidays, Pop took her into Chichester for lunch. She was pleased to see him, but it was as though a piece of ice lay in her stomach – cold and hard. If only one of her parents had come.

She tried to hide her disappointment from Pop, but she could see from his pained expression he knew how hurt she was.

"Papa would have come himself, darling, but there's been an outbreak of diphtheria, and he's really busy at the hospital. And Mama's got a sore throat, or she'd have come to pick you up. We're hoping she's not going down with anything nasty. But at least she sat her exam a few days ago, and she thought it went well."

"How's Jack?" Rae asked, waves of homesickness now washing over her.

"The last time I saw him, he was elbow deep in flour in the kitchen, making pastry for mince pies."

"Mrs Bolton's allowed Thérèse into her kitchen?" Rae asked in amazement. So, the elegant French woman had even wormed her way into Mrs Bolton's good books, thought Rae with disappointment.

"No, darling, Thérèse isn't there. She's gone home to Paris for Christmas. Mrs Bolton's looking after Jack while your mama's not well. You know how she dotes on him."

"Really?" Suddenly, Rae longed to be home. The prospect of Christmas wasn't so gloomy after all.

Mrs Bolton greeted Rae the following morning when she went into the kitchen.

"Yer mam's not feeling too good. That sore throat's got worse, and she wants you and the little man out of the house so neither of you catches it. Why don't you poke your head around her bedroom door and say 'hello'? I know she'll be pleased you're home. But she said you can go down to the harbour today if you want – so long as you don't get into mischief – or you can come with us to feed the ducks." She patted Jack on the head.

Rae decided she was much too old for a trip to the village pond to watch Mrs Bolton and Jack throw bread at ducks. Perhaps she'd go and see *Wild Spirit*. After dressing warmly, she cycled carefully through the lanes, avoiding the ice that had appeared overnight. Idly, she wondered if Jamie would be waiting outside the boatyard.

Of course, he won't, she told herself. How would he know she was coming? Indeed, how would he know she was home from school? She hadn't heard from him all term and she wondered whether she dared to peer through the gates of the boatyard to see if she could catch his eye.

No, she decided, she didn't dare. The only person's eye she was like ly to catch was Mr MacKenzie's, and she didn't want to face him. Even if it would have been satisfying to tell Jamie off for wasting her time. What had he been thinking, asking her to write and then completely ignoring her? What a nerve. The disappointment of those early weeks when she'd waited eagerly for a letter from him still weighed heavily. If only he hadn't asked her to write.

She wondered if he'd written to Joe. If so, he might know when her holiday started. That was unlikely, though. If Jamie and Joe had written to each other, they probably hadn't mentioned her.

She stopped outside the harbour café and looked at her reflection in the window. Removing her hat, she pulled her hair into some sort of order with her fingertips. It was a shame her cheeks and nose were bright red after her ride through the chilly lanes, but there was nothing she could do about them. Anyway, what did it matter? No one would notice.

She cycled slowly towards the corner. If Jamie was waiting outside the yard, she decided she'd pass by as if she'd forgotten him. If he spoke, she'd pretend to wonder who he was and then, perhaps, she'd make a show of remembering. Rae wished she'd rehearsed the whole sequence at home in the mirror because she wasn't confident she'd look believable. Perhaps she'd simply cycle past him and not stop.

Yes, that was best.

Anyway, he'd probably gone to Scotland for Christmas. A hollow feeling crept through her, leaving her cold and empty.

As the boatyard came into view, she saw someone leaning against the wall, with one leg bent and his foot pressed against the bricks.

Her heart soared.

Was it Jamie? Surely not. This boy was taller than Jamie had been in September.

When he saw her, he sprang forward and ran towards her – a joyful smile on his face. He was taller and thinner. More grown up than he had been the last time she'd seen him.

"I wasn't sure you were coming," Jamie said, still grinning.

The breath caught in her throat.

He was pleased to see her.

"Where's Joe?" He peered around her towards the corner.

Joe? He wanted to see Joe? So, he hadn't been pleased to see her after all.

It felt as though the breath had been squeezed out of her. "He's gone to stay with a friend." If only she'd cycled past him as she'd planned.

"I've been keeping an eye on the *Wild Spirit* for you," he said, still smiling. "D'you want to go and see her?"

He appeared to be unaware of her annoyance. Well, she'd show him.

"No thank you, I don't. Not with you, anyway. I'll go on my own."

His smile faded, and he looked so hurt, she regretted her words. Why hadn't she thought before she'd spoken?

Out of the corner of her eye, she saw Mr MacKenzie at the gate. He took the pipe out of his mouth and said, "Mornin' lass. I thought I heard voices. I wondered if it were you."

Her cheeks flared red. "Good morning, Mr MacKenzie."

He continued to stare at her, his message clear. *Leave my son alone.*

"Well, I'd better be off." Rae pedalled away as fast as she could.

By the time she'd reached *Wild Spirit*, Jamie had picked up his bicycle and had caught up with her.

"I don't understand, Rae..." he gasped, trying to catch his breath. "Why're you so cross with me? I thought we were... friends."

"Cross? I'm not cross... no, I'm *furious*," she said, using one of Bobby's favourite words. "You asked me to write to you. And I did. Four long letters and you didn't bother to reply." What was it about this boy that made her feelings explode inside?

"Ah." His brows drew together over sad eyes, and he swallowed.

"*Ah?* Is that all you've got to say?" Her voice rose in outrage.

"Come with me to Cranston's Point, and I'll explain," he said without meeting her eye. "Please, Rae."

The rock was still in shade when they arrived at the beach and propped their bicycles against the ruins.

"So?" she demanded, still out of breath after their dash through the lanes.

On the journey there, she'd wondered why she'd done as he'd asked. She should have simply ridden home. But she wanted to hear his explanation. Even if only to shout at him again.

No, be honest, Rae. You simply want to spend time with him. And it's not his fault you were so disappointed when he didn't write. He has to help his dad in the boatyard...

He looked down and dug the toe of his boot into the wet sand. "Well, I did try to write you a letter," he began. "I started lots of them. In the end, Dad told me off for wasting good writing paper. But... well, I just couldn't think of anything to say. You told me about all sorts of things at your school, but there was nothing to tell you. I went to school. I helped Alex and Dad and then I did it all over again the next day. My school's not a fancy place like yours."

"Oh," she said in a small voice. He looked so sorry; it was hard to be angry. "But I didn't even know you'd got my letters. You could've just written and told me not much was going on."

He hung his head. "Well... there's another reason..." He crouched and picked up a flat pebble. After inspecting it, he skimmed it across the water, shielding his eyes with one hand, watching it bounce.

"Yes?"

"It's just that I'm left-handed."

"So?"

"Well, my writing's awful and I smudge a lot of it. I didn't want your friends at school to laugh. I couldn't even address the envelope properly. I asked Alex to do it, but he told me to get lost and do it myself."

With his head still lowered, she couldn't see his face, but she could hear the embarrassment in his voice.

"Oh. I wish I'd known," she said finally. "Only it felt like you'd forgotten..." She wanted to say, 'It sounded like you'd forgotten *me.*' But that was too... too what? Too conceited. As if she'd expected him to think of her. Too demanding. As if she had some right to be remembered. In the end, she finished, "...like you'd forgotten you asked me to write." Almost in a whisper, she added. "Like you didn't care."

He fished in his pocket, withdrew four dog-eared, folded sheets of paper and opened one out. It had almost torn in two. They were the letters she'd sent him.

"I do care." He pressed his lips tightly together.

"You've still got them?" she asked, incredulous he was carrying them in his pocket.

"Of course."

"But why?"

He bent to pick up another stone, then crouching low, he skimmed it across the water. "I just have."

He looked up at her, his eyes questioning, pleading to be forgiven. She smiled at him. How could she be angry after his explanation?

"Am I forgiven?" He pulled a silly face.

She pretended to consider and then nodded grudgingly.

He grinned and leapt up. "So, tell me about Hong Kong. Your friend, Bobby, sounds so lucky."

Before long, they were chatting as easily as they had in August. Jamie's Scottish accent had almost disappeared, as he'd said it would. When she remarked on it, he assumed a very strong accent and made her laugh. They planned to go to all the places Bobby had told Rae about and some more that Jamie had seen in his atlas.

As the sun dipped towards the west, Jamie reluctantly said they'd have to go.

"It'll be dark soon."

Rae nodded, disappointed at the shortness of the day.

"Will you come tomorrow?" he asked. His words were casual, but his eyes pleading.

"I'll try."

"Will Joe come?"

"No, he's staying with his friend for a few days."

Jamie smiled a slow smile, and, for some reason, her heart skipped a beat. *He was pleased she'd be on her own.*

The next day when Rae arrived at the boatyard, Jamie was waiting outside, already mounted on his bicycle and he rode off, leading the way to their beach.

"I can't stay long," Rae said when they dismounted at the ruined tower. "Mama told me off for getting back after dark yesterday. She made me promise to be earlier home today."

"I can't stay long either," said Jamie. "Dad wants me to help him with something after lunch. But we've got a few hours together."

Rae looked up at the heavy grey clouds that promised snow. "I'm not even sure we've got a few hours."

"Well, I'd better give you this now, then," he said, taking a box out of the bag he'd slung over his handlebars, "Dad, Alex and I are off to Scotland for Christmas and Hogmanay. As soon as we get back, I start school."

"Oh." The day had looked so promising. Now her mood matched the steely clouds that were rolling towards them.

He looked down as he held a small box out to her, unable to meet her gaze.

"What is it?"

"Open it and see."

Rae raised the lid and saw a tiny boat inside. She lifted it out, and placing it on her palm, she inspected the tiny model.

"It's the *Wild Spirit*." She gasped with pleasure.

"It's for Christmas. D'you like it?" he asked shyly, still not able to look her in the face.

"I love it. Did you make it?"

He nodded, blushing.

And then, without thinking, she threw her arms around his neck and kissed him on the cheek.

Jamie grunted in surprise and Rae leapt back, horrified at her impulsiveness. "I'm so sorry." Her hands flew to cover her burning cheeks. "I wasn't thinking."

Stupid, stupid.

What must he think of her? And then another embarrassing thought occurred to her – she hadn't brought him anything for Christmas.

She groaned.

"What's the matter, Rae?"

"I haven't got anything to give you." She sighed. If only she'd known, she'd have brought him something.

Jamie held his fingers to the place on his cheek where she'd kissed him. "You've given me something special I'll remember all over Christmas," he said, and his face lit up with pleasure.

Chapter Eleven

♥

For once, life in the Kingsley household passed by without a cross word and Rae enjoyed Christmas far more than she'd expected. As the start of the new term approached, she was surprised to realise she wasn't filled with dread at the thought of going back to school because it meant she'd see Bobby again.

Of course, she wasn't looking forward to resuming lessons, but with Bobby sitting at the desk in front of her, even classes were more enjoyable as the two girls passed notes back and forth. The time was no less dull, but at least it appeared to go by faster. And on the odd occasion when Bobby skipped a lesson, at least the other girls were pleasant to Rae. That was only because they wanted to please Bobby – they weren't really bothered about Rae – but so what? Life with Bubbles was always fun. She had a clever way of bending the rules without actually breaking them.

How lucky Rae was to have found Bobby. Or more accurately, how lucky Rae was that Bobby had found her. No longer drifting aimlessly on a dark sea, now Rae had direction and purpose.

And even better, the days were lengthening. Soon, she'd be home for Easter. At long last, she'd be able to go to the harbour again and sail in the *Wild Spirit*. However, whenever she conjured up pictures in her mind's eye, it wasn't Joe she was sailing with. It was Jamie.

And more often than sailing, she imagined sitting with Jamie on their rock at the edge of the sliver of beach at Cranston's Point.

Rae had hidden Jamie's Christmas present in a cupboard, although she often took it out and marvelled at how detailed the model was with its tiny portholes and intricate decking. If Joe were to see it, he'd only ridicule her and tell Mama and Papa. And then there'd be lots of teasing. No, it was best she kept it to herself. A secret to be savoured. Jamie had made it for her – and not only made it; he'd thought about what she enjoyed most and had seen it was the boat. Then, he'd painstakingly carried out the delicate carving, sailmaking and painting. Just for her. No one had ever put as much thought or care into giving her something.

She often thought about Jamie, trying to imagine what it was like for him in Scotland. Never having visited the country, she had no notion of what it looked like. Other than the postcard with the lone stag in the heather which he'd sent during the summer, she had no mental image at all. So, in her mind's eye, she saw Jamie out on those hills.

He'd promised he'd write to her at school. But wanting to save his embarrassment, she told him she wouldn't mind if he didn't.

That hadn't been true. She knew she'd be dreadfully hurt, but she couldn't bear to think of him worrying about what to say, so she'd resigned herself to writing the occasional letter to him, containing nothing that might make his day appear less interesting than hers. She'd resigned herself to waiting until Easter to see him again and hear what he'd been doing.

However, the first day she'd returned to school, there'd been an envelope with a typed address, a Scottish stamp and postmark waiting for her. She'd hidden it away until she'd been alone, then had torn the envelope open. Inside was a postcard. She read the message:

Wish you were here. J

She turned it over and admired the photograph of green hills reflected in what looked like a large lake. Printed at the bottom, it said *Greetings from Loch Lomond*. On the shore of the loch were two squiggles. Rae screwed up her eyes at the two spirals Jamie had drawn in ink. Closer inspection showed each shape had two small lines at the front of each. Suddenly, she realised they were two snails crawling along with their belongings on their back, one following the other.

She wrote Jamie a long letter, drawing two similar snails at the bottom of the page.

Several days later, she received another envelope with a typewritten address, this time with an English stamp and postmark from Chichester. Inside was a postcard of the harbour, near MacKenzie & Sons, and at the bottom, Jamie had drawn two snails. By the time the Easter holidays arrived, she had a pile of postcards, each with two snails at the bottom.

Chapter Twelve

1937

Rae's fifteenth birthday was a turning point in her life. She was another year older, but she certainly hadn't expected things to change so quickly. Neither had she expected it would be her best friend, Bobby, who inadvertently brought about those changes.

For years, Rae had begged her friend to stay at her house, and finally, Bobby had her parents' permission to go to Barlstead for a few days at the end of the Easter holidays.

"We can sail the *Wild Spirit*, and you can meet my friend Jamie."

"Is he the one who sends you those mysterious postcards?"

Rae nodded. "You'll like him. He's really good company. And they're just postcards. Nothing mysterious about them." She turned to hide her blushes.

"Will Joe be there?" Bobby asked, apparently not noticing Rae's embarrassment. Bobby had met Joe on several occasions and had told Rae she thought he was very handsome. "Just like Errol Flynn, but obviously without the moustache," she said, pretending to swoon like a Hollywood actress.

Bobby had pouted when Rae told her Joe would be staying with a friend, although she cheered up when Rae said he might return early.

And at last, Bobby came to stay with Rae.

They'd been such good friends at school, it hadn't occurred to Rae that things would be different at her house.

The first surprise was Bobby's reaction to the nanny.

Rae had almost got used to Thérèse's presence at home. Jack adored her and Mama was grateful she was there to take over when she was studying, so the household benefited from her presence.

Even cranky Mrs Bolton had mellowed over the years. There was a thinly veiled truce: Mrs Bolton only concerned herself with the care of Jack when the nanny wasn't there, and Thérèse didn't interfere in the kitchen.

When Bobby arrived at the house, Rae had briefly introduced her to Thérèse and expected her friend to follow her lead and ignore the nanny. However, to her surprise, Bobby was fascinated by the young French woman and soon discovered Thérèse's family home was near the house where her Papa stayed when he was working in Paris. They discussed the delights of the city, like old friends.

"She's so fashionable," Bobby said enthusiastically afterwards. "You can't beat the French women for style."

"You can't?" Rae suppressed her irritation. She didn't want to talk about the nanny. Bobby was her friend, and she didn't want to share her with Thérèse.

"Oh, no, definitely not. They have a certain *je ne sais quoi.*"

"What's that?" Rae asked.

"Oh, Rae, you're so funny."

Rae joined in laughing with her friend, although she had no notion what the joke was – 'They have a certain *I don't know what,*' wasn't a sentence that made sense, especially since half of it was in English and the other half in French.

"You're so lucky having Thérèse here. I bet it's simply glorious to go on shopping trips with her. D'you think she knows how we can make our uniforms look more fashionable?"

"I don't suppose so," said Rae, who wasn't very interested in clothes. "It's called a uniform for a reason, you know."

"But it won't hurt to ask, will it? D'you think she's too busy to talk to us now?"

And to Rae's amazement, she discovered Thérèse was actually friendly.

The second surprise was Bobby's opinion of Jamie.

The two girls set off early the following morning to go sailing. She'd written to tell Jamie about their plans, and he was waiting for them by the *Wild Spirit*.

"It's going to blow up this afternoon, so we've only got a couple of hours," he said, helping Bobby aboard.

It soon became clear Bobby was not a natural sailor. She demanded to know where they were going and how long it would take to get there. When she realised they were simply sailing for the fun of it, she couldn't understand why they went back and forth, rather than going in a straight line like the cruise liners she'd been aboard. Jamie tried to explain about tacking, but she'd begun to turn pale and complain she felt sick.

Reluctantly, Jamie and Rae sailed back to the harbour and helped Bobby out of the boat.

"And as for that beam swinging about," she said crossly.

"Boom," Jamie and Rae said together.

Bobby scowled. "Beam, boom. I don't care what you call it. It's not sensible to have something waving about that threatens to take your head off when you least expect it."

The girls cycled home and Rae was relieved that by the time they reached the house, Bobby had recovered.

The following day, Jamie was waiting for them outside the boatyard.

"I wasn't sure you'd come," he said, glancing at Bobby doubtfully. "Are we sailing today?"

Rae shook her head. "No, I thought we could show Bobby Cranston's Point."

He frowned and his eyes opened wide in surprise. "B... but I thought that was our..." He paused and before he could finish, she'd mounted her bicycle and set off, followed by Bobby.

Rae had deliberately avoided looking at Jamie, knowing from the regret in his voice, he'd be disappointed. But what could she do? Surely Jamie could share the place for a short time. Then, the next time they went, it would be theirs again.

It was unlikely Bobby would hurry back to stay with Rae in Barlstead, so she probably wouldn't want to go to Cranston's Point again. The friendship that had been so easy at school had changed since Bobby had come to stay, and for the first time, Rae was aware her friend was older and more experienced. Staying with Rae in her family's home had merely underlined the differences between them, and more than anything, Rae wanted to keep the friendship.

Bobby grimaced every time Jack cried, which was whenever he saw her. "What's wrong with that child? Doesn't he get on your nerves?" she asked, a look of disbelief on her face.

Rae had never thought about it like that before. The household revolved around Jack, and no one had ever criticised him like that. She'd wanted to stick up for her baby brother, but for the first time, she saw how much noise and fuss he made. It wasn't pleasant. So, how could she disagree with Bobby, who was seeing things as they really were and voicing her opinions? Anyway, Rae always agreed with her friend, and she suspected Bobby wouldn't be happy if she didn't.

What would happen if Bobby found another friend? There was no doubt the other girls at school wouldn't want to know Rae any longer. How would she cope with being alone while the other girls gathered around Bubbles, and they all laughed at Rae?

No, she'd had no choice other than to take Bobby to Cranston's Point. Jamie would understand. Rae was simply being a good host, sharing all the good things with her best friend and if Jamie didn't feel the same... well, he didn't own the beach.

Nevertheless, she felt as though she was being torn in two.

"Is this it?" Bobby asked when they arrived at the ruined tower. "Is the tide in or something? There's nothing here."

"It's only small." Rae stared at the sliver of sand, seeing it through more grown-up eyes.

"You can say that again. There's absolutely nothing here." Bobby wrinkled her nose in distaste. "And it smells of seaweed. How about we find a proper beach and get some ice creams?"

Bobby whispered to Rae while they sat on the rock getting their breath back. "Your Jamie's a bit immature, isn't he? I mean, you wouldn't get Errol Flynn skimming stones or Clark Gable chasing a girl with a bit of seaweed."

Rae couldn't disagree with Bobby. There was no comparison between Jamie and a Hollywood star. "Well, he's..." Rae paused, wracking her brain to think of a way of describing Jamie that would impress Bobby. But what was there to say? Best to keep quiet and hope her friend found something she liked. How awkward would it be if they fell out while Bobby was staying with her?

And actually, Bobby had a point. Rae had never noticed it before, but Jamie seemed incredibly young compared to them. Rae had learned so much from Bobby, perhaps it was time to accept she'd outgrown Jamie. He was nothing like the handsome actors who she and Bobby keenly watched at the cinema or whose posters hung on the walls in their shared room at St Helena's. He was just a boy.

Why was life full of difficult choices? If she sided with Jamie, Bobby would be annoyed and then school would be a problem. If she sided with Bobby... Need Jamie know? He appeared to be so involved in skimming stones; he wasn't taking much notice of them.

When Bobby announced she was hungry and simply must have ice cream, Jamie said he'd have to go because he'd forgotten to do something for his father. Rae knew he wasn't telling the truth, but what did it matter? She and Bobby could do as they pleased without him trailing behind them. It was a relief. She obviously couldn't please both of them, so, thankfully, Jamie had saved the situation.

The following day, Mrs Bolton offered to look after Jack, and the girls went shopping in Chichester with Thérèse, which Rae found surprisingly enjoyable.

A doorway had opened into a different world, and she could see things she hadn't noticed before.

I've grown up, she thought. In the depths of her heart, she felt a sharp pang of sadness as if she'd lost something precious. She wondered whether to ask her mother but decided against it. The gnawing feeling was too hard to explain. Should she ask Bobby? No. Rae suspected she'd laugh if she mentioned it to her. Perhaps everyone felt like this when they left childhood behind. There wasn't any choice, anyway. Rae couldn't stop the clock. It was inevitable, and Bobby had made it clear she had no time for babies. This must be how everyone felt...

Chapter Thirteen

How could things have gone so completely wrong? Jamie wondered.

First, he'd lied to Rae. He'd never done that before. But he'd only been able to bear so much of that girl, Bobby, before he'd made his excuses and left Cranston's Point. Rae would have known he hadn't forgotten something he needed to do in the boatyard, but she'd probably have been grateful he'd gone. She'd appeared very uncomfortable.

If he hadn't recognised how confused she was, he'd have been pleased she wasn't happy, fawning over that dreadful girl. But he'd always been able to see how fragile she was, despite her – sometimes – hard exterior. Just like a thistle. If you wanted to get to know Rae, you had to put up with the spikes before you got to the beauty. No, he'd been sad she'd been unhappy, but he hadn't been prepared to be ignored.

Not wanting to go back to the boatyard, he'd doubled back after the girls had left Cranston's Point and sat alone on what had once been their rock – his and Rae's. Now, it was just a slab of stone. He'd watched the wavelets lapping the sand along the tiny strip of beach that had once been his favourite place in the whole world. It had been their secret place – his and Rae's. It was so small, no one bothered to visit it when there were so many other beaches nearby, so every time they'd cycled to it, they'd been alone – well, until today. He'd found it hard to believe that after the girl had sneered at the *Wild Spirit* and sailing in general, Rae had wanted to take her to their private place.

His eyes roved over the entire view – the ruined tower, the pebbly sand and the scrubby grass that edged the strip of beach. He wasn't surprised Bobby had scoffed at Cranston's Point, especially if she was used to long stretches of tropical sand on foreign shores. This was a joke of a beach. He kicked at the sand, sending a cascade of fine grains into the air, to land in the wavelets and sink.

The awful thing was that Rae had appeared to agree with Bobby. That had hurt more than the time she'd punched him. More than the time they'd clashed heads. This had been like a knife twisting in him. He hadn't thought he could feel worse, but then he'd overheard Bobby criticising him for being childish. He hadn't reacted to her comments. Let her think what she liked – he didn't like her either. However, he'd expected Rae to disagree and to stand up for him. She hadn't, and that had felt as though the knife had sliced him in two.

Rae was turning into a different person thanks to her friend.

Bobby had thought he was childish, and Rae obviously agreed with her.

Jamie leapt off the rock and stood tall; shoulders back and head up, as if standing on parade. He might not be old enough to call himself a man, but he was strong – he was nearly as strong as any of the men who worked in his father's yard. But he knew deep down Bobby hadn't been referring to his muscles. Exactly what she had meant, he wasn't sure, but more importantly, he didn't know what to do about it – if indeed, anything could be done.

His shoulders slumped. He might as well go home.

When he arrived back at the boatyard, Jamie found his father in the office. "Am I childish, Dad?" The words tumbled out before he'd had a chance to think.

Mr MacKenzie removed the pipe from his mouth and considered the question for a second. "Is that what the Kingsley lassie said?"

Jamie wished he hadn't asked. Why had his father linked his question with Rae? But having asked it, he pressed on. "No, Rae didn't say it, but her friend did."

Mr MacKenzie nodded and frowned. "I know you like Rae, son, but she's not a suitable friend for you."

"But it was Rae's friend who said it."

"And did the lassie put her friend straight?"

Jamie hung his head. "Well, no…"

"Best forget her, lad. She's too wayward. Too pig-headed. And she's not of our class. Sooner or later, your friendship would've ended. Looks like it's sooner. And I can see you're upset. But believe me, laddie, it's for the best."

Jamie walked out of the office before his dad saw how upset he was. Tears pricked his eyes. Oh, yes, he was childish, all right. He needn't have asked his father; the proof was trickling down his cheeks and drying in the wind as he cycled back to the cottage where he lived with his father and brother. He'd asked Dad a question about himself and had received an answer about Rae being an unsuitable friend. How had that helped him?

But it wasn't surprising. He'd known his father had never liked Rae.

As Jamie's legs pumped up and down as fast as he could pedal, he recalled the day he'd first set eyes on her. He could still remember how wonderful she'd looked in her red coat and hat. Never had he seen anything so beautiful, and he'd stared at her in adoration. He'd even got that wrong because, for some reason, he'd upset her. It'd seemed so unfair – he couldn't believe she hadn't recognised how much he'd admired her. Why hadn't she been able to see? But he'd obviously done something wrong because her response had been to poke her tongue out at him. To his shame, in his embarrassment and confusion, he'd stepped towards her.

Later, he couldn't remember why he'd done that. Perhaps to tell her she'd behaved unfairly. Perhaps to explain he'd meant no harm. He certainly hadn't foreseen she'd back away and fall over. But once she'd got up, she'd been furious... and then she'd punched him.

He'd often asked himself why he was still drawn to her, but when he'd looked into her eyes, he'd seen sadness and confusion. It was something he saw when he looked in the mirror. She was like a hurt animal and, as hard as he'd tried, he hadn't been able to forget her. Later, when he'd got to know her a little, he'd seen he'd been right. Inside, she was lost. Just like him.

But Dad hadn't seen how much she needed a friend. He'd been there when Rae had punched his son and he'd never forgiven her for that.

"They let that Kingsley lassie run wild," he'd say whenever Rae's name came up until Jamie didn't mention her at all unless it was unavoidable. But it wasn't simply that he wanted to be her friend and ease away her pain; since the first time he'd laid eyes on her, the word that came to mind when he thought of Rae was 'splendid'. He wasn't even sure what he meant by that, but he longed to spend time with her to find out, despite Dad's doubts.

He'd tried to work out how he felt about her, but he didn't know how to describe his feelings.

There must be words for how he felt. Someone must be able to explain it to him. If his mother had still been alive, he would've asked her, although he had no idea if she'd have sided with his father and taken a dislike to Rae too. He liked to believe she'd have been fairer and would have given Rae a chance. But she had died many years ago, and although he knew his brother still retained memories of her, Jamie had none.

How had Alex navigated through feelings such as Jamie had for Rae? Or perhaps his brother didn't have complicated thoughts. Maybe this wasn't normal, and there was something wrong with him.

During the next few days, after his disastrous outing with Rae and Bobby, he listened carefully to conversations between the men who worked in his father's boatyard. Two of the younger ones were about to get married and Jamie had eavesdropped, remembering comments he wouldn't have noticed before.

He began to get the picture that girls liked a decisive man – a leader – and one who told them what to do. He wasn't sure Rae would be one of those girls, and he'd wondered if his father had treated his mother like that.

No one would know except his dad, so he waited until they were alone in the office and casually asked, "Did Mum like it if you always told her what to do, Dad?" He was prepared for his father to avoid answering the question because he was always uncomfortable when anyone mentioned Mum. But who else could Jamie ask?

Dad cleared his throat and Jamie thought he was going to send him on an errand, so he didn't have to answer, but to his surprise, his dad said, "No, son. No one always likes to be told what to do by someone else. Who's been filling your head with nonsense?"

"Oh, it's just something I overheard."

"That wouldn't be young Arthur and Pete, would it?"

"Well..."

"I should take whatever those lads say with a wee pinch o' salt."

And that had been that. Dad walked out of the office and back into the yard. And Jamie was still none the wiser.

And then Susannah Turner had started to take an interest in him. She was two years younger and still attended the school where he'd once gone, but she passed the boatyard every day and always waited by the gate so she could wave to him. She was pretty enough, but she didn't compare to Rae in Jamie's opinion.

One day, his father and Alex had gone to Chichester for the afternoon, leaving Jamie to walk home on his own after work. Susannah had been waiting for him and said she was going his way, so she'd walk with him. She took his arm, and he'd been too embarrassed to push her away – it would have been unkind.

And then she'd suggested a shortcut through the woods. There was no shortcut as far as he knew, but she insisted, and again, he didn't want to hurt her feelings, so he followed her.

There had been something forbidden, and therefore exciting, about being with her, although he wasn't sure why. Perhaps it was the way she glanced up at him through her lashes with… With what? It appeared to be admiration.

She led him into the undergrowth and suddenly exclaimed she had something in her eye. While he'd gently steadied her face with his hands and peered into her eye, she stood on tiptoes and kissed him on the lips. He'd been so shocked he'd forgotten to worry about offending her and had turned away. Then, with flaming cheeks, he'd stomped off towards home. Susannah had run after him and, to his amazement, appeared keener on him than ever, plucking at his sleeve and begging him to meet her again.

Perhaps Arthur and Pete were right – girls liked to know who was boss.

He thought about being in the woods with Susannah that evening as he lay in bed. How stupid to have reacted like that. He was flattered that she liked him. But it was as though she'd stolen something from him. He hadn't wanted to kiss her although he'd wondered what a kiss might feel like, but it had always been Rae in his mind when he'd wondered that.

That would never happen now. It probably wouldn't have happened anyway. Bobby had seen to that.

Chapter Fourteen

During term time, Rae and Bobby couldn't wait for their Saturday afternoon trip to town. The cinema wasn't out of bounds, but it wasn't considered a 'proper' place to go by many of the teachers. That disapproval added a hint of defiance that made their outings even more pleasurable and exciting.

On Saturday, shortly after the Easter holidays, they went to see *The Amazing Quest of Ernest Bliss*.

"Oh," Bobby sighed, taking Rae's arm as they came out of the auditorium. "Cary Grant is so divine, isn't he?"

They emerged, blinking, from the dark cinema into the afternoon sunlight, and Rae noticed two boys waiting by the box office.

The taller one walked towards them. "Don't you two go to St Helena's?"

Rae's cheeks flamed. She wasn't used to older boys speaking to her, and she was grateful Bobby chatted to them with ease.

Philip and Andrew went to Bishop's Hall School, which was several miles away from St Helena's. They professed not to know any of the younger pupils and shook their heads dismissively when she nervously asked if they knew Joe.

If anyone saw her and Bobby with the two boys and reported them to the headmistress, they'd be in trouble for unseemly behaviour. Rae's heart raced with exhilaration. It was exciting yet, at the same time, terrifying.

Philip and Andrew offered to accompany Bobby and Rae back to school. They sat on the seat behind the girls on the bus, and Philip leaned forward to whisper in Bobby's ear, making her laugh. Andrew simply stared out of the window.

It's almost as if he's bored, thought Rae. But she was so self-conscious and afraid of saying something silly, it was almost a relief he didn't speak to her.

By the time they arrived at the bus stop near St Helena's, Philip had suggested they meet up that evening and Bobby had agreed.

"Why did you let them think we're going to meet them tonight?" Rae asked incredulously once they were off the bus. It would be impossible, and it was mean of Bobby to make plans with the boys they wouldn't be able to keep.

"Because we *are* going to meet them, silly." Bobby laughed.

"But how're you going to get out of school?"

"How're *we* going to get out, you mean? I'm not sure yet. But there must be a way. Say you'll come with me," Bobby begged.

"I… I don't know." Rae's heart was now beating out a rhythm of danger, not excitement. She was sailing into unknown waters. While she'd thought everything was under her control, she'd enjoyed it. Now, the currents and winds were taking over, dragging her off course.

"You're not going to pass up a chance for a bit of fun, are you?" Bobby's mouth had become hard and pinched. It was an expression she increasingly used when Rae didn't immediately do as she wanted.

"I'm not sure, Bobby…"

"Come on! Let's imagine we're starring in our own film and we're off to meet two handsome heroes. It'll be such a lark."

"Well…" Rae tried to convince herself, but could find nothing about the situation that was like taking part in a film.

Bobby ignored her hesitation. "Good. That's settled then. Promise?"

"Yes, promise." Rae sighed. Well, what did it matter, anyway? It was best Bobby thought she'd agreed to go. Then, when they couldn't get out of school after the doors were locked, Bobby would believe she'd been game to go on what she kept calling their dates.

At bedtime, Bobby put her nightdress on over her dress and told Rae to do likewise.

"We'll get into bed and then, after Miss Tansey checks us, we'll go."

"Go where?" Surely Bobby had worked out by now they wouldn't be able to open any of the doors without being seen.

"Oh, Rae! Keep up, will you? We'll meet Philip and Andrew in the woods as we arranged. And then who knows where they'll take us? Philip told me he can drive, and his father often lends him his car."

"But how're we going to get out?" Rae bit the inside of her cheek. How could she stop this?

"We'll go out of the window. There's a flat roof not far below and then it's just a short climb to the tree outside the library. I'm sure it's possible."

"But how d'you know?"

"I don't. But that's not going to stop me. It simply must be possible." Bobby squeezed her lips together in the thin, hard line that Rae dreaded.

"But things don't become possible just because you make up your mind they should be."

"Oh, don't be such a wet blanket, Rae. How hard can it be? And if it can be done, we're the girls to do it."

After Miss Tansey had checked them, Bobby opened the window and straddled the sill. She swung her other leg over and twisted around. Then, after dangling by her hands for a few seconds, she dropped, landing softly onto the roof. Rae rushed to the window and looked down at her with wide eyes. While she'd been lying in bed, she'd hoped Bobby would have reconsidered.

Bobby beckoned her. "Come on, Rae. It's easy. I've never known you to be a sissy."

Rae wasn't afraid of the drop. It was what might come after that frightened her.

It was madness, but surely once Bobby saw how far it was to the ground, she'd change her mind. Nevertheless, until she decided to give up, Rae would have to appear willing. After all, she had promised to go, and if she didn't at least attempt it, Bobby would sulk. She might even carry out her threat to find someone else who was more grown up. Recently, on several occasions, she'd warned Rae not to act like a child or she'd be forced to find a new friend.

Rae climbed over the sill, and with closed eyes, dropped to the flat roof. She paused, straining to hear any sign they'd been heard, but the only sound was a burst of laughter from the other side of the building and the mournful wail of the wind in the trees. Bobby beckoned her to follow as she climbed over the library roof towards the tree at the far end.

There was nothing for it. Rae had to follow Bobby down through the branches until they jumped to the ground, scratched and grazed.

There was no turning back now.

By keeping to the shadows, they made it to the woods on the far side of the playing fields.

"Suppose Philip and Andrew haven't come?" Rae whispered, hoping desperately they hadn't.

"Of course, they'll come. Philip told me he'd fallen in love with me.

He said it was love at first sight. He's so romantic."

Jealousy sliced through Rae. Andrew had shown no interest in her, although, to be fair, she hadn't been friendly to him. Perhaps if she hadn't been so embarrassed... No, the truth was, she hadn't liked him very much. But that wasn't the point. How exciting it would have been if he had fallen in love with her.

She dared to hope that even if Philip had come, Andrew hadn't. Then perhaps she could steal back into school. Bobby would probably be grateful if she left the two of them together.

A low whistle pierced the evening air.

Rae's heart sank as both boys crept out from behind a bush.

Philip swaggered to Bobby and put his arm around her shoulders. "Wasn't sure you'd come."

"I wouldn't have missed it," Bobby said.

Rae stared at her. She'd never seen Bobby behave in such a way – fluttering her eyelashes and simpering.

"Drink?" Philip offered his hipflask to Bobby.

She took a mouthful and gasped as she swallowed.

"Here, have some more." He drank some, then passed her the flask again. She took another mouthful and wiped her mouth with the back of her hand as he'd done.

"I didn't think you'd come," Andrew said to Rae. But his expression wasn't appreciative. He surveyed her coolly.

"Drink?" Andrew handed his hipflask to Rae.

"What is it?"

"Taste it and see."

Common sense told her to say no. It was undoubtedly alcohol – something her parents had always forbidden her to try. But perhaps it was time? She'd have to drink it one day, so why not now? And anyway, she longed to see Andrew's superior smile slip. If she drank some, would he show admiration for her like Philip was showing for Bobby?

She took the flask and pretended to take a large mouthful. Having blocked the opening of the flask with her tongue, only a small drop went down her throat, but it was enough to make her splutter and choke. A dribble ran down her chin onto her collar and she wiped it away with the back of her hand.

Andrew laughed. However, to her satisfaction, his face had lit up with approval.

"Brandy's an acquired taste," he said pompously, seizing the flask and taking a mouthful.

Rae held out her hand for the brandy and took another few sips, then forced her lips to curve upwards into a smile. It was revolting. The liquid left a fiery trail all the way down to her stomach.

"Come for a walk with me," Andrew said and took Rae's hand.

He wanted to walk with her. Did that mean he liked her, after all?

"I'll just tell Bobby we're going," she said, not sure she liked him grabbing her like that, but afraid to pull away in case he thought her childish.

"She won't be interested." Andrew jerked his head towards the other two.

Rae turned to see Bobby and Philip kissing, just like she'd seen in the Hollywood films. Except it wasn't exactly like in the movies. That was glamorous and charming. The hero and heroine were usually in elegant surroundings, and everything was perfect. He would have his arms around her and would be... well... respectful. Gentle. Philip was pushing Bobby against a tree trunk.

This isn't what I was expecting at all.

Rae shivered. Everything was out of control. She'd done her share of foolish things before – rash, impulsive moments she could laugh about later – but nothing had ever led her into a situation that whispered danger like this.

Danger? No, she was exaggerating. She wasn't in danger. What could possibly happen to her? The worst was that if she ran off, the others would laugh at her for being a baby.

So why was her heart racing and her mouth dry? She'd broken rules before and she'd been told off when she'd been caught, but they'd been larks. This felt as though it was serious in a way she didn't understand, and the brandy that had dripped onto her collar gave off fumes reminding her she'd walked into something more adult than she'd been prepared for.

Andrew led her away to a clearing not far from Philip and Bobby. *Perhaps he's got more manners than his friend,* Rae thought. *We'll just find something to sit on and talk,* although what they'd talk about, she couldn't imagine.

Well, she was sure she'd think of something.

He stopped abruptly and dropping her hand, he snaked his arms tightly around her waist, then lowered his mouth to hers. It took her by surprise, and she froze for a second, but that was enough for him to place his brandy-flavoured lips on hers. He pressed hard, his nose colliding with hers.

So, this is what it's like to be kissed?

What was all the fuss about? Rae's eyes opened in alarm. Although the smell of brandy filled her nostrils, beneath that odour was something more unpleasant. Sweat. Andrew smelt like Joe after he'd been playing rugby.

Surely this couldn't be all there was to kissing? Greta Garbo and Robert Taylor had looked as though they were enjoying it. Robert had held Greta as though she were precious. As though he cared about her.

Perhaps it took practice. You couldn't just pick up a tennis racquet and expect to play perfect tennis immediately. Maybe kissing was the same.

When will he stop?

Andrew's hand slipped downwards and with shock, she realised he was pulling up the skirt of her dress. She slapped him away, wondering if he'd somehow got caught up in the fabric. Perhaps his watch had snagged on the material.

But when he pushed his hand back and his fingers brushed her leg, she brought her knee up to his stomach. He grunted and doubled over, his hands now clutching himself.

Rae backed away. She felt sick. Andrew was bent over, groaning and gasping. She hadn't wanted to hurt him – just stop him pawing at her.

Once, she'd accidentally kicked Joe between the legs and he'd howled with agony.

"But I hardly touched him, Papa," she'd wailed to her father, expecting a telling off.

Papa had explained that men were very sensitive in that area and that she must be more careful in the future.

If only she'd thought first. It was dreadful to see Andrew in such pain and know she'd caused it. Should she help him? She'd find the other two. Bobby would know what to do.

"Bobby!" she called as loudly as she dared and stumbled to where she'd last seen her friend. She stopped still when she saw them. Philip was lying on top of Bobby.

What was he doing? Was he hurting her? Had the world gone mad? Rae's heart beat furiously. She'd pull him off her friend. She'd...

At the instant Rae decided to run to them and grab Philip by his pullover and push him away, Bobby saw her, and locked eyes. To Rae's amazement, she angrily waved her hand in a gesture of dismissal.

Bobby didn't want her help.

With blood pounding in her ears, Rae ran. She'd never run so fast or so hard. Not bothering to keep to the cover of the trees, she flew across the field. Gasping for breath, she scrambled up the tree, heedless of scratches and scrapes. Back across the library roof to their bedroom. She was sobbing by the time she reached the open window.

Safe.

Then realisation hit her – she wasn't safe at all. The window was too high for her to climb into.

Her breath came sharp and ragged. How would she climb into their bedroom? On their way out, they'd dropped from the window to the flat roof, but now, there was nothing to climb onto to get back. If she stood on tiptoe, she could just touch the windowsill – but not enough to grip it. And even if she had been tall enough, she didn't have the strength in her arms to heave her body up until she could straddle the windowsill.

Sobbing, she sank onto the roof, her arms wrapped around her legs, chin on her knees. Panic had numbed her brain.

Think!

Suppose Bobby didn't come back? Rae couldn't spend the night on the roof. But if she shouted and raised the alarm, she'd have to tell her rescuers where Bobby was. If they found her with Philip, Miss Frost would certainly expel her.

Think!

If only Bobby would come.

She could link her hands and boost Bobby upwards, giving her the height she'd need to climb into their room. Once she was in, she could lean out and haul Rae up. Yes, that would work. But only if Bobby came. Where was she?

Rae watched the last of the light fade, straining to catch sight of a figure slipping out of the woods. The cuts and scratches she'd gained during her frantic scramble up through the tree now throbbed and stung. They weren't painful enough to make her cry, so she didn't know why she'd started sobbing, but once she'd started, she carried on until there were no more tears.

It was completely dark by the time Bobby returned. Rae had expected her friend to treat her with scorn for having run away. Andrew would surely have told her and Philip what she'd done, and Bobby would be angry. But she was remarkably quiet, especially when she realised they couldn't easily climb back into their room.

Rae explained her plan and after linking her hands together for Bobby to stand on, she pushed her into the bedroom. Once inside, Bobby reached out and hauled Rae up. More scratches and scrapes as Rae slid up the bricks. But she was so relieved to be back in the safety of their room, she didn't bother to look at the grazes. She simply wanted to curl up in a ball in bed and cry.

Both girls went to bed in silence, and Rae knew Bobby had lain awake until the early hours, just like she had. It felt as though something precious had broken that could never be mended.

After that, Rae refused any more night-time sorties with Bobby, who declared she'd do whatever it took to be with Philip. "We love each other passionately," she said.

Rae was puzzled. People in Hollywood films appeared happy when they were in love, but since Bobby had met Philip, she'd become distracted and distant. She'd always been the one to take control and make things happen, but now, it was as if she lived to please Philip. Perhaps that was what being in love was all about?

Rae wanted to ask Bobby, but the closeness they'd once shared had gone. They were polite to each other, but there were no more shared secrets or laughter. The only good thing was Bobby no longer suggested she'd find another friend if Rae didn't fall in with her plans

– presumably because she needed her each night to climb back into their bedroom.

Rae was torn. She didn't like the deceit, but what could she do? Bobby would never forgive Rae if she betrayed her. On the other hand, they no longer had a friendship. Hopefully, Bobby would get fed up with Philip and then things could go back to normal.

Yes, that was it. She'd wait for Bobby to come to her senses.

Chapter Fifteen

♥

Weeks after they'd first met the boys outside the cinema, Rae awoke to hear muffled sobs from Bobby's bed.

"Bobby? Bobby, what's wrong?" Rae got out of bed and crouched next to the weeping girl.

"Oh, Rae! I don't know what to do. I'm late." Bobby wiped her eyes with the back of her hand.

Rae looked at her clock. "Late? It's not late. There's still half an hour before we need to get up. I think you've had a nightmare."

Bobby reached out and gripped her wrist, "I mean I haven't had…" Her eyes were enormous.

"What? What haven't you had? Bobby, you're frightening me! You're not making any sense."

Bobby buried her face in her hands. "Rae, I think I… I might be pregnant." Her body shook silently.

The only time Rae had heard the word *pregnant* before was when Mrs Bolton's dog had a litter of pups. Bobby must be confused and had used the wrong word. Yes, she'd definitely had a bad dream.

"Bobby," Rae said in a gentle, calming voice. "You've had a nightmare, that's all. Everything's all right."

"Rae!" Bobby wailed, burying her face in her hands. "For goodness' sake! Don't you understand? I'm going to have a baby."

Rae placed a hand on her shoulder. "Don't be ridiculous, Bobby. You can't be. You're not married."

"Oh, Rae, you're such a child. You don't have to be married to have a baby." Bobby shrugged her hand off.

Rae was certain you *did* have to be married to have a baby. She didn't know of anyone who was still single with a child, but she didn't want to upset Bobby further. In gentle tones, she said, "What makes you think it's possible?"

"Because..." Bobby sat up and sobbed into her hands. "Because... Philip and I... we... well, we kissed... and things."

No. It was nonsense. Bobby was mistaken. But how could she convince her? "Shall I get Nurse?" she asked finally.

Bobby nodded. "Yes, please. Just tell her I feel ill. Don't tell her about... you know. I don't want her to find out. It's going to be bad enough telling my parents. Papa's going to have an absolute fit. And as for Mama..."

Later, Rae attended her lessons and didn't see Bobby for the rest of the day. She assumed her friend was sick and had been sent to the sanatorium to rest.

However, after lessons the following afternoon, Rae went back to her room and found Bobby packing her things. Her parents had arrived and after a long meeting with the headmistress, Bobby said she was being taken away and wouldn't be back. They'd make arrangements for the birth.

So, it was true? She really was going to have a baby? It was unbelievable.

Bobby's face was white and pinched. "I'm sorry, Rae, I had to tell them you helped me back into the room each evening. They'd have worked it out, anyway. But I didn't tell them about you meeting

Andrew. I said I'd always gone on my own. Just keep quiet and they'll never know. Stick to the story. I'll write when I can. Now promise me you won't tell them about Andrew."

Rae was close to tears. Her friend was leaving, and the guilt weighed heavily. Why hadn't she stopped Bobby? Should she have tried harder?

"Promise you won't tell them about Andrew!" Bobby's eyes were hard and determined.

"All right, although I don't want to lie."

"Do as you're told, Rae. You'll make me look a liar if you tell."

The following day, a prefect knocked at the bedroom door and told Rae to go to the headmistress's office. She dawdled in the corridor as much as she dared, then hesitated before she knocked, wondering if she could convince Miss Frost she hadn't been aware of what Bobby had been doing. It was true; she hadn't known exactly what Bobby had been doing, although judging by what she'd seen during her outing in the woods, she might have guessed. Kissing and things...

Miss Frost's stern voice bade her enter.

Rae took a deep breath, swallowed and opened the door. Rae gasped. Opposite the headmistress's desk sat Mama and Papa.

She hadn't realised her parents would be told, much less that they'd be summoned to the school. The weight of guilt and disgrace felt as though it was crushing her soul as she walked to the spot Miss Frost had indicated. She stood, head lowered, and sweaty fists clasped behind her back.

A handkerchief peeped out of Mama's clenched fist and her eyes were glistening and red-rimmed. Papa's eyes were heavy with disappointment.

"Hannah-Rae," Mama said in a tiny, strangled voice. Not tinged with anger, as Rae expected, but with what she recognised as shame.

Rae bit down hard on her lip, trying to keep back the tears. How had her life unravelled so quickly? Not long ago, life had been difficult but manageable. Now it was a whirlwind of chaos.

Miss Frost steepled her fingers and rested her chin on the tips. "Perhaps you'd care to tell us what you know, Hannah-Rae."

Swallowing back the lump in her throat, Rae told them how she'd helped Bobby back into the room each evening, but she left out her part in the first outing. She pretended to know nothing more, and although her story was completely unbelievable to her ears, Miss Frost appeared to accept her story.

"The fact remains, Hannah-Rae, that you should have alerted a member of staff as soon as you knew Roberta was playing truant. I realise you are an impressionable and innocent girl, but even you should have questioned her story about having acting lessons in town."

"Acting...?" Rae looked up in surprise. What had Bobby told everyone?

"We have a perfectly good drama department in the school. Did that not occur to you? Why would Roberta have engaged the services of a retired Hollywood actress?"

Rae stared at the headmistress.

"It was utter nonsense, of course," Miss Frost continued. "I know both of you had your heads in the clouds with your interest in the American film industry, but surely you could see Roberta was lying?" Miss Frost pursed her lips; it wasn't clear what she believed.

Rae hung her head further. She was so far inside Bobby's web of deceit; there was no escape, only the possibility of becoming entangled further.

Miss Frost turned to Mama and Papa. "In conclusion, I feel that under the circumstances, it would be best for everyone if Hannah-Rae goes home immediately and doesn't return this term. There are parts of Roberta's story that make little sense, but she took full responsibility for her actions and claimed she lied to Hannah-Rae. Roberta will not be returning to school. However, I find it hard to believe Hannah-Rae didn't suspect something. Innocence is one thing. Turning a blind eye is quite another. I cannot prove exactly what went on, but since Roberta confessed her guilt, I must accept that. However, if you knew what was going on..." Miss Frost turned to Rae. "Then it will forever be on your conscience. Had you come to me, I would have treated the matter in confidence. And had you done so, a disaster might have been avoided."

The trip home had been silent, but Rae knew that once the shock had worn off, she would be in serious trouble. She felt sick with guilt, shame and disgrace. In the past, she'd been naughty and had taken her punishment. But she hadn't planned any of this. She hadn't wanted to be part of Bobby's adventures. So why did she feel so wretched and responsible?

What had happened to the world? Once, if she'd been told she would be sent home from school until September, she'd have been overjoyed. All those weeks off school. But now, it would simply give her time to remember. If she hadn't deliberately lied about Bobby, she'd kept quiet about Andrew, and that was the same thing as a lie. That would forever be on her conscience.

And it had all been for what? It wasn't as if she'd wanted to meet him. She certainly hadn't enjoyed being with him.

There was no shouting when they arrived home. Mama went to bed without saying anything and Papa looked at her with such disappointment, it nearly broke her heart. What would they think if they knew she'd gone with Bobby that first time and met Andrew?

Rae went to her room. She knew it was unlikely she'd sleep.

Chapter Sixteen

♥

Shortly after midnight, a terrible thought gripped Rae, squeezing the breath from her lungs. Bobby had said she was going to have a baby because she'd been with Philip and... what was it she'd said? 'Kissed and things'.

Andrew had kissed her. True, it hadn't lasted very long. But how long did it take? Why hadn't she known about being pregnant and kissing and things? And, anyway, what were 'things?'

Suppose she was pregnant? How would she know? What should she do? One thing was certain, she couldn't ask Mama or Papa – it would break their hearts. A few months before, she'd told Mama she must have cut the top of her leg, although she couldn't see where the cut was. Mama had told her it wasn't a cut and that from now on, she'd see blood each month.

"But why?" Rae had been aghast.

"It's a sign you're now a woman," Mama had said in a way that appeared to close the conversation.

Rae could tell her mother was uncomfortable, but she'd pressed on, trying to find out more.

"You're too young, Rae. There's plenty of time for those sorts of things," Mama had said as she bent to pick up Jack, who was crying.

Those sorts of things.

More things. Or the same things?

Who would tell her?

There was only one other adult in the house – Mrs Bolton.

Should Rae ask her? No, she'd be sure to tell her parents.

Rae lay awake the rest of the night, crying and fretting about what would happen if suddenly a baby burst out of her. Everyone would know, and her disgrace would be complete. And how could she look after a baby?

In the morning when she finally got up, Mama had taken Jack to the doctor's surgery in the village because he'd developed a rash. Papa had gone to work and Mrs Bolton was in the kitchen, humming tunelessly.

During the night, Rae had remembered Thérèse. She'd got so used to ignoring the French woman, she hadn't considered asking her, but Thérèse was much older than Rae and, therefore, might know about 'things'.

There was no one else.

Rae decided she'd tell Thérèse she had a friend with a problem – that much was true – and she'd say her friend didn't know what to do and she needed help.

Rae got as far as Thérèse's room three times before she summoned the courage to knock. If she didn't hurry, Mama would be back, and the opportunity would be lost.

She took a deep breath and tapped on Thérèse's bedroom door.

"Come in."

Thérèse was sitting in front of her dressing table, combing her hair and arranging her kiss curls.

She gasped and stood up when she saw the girl's swollen eyes and blotchy face. "Are you unwell too, Rae? Do you have a rash like Jack?"

"No... I don't think so." Then remembering she didn't want

Thérèse to know she needed the information herself, she said, "I hope I'm not disturbing you, but I have a friend and she's in trouble... well, that is, she might be in trouble... and I really want to help, but I don't know what to do, that is she doesn't know..."

Thérèse put down her comb and stood to face Rae. As she focused on the gibbering girl in her doorway, her head tilted to one side and her eyes narrowed slightly, the way Mama might have looked at Rae when she was confessing to something trifling. But Thérèse's eyes were filled with concern, not suspicion or anger. She appeared to be taking Rae seriously, which was strange because – even to her own ears – Rae was talking nonsense. Switching from 'I' to 'she' and not even having the right words to ask the questions for which she was desperately seeking answers.

Thérèse gently held up one long finger for Rae to stop. "Now, chérie, I think I understand what you are asking. You are asking for you and not for a friend. I am right, *n'est-ce pas?*"

Rae nodded miserably, her cheeks burning with shame.

"Then, Rae, you must tell me everything, down to the tiniest detail. Do not be afraid. I will not judge you. Come, sit." She moved the dressing table stool closer to Rae and patted it in invitation to sit. As soon as Rae was seated, she perched on her bed, hands folded in her lap, a kindly smile of acceptance on her face.

With downcast eyes, Rae poured out the entire story of that first meeting with Andrew and Philip and what Bobby had said.

Thérèse leaned forward and lifted Rae's chin with her finger as she looked into her eyes. "And you say he just kissed you?"

Rae hung her head again and nodded. "J... just for a second. Well, perhaps a few seconds. But not much longer than that."

"And he tried to put his hand up your skirt, but you pushed your knee into him and then he stopped?"

Rae nodded again, tears streaming down her face. "Does it matter how long he kissed me?"

Thérèse shook her head. She rose and put her arm around Rae's heaving shoulders. "There's nothing to cry about, chérie. I can assure you if you've been honest with me, there is no possibility of you being pregnant."

Rae could scarcely breathe. "Are you sure? Even though he kissed me?"

"*Certainement.* A kiss alone will not make you pregnant, however long it carries on."

Rae buried her face in her hands. She sobbed with relief.

"Your mother didn't tell you how babies are made?" Thérèse asked in disbelief. She placed a reassuring hand on Rae's shoulder.

"No. She said I didn't need to know yet."

"I have heard that many English ladies do not speak frankly to their daughters, expecting them to find out everything on their wedding night. Nevertheless, I find it a terrible shame, and I will tell you all you need to know. But I warn you, it may come as a shock. Do you want me to carry on?"

"Yes, please, Thérèse. I would like you to tell me very much."

Thérèse had been right, Rae was shocked. But what surprised her most was that she'd been living in a world where, despite believing she was grown up, so many things had been happening to the adults around her – and she'd been unaware. The girls at school had often whispered about things behind cupped hands, but Rae hadn't tried to find out what they were talking about. She hadn't wanted to know. The sniggering had suggested something unpleasant.

How had Rae not known the risk she'd put herself in by going out with Bobby that evening to meet those two boys? She wondered if Bobby had truly known how foolishly she'd behaved. She'd always described herself as 'worldly-wise', but Rae suspected her wisdom about the world hadn't been as complete as she'd assumed.

Thérèse's long explanation took in all sorts of surprising things – love, men's and women's bodies, where babies grew, how to avoid having babies – to name a few. When she'd finished, Thérèse put her hand on Rae's.

"That's a lot to take in, chérie. I'm greatly saddened your mother didn't think to tell you any of these things. But perhaps she hasn't realised how fast you're growing up. This is something you wouldn't tell a young child, and she may not have realised you're ready to know. Since she is training to be a doctor, I would have thought she'd be different from other mothers. But perhaps her embarrassment is too great."

Yes, that made sense. Mama had been uncomfortable when she'd explained about Rae's monthlies, but it hadn't occurred to Rae she'd been embarrassed. Perhaps knowing about these things as a mother and a doctor was very different from having to explain to your daughter. Had Grandmother Ivy explained to Mama what she'd needed to know? Rae doubted it. Perhaps that had raised memories in Mama's mind.

The lump in Rae's throat threatened to choke her. She simply nodded and thanked Thérèse. Thoughts and images swirled in her mind; if she'd been able to speak, she wouldn't have known what to say.

All those Hollywood movies she and Bobby had adoringly watched had been a fairy tale. She'd dreamed of sweeping into a room in a glamorous gown, or dancing on a moonlit lawn with a handsome suitor and receiving enormous bouquets of red roses. But that was all make-believe and had nothing to do with real life.

Now she thought about it, the idea that real people behaved like the actors in films was absurd. When had Papa ever serenaded Mama from the garden? She'd have told him to be quiet, or he'd wake up Jack. The last time her parents had dressed up in glamorous clothes was for a cousin's wedding months before. Jack had been sick down the front of Mama's gown, and they'd all gone home early.

And now Rae had discovered that eventually, kissing led to the man and woman taking off all their clothes and... things. She shook her head in disbelief. It wasn't romantic at all. It was shocking. She'd been tempted to believe Thérèse had her facts wrong. Perhaps things were done differently in France? But the vision of Bobby and Andrew in the woods continued to appear in her mind like a movie she couldn't switch off, and that had apparently led to Bobby expecting a child.

Thérèse must be correct.

Rae wanted to get away, to think and to absorb all she'd learned. Stealing into the kitchen while Mrs Bolton was in the garden hanging out washing, Rae took a few apples and two of the biscuits that were cooling on the rack. After quietly wheeling her bicycle across the front lawn so it didn't crunch on the gravel of the drive, she climbed on and started to pedal.

There was no plan in her mind other than to ride until she was exhausted. But at the crossroads, she turned towards the harbour. Perhaps she'd sit on *Wild Spirit*. She'd stare at the water while she tried to make sense of what Thérèse had told her, and of the betrayal she felt at her mother's lack of guidance.

Her parents had told her she must do well at school, mind her manners, eat healthily because in the future she'd be a woman in the grown-up world – as if she'd be awarded a prize. But her new knowledge had destroyed romance, robbing life of its gentleness and colour. She'd been deceived. The world had once appeared bright and shiny, but now it was tarnished and soiled. And the thought that one day she'd be married off and expected to do with a man what Thérèse had described was too much to bear.

If only she could go back to a time when things had been simple. In the past, all she'd had to worry about were the tides and the weather forecast for a day of sailing.

When she reached the boat, she had the urge to rig her and sail away. She wouldn't, of course, because she recognised that as a fanciful, romantic impulse. Something someone in a Hollywood movie might do. The hero and heroine would sail towards the sunset... And then what? That had never occurred to her before. What happened after the movie's closing credits? Well, obviously, it would mean real life for the hero and heroine, and that's why the film always stopped there. Because everyone knew about real life. It was just regrettable Rae hadn't worked that out before. She definitely wasn't a heroine. And she didn't have a hero.

Bobby hadn't appeared to understand the difference between make-believe and real life, either. But the only other person she'd thought of as a friend did. Jamie.

He'd wanted to go to college, but Mr MacKenzie had decided both his sons would run the boatyard, and before they could do that, they needed to know how to do everything – from the lowest jobs to the highest. College was out of the question. Simply a waste of time. Jamie wouldn't have any foolish notions in his head. He'd see life as it was. She wondered what he was doing now, and suddenly, she longed to see him, to check he was still the same.

School had changed. Home had changed. Bobby had changed.

But surely her friendship with Jamie would still be the same?

Yes, she needed to see Jamie. She needed some reassurance the entire universe hadn't gone mad.

But she couldn't wait in the harbour and simply hope he'd come out of the yard. He might not appear for hours and if he did, he might be with his father. If she wanted to see Jamie alone, she'd simply have to go in and ask for him. But as she neared the gate and heard several of the men calling to each other, she wondered if perhaps it would be better to hover by the gate and hope Jamie saw her.

"'Ello, love, waitin' for me, are you?" one man called good-naturedly when he saw Rae at the gate.

"I was hoping to talk to Jamie, please," she said, aware her cheeks were flaming.

"Jamie!" he yelled. "There's a lovely young lady waitin' for yer. If yer don't hurry up, I'll be happy to take 'er off yer hands."

When there was no response, an unseen voice called out, "Jamie! Sam's yellin' for yer. That Susannah's waitin'. Get a move on!"

"It ain't Susannah," the first man yelled. "It's another lass."

There was a chorus of "Ooh!" from several of the others and finally, Jamie appeared at the gate, an anxious look on his face that was replaced by a smile when he saw her.

"Rae! What're you doing here? Have you broken up already?"

"Ooh! It's Rae! He's got another girl," one of the men shouted. "Ain't Rae a boy's name?" They all laughed. "I'd stick with Susannah, Jamie lad. She's mighty keen on you," someone called after him.

"Let's go down to the harbour." Jamie glanced over his shoulder at the men.

He was taller and broader than when Rae had last seen him – less like the boy she remembered.

"So, come on, tell me. What're you doing here?" he asked eagerly.

"I... I..." Rae didn't know how to start, nor where to begin. But she wanted to get away from the boatyard. "D'you think we can go to Cranston's Point?"

He frowned. "I can't leave work yet, but as soon as I can, I'll get away. Can you wait for me?"

Rae nodded.

She sat on the harbour wall, dangling her legs over the edge, and watched *Wild Spirit* rock gently on the water until Jamie appeared with his bicycle, and they set off.

Her stomach sank as she remembered the last time they'd been to the beach with Bobby and how it had appeared so dull. Would it be the magical place it once had been, or would it, too, be spoilt?

They propped their bicycles against the ruins, and Jamie led the way to their large rock and sat down. He remained silent, waiting for her to speak, and then, as she began to cry, he put his arm around her shoulders. It was quite unexpected, but strangely comforting.

She started, hesitantly at first, telling him she'd been sent home from school in disgrace until the end of the summer term.

"So, you're back until September?"

She couldn't see his face, but he sounded pleased. "Yes."

"That's good," he said.

"Don't you want to know why?" She could barely force the words out, not sure if she'd have the courage to describe her shame. Would he be on her side? No one else had been.

Please, please be on my side.

He shrugged. "D'you want to tell me?"

Nestled in the comfort of his arm, she decided to take a chance; desperate for someone to sympathise with her. Thérèse had been kind, but she wasn't exactly a friend, and Rae needed someone special to accept her and show understanding. If he showed her he didn't care she'd been with Andrew in the woods, it would be as if it had never happened. If they could laugh about it... If, if...

Yes, she needed someone special. She needed Jamie.

Rae turned towards him, wanting to see his expression. She told him she was in trouble because she'd helped Bobby get back through the window into their bedroom, and that as a result of those trips out of school, Bobby was now expecting a baby and had been removed from school by her parents.

"I'm not surprised," Jamie said, his brows drawn together. "She seemed a bit of a flirt."

Rae's jaw dropped open. "What makes you say that?"

"Because when she came, she kept fluttering her eyelashes at my brother. He told me."

It stung that Jamie had been so quick to criticise Bobby. Did he think badly of Rae too? She couldn't bear it if he did. Perhaps if she explained. "I don't think Bobby was flirting. She was trying to look like Jean Harlow. She practised in the mirror. She didn't mean any harm."

Jamie frowned. He wasn't convinced. "I think anyone who sneaks out of school to meet a boy in the woods is asking for trouble."

Rae lowered her head and allowed her curls to hide her face. She felt sick. Sneaking out to meet a boy was exactly what she'd done, although she hadn't been happy about it and she hadn't known she was asking for trouble. She'd wanted Jamie to see everything through the haze of Hollywood glamour as she once had. Only then would he understand her reasoning. But how could she explain it to him? Judging by his few words, he could see what everyone saw – two silly schoolgirls who couldn't tell the difference between romantic notions and real life. And to her dismay, that was now all she saw, too. How could she have been so blind?

"I'm really sorry you've lost a friend," Jamie said. "It was unfair of her to get you mixed up in her bad behaviour, so you got punished, too. But perhaps you'll be able to come down to the harbour more often now. When I finish work tomorrow, we could take *Wild Spirit* out. What d'you think? Or we could come here. I'll try to get off early..." He pulled her closer, but this time, he'd turned towards her; his face now inches away.

What was he doing? Rae wanted a friend; someone to comfort her and make her forget her stupidity. Someone who'd take her back to the world before she'd learned about *things*.

But Jamie was close. Too close. And there was a strange look in his eyes she didn't recognise. She didn't want someone to pull her about like Andrew had done. He'd pressed his face towards hers and pulled her tight without giving her a chance to get used to it. Without even finding out if she minded. He hadn't considered her at all – simply tried to use her as she now understood Philip had used Bobby.

She shuddered and Jamie's arm tightened around her.

This wasn't what she wanted. Why couldn't he see she longed for the easy friendship they'd once shared? She wanted his understanding, but in condemning Bobby, he was condemning her. Rae pushed him away.

"So, anyone who sneaks out of school to meet a boy is asking for trouble, is she?" Shame and the unfairness of life bubbled up inside her and exploded into rage. Unable to stop herself, she added, "Well, I'll have you know, I wasn't asking for trouble when I went out with Bobby."

His mouth opened, but no sound came out. He drew away from her and whispered, "What are you saying?"

"I'm saying the first time Bobby went out, I was with her. And I met a boy called Andrew. And he kissed me, and it was horrible. And I never want to kiss anyone ever again. *Ever.*"

She leapt from the rock. Why had she been so unfair to Jamie? It wasn't his fault. But why had he been so judgemental? She ran back to her bicycle, then climbing on, she pedalled as fast as she could away from Cranston's Point... and away from Jamie.

How could that have gone so wrong? Thérèse had told her it wasn't only girls whose bodies and outlook changed when they reached her age – boys changed too – although not in the same way. Rae wondered if both she and Jamie had become different people, and now, he wasn't capable of being the childhood friend he'd once been. The one she needed. Thank goodness she'd left him before he'd tried anything like Andrew had done.

It was hard to imagine Jamie treating her like that, but she suddenly recalled earlier when the man in the boatyard had thought she was Susannah. Who was she? A girl Jamie was interested in? Icy fingers clutched at her heart at the thought of Jamie with the faceless Susannah.

Rae was pedalling so furiously she could scarcely breathe. She didn't want to think. She didn't want to feel. She wanted to turn everything off.

What was the matter with her?

Chapter Seventeen

Jamie sat with his head in his hands, the cold from the large rock chilling his legs. What was the matter with him? How could he have got it so wrong?

When Rae had appeared earlier, he'd been surprised because he hadn't expected to see her before the start of the summer holidays. After that disastrous time she'd brought Bobby, he wasn't sure he'd ever see her again, although he'd hoped she'd be back, even if only to sail *Wild Spirit*. And if she came, he'd wondered how he ought to behave towards her.

She'd been troubled about something, and he'd been glad she'd suggested they go to their private beach. He'd been determined to be grown up. He wouldn't skim stones. He wouldn't chase her with dripping seaweed. He'd show her how wrong Bobby had been.

So, he'd put his arm around her like Arthur had told Pete he'd done when he'd first met his girl, and Rae had appeared to like it.

If only he'd known how he ought to behave before.

It had then crossed Jamie's mind that if she'd liked that, perhaps Arthur, Pete and the others in the boatyard were right. She'd expect him to kiss her.

He'd decided to wait until she'd finished explaining why she was home so early from school – that would be polite, and then he'd summon every ounce of courage and kiss her. He had a rough idea of what to do from Susannah's attempt to kiss him. And it didn't appear to be very difficult.

But Rae had taken him completely by surprise when she'd told him why she'd been sent home from school. And when she said she'd kissed that boy, he'd felt a stab of jealousy so intense, he'd almost doubled over in pain. She'd looked at him as if waiting for him to say something, but what could he say? He'd stared at her. Stupidly stared at her.

Then she'd said she never wanted to kiss anyone again, and she'd gone, the sound of her bicycle tyres sliding over the patch of gravel near the ruins.

Jamie raised his face and looked up in case she'd returned. But of course, she hadn't. He'd somehow upset her. So why would she come back?

On his way home, he'd decided he would go to Rae's house the following day and apologise. What he'd be apologising for, he didn't know, but that wouldn't stop him. He'd admit to anything if Rae would smile at him again, and if they could be friends.

When Jamie arrived home, Alex was working in the vegetable plot.

"Alex, have you ever been keen on a girl?" he blurted out.

His brother looked up in surprise. "None of your business," he said sharply and carried on digging.

"But Alex, there are things I need to know and I've no idea who to ask."

Alex was silent for a while, then he said, "D'you remember Aunt Lily?"

"Mum's sister?"

"Yes."

Jamie nodded. Of course, he remembered her, although he hadn't seen her for several years. There had been a disagreement between her and his father, and all visits to her had stopped.

"Go and see her," Alex said. "She'll sort you out. But don't tell Dad you've been. And don't tell him I told you to go."

"Jamie! How lovely to see you!" A huge smile lit up Aunt Lily's face when she opened the door to her cottage and recognised him. "Come in, come in. My word, how you've grown."

She led Jamie into the parlour and once she'd made sure he was comfortable, she busied herself in the kitchen making tea. He looked about the room and was surprised at how different it was from his father's home, which was plain, drab, and often untidy.

In his aunt's house, everything was neat. There were embroidered cushions on the chairs and lace runners on the sideboard and the small tables, all of which were covered in china ornaments and photographs in silver frames. He glanced at the one closest to him, which showed two young girls sitting on a furry rug in a photographer's studio. It was obvious from the similarity in their features; they were sisters. In fact, they could have been twins, although one girl appeared to be slightly younger than the other.

He looked at the other photographs and saw that, mostly, they featured the two girls at different stages of life and as the pictures of the girls showed them approaching adulthood, he could see the slightly taller one was his aunt. That, of course, meant the other girl was his mother. He swallowed hard and tears came to his eyes. There were no photographs of Mum in his father's house; no memories of her at all – well, none that were obvious to him, anyway.

Standing on the mantelpiece was a wedding photograph and, for a second, he thought his aunt was the bride, which was strange because he'd never heard he had an uncle. Then he realised the bridesmaid was slightly taller than the bride. It was his parents' wedding, and the bridesmaid was Aunt Lily. How happy everyone appeared, how young and hopeful his parents looked.

"I love that photograph," Aunt Lily said, returning with a tray on which she had a fancy teapot and delicate cups and saucers. "It was such a wonderful day."

"We don't have any photographs like that," said Jamie.

Aunt Lily nodded; her eyes downcast. "That's a shame, love. A real shame. But I suspected as much. Your father couldn't bear anything to remind him of your mother after she passed away – not even me, in the end."

"Is that why we don't see you anymore?"

She nodded and bit her lip as if fighting back tears, then busied herself pouring tea. By the time she'd finished, she'd composed herself. "Now, to what do I owe the pleasure of your visit?"

He stared at her for a moment. "I'm not sure where to begin, Aunt..."

"I always find the beginning is the best place to start," she said and smiled encouragingly. "I've got a pot of stew cooking and there's plenty for two, so we have as much time as you need..."

When Jamie finished explaining about Rae and how he'd tried to be what he thought she wanted and how upset she'd been when he'd pulled her to him, Aunt Lily nodded sympathetically.

"Everyone treats me like a child," Jamie said, "and no one'll talk to me about anything, so how can I ever learn? All Dad wants to do is warn me off Rae. Alex is too embarrassed to say anything, and the men in the yard just laugh at me. I rarely see men and women together other than in the town. And when I listen to the men in the yard, they talk about women as if... well, as if they don't really like them very much. Well, that is to say, they do like them – sometimes that's all they go on about, but I want to know how to talk to someone, how to spend time with someone, not just get them into bed..." He gasped. Had he really said that? Turning red, he looked at her in exasperation, knowing he should have minded his manners. It had been unacceptable, and he started to rise, ready to apologise and leave.

But rather than expressing shock or anger, Aunt Lily nodded sympathetically and raised a hand, gesturing for him to sit. "Yes, I know what you mean, love. Men can sometimes be rather bad at expressing their feelings."

She didn't appear to be offended at all. Dare he keep asking questions? Jamie feared this may be his only chance to find out so many of the things he wanted to know. He took a deep breath and pressed on. "How do men know what they're supposed to do when they grow up?"

"How indeed?" she said, shaking her head sadly. "But actually, Jamie, I think you'll find that many of them don't. They are the men who bottle everything up and never discuss things. Those, like you, who try to understand themselves and question everything, usually do very well in love and in their lives in general."

"Do you think that I...?" Jamie hesitated. He bit his lip. Dare he ask? Would he shock her?

"Yes?" Her face was gentle and understanding.

"Well, d'you think I could be in love?" He blushed. There, he'd said it.

"It's not possible for me to say, Jamie. Only you would know."

"But how would I know?"

"Hmm, that's a tricky one." She sighed. "Everyone is different, but in my experience, you know you love someone when they're the first person you think about when you wake up in the morning and the last person on your mind when you go to sleep at night. When you find things are meaningless unless you're sharing them with that person and when you feel as if you're half-alive when they're not there. If that's how you feel, I'd say it's most likely you're in love."

"That is how I feel about Rae," Jamie whispered. "But isn't being in love supposed to be happy? I feel miserable. Rae was so upset with me and I'm not sure she'll ever speak to me again. I can't tell Dad about how I feel because he doesn't like her and if I tell anyone else, they'll just laugh and say I'm too young to know what I'm talking about."

"The best thing is not to tell anyone else. It isn't anyone else's business. But it would be a good idea to talk to Rae and find out how she feels. That won't be an easy conversation because she may not share your feelings. Remember, she is younger than you, although girls mature earlier than boys. If you're ever going to have peace of mind, it's a discussion you need to have. But never let anyone tell you you're too young to fall in love and that it won't last. I fell in love when I was about your age. He didn't feel the same about me and he married someone else. But I still love him. I always will." Her eyes filled with tears, and she looked towards the wedding photograph on the mantelpiece.

Surely, she couldn't mean she loved Dad? Was that why they'd all stopped visiting Aunt Lily? Jamie wasn't sure if he should say something or pretend he hadn't noticed her tears. But if it was Dad she loved, how terrible for her because once Dad made up his mind about something, he was very hard to shift. They must both once have shared a love for his mother; surely, they could have consoled each other and made each other happy?

Finally, Aunt Lily dabbed her eyes with a handkerchief and suggested they have supper. Jamie helped her to set the table.

"Your father has raised you to be a polite young man, Jamie. Your mother would be so proud. You said you were worried about how to behave towards girls, but I think it's inside you already. Forget all the things you've heard in the boatyard about women liking a strong, domineering man. I think you'll find women like a man who makes them feel like they're the most precious person in the world and who lets them know they're appreciated and respected. If you keep that uppermost in your mind, you won't go far wrong."

Dad was reading his newspaper in the parlour when Jamie arrived home that evening.

"You were out late, laddie."

"Yes, Dad."

"Have you been with the Kingsley lass?"

"No!" he snapped, and then, although he hadn't intended to tell his father, he added, "I've been with Aunt Lily."

"Oh!"

Jamie had expected anger – in fact, there was nothing he'd have liked more than an argument with his father for always being so set against Rae, but Dad's gasp had been of surprise, and Jamie saw that when he laid his pipe in the ashtray, his hand was shaking.

"And how is your aunt?" Dad folded his arms and stared at the floor.

"Fine. Although I think she's lonely." Now Jamie wished he hadn't mentioned her. He hadn't wanted to hurt his dad.

"Did she say as much?"

"No, but I could tell."

Dad was silent for a few moments, and Jamie thought the conversation was over, when his father added, "She's living alone then?"

"Yes... Dad?"

"Aye?" His voice was guarded.

Jamie wondered whether to ask, but why not? Dad could always refuse to answer – indeed, probably *would* refuse to answer. "Why doesn't she come here now? She used to visit. I remember."

His father sighed. "Some things are best left alone, laddie. Now, you'd better get off to bed. We've got a busy day tomorrow."

The following morning, Jamie got up very early and cycled to Rae's house in Barlstead. He'd be late for work, but he'd just have to put up with his father's anger.

With any luck, he could apologise to Rae and be back at the boatyard before his father noticed, although he doubted it. Even if Dad was angry, it would be worth it.

Jamie knew the way to Rae's house. He'd been there once with his father when he'd dropped something off for Dr Kingsley, although they hadn't been at the house long, having knocked at the door but not been invited inside.

The journey was imprinted on Jamie's memory, and he cycled straight to it, stopping outside the gate to smooth his hair back into place and to give him a few moments to gather his thoughts.

He'd tried to rehearse a speech, but nothing sounded right, and he hoped if Rae gave him the chance, the right words would come. Leaning his bicycle against the gate, he walked up the gravel drive. Dad was right about one thing – the Kingsleys were much wealthier than his family. But did that matter?

He took a deep breath and tapped with the knocker.

After a few seconds, a stout woman who was drying her hands on her apron opened the door. "Yes?"

"Please, would it be possible to see Rae?" he asked, assuming this must be Mrs Bolton.

"I'm afraid she's not here." She finished drying her hands and smoothed the apron.

"Please can you tell me when she'll be back?" he asked politely.

Mrs Bolton sniffed. "I've no idea. Possibly August. I don't know. No one tells me anything."

"August?" he asked in surprise. Was Mrs Bolton joking? But her frown suggested she wasn't.

"Yes, she's gone to stay with relatives."

"I'm sorry to trouble you, but do you have an address, please?"

She snorted. "Address? As if anyone would give me an address..." Turning, she began to shut the door.

"Please!" His voice cracked in desperation.

"I told you; I don't have an address." She closed the door firmly.

Jamie felt as though he'd been punched in the stomach. He couldn't breathe. Rae had gone? He'd missed her? No, it wasn't possible.

As he trudged down the drive, the door opened, and he turned back to see if Mrs Bolton had suddenly had second thoughts. However, it wasn't the housekeeper; it was a smart young woman with what looked like curls stuck on her face who was beckoning him.

"You are Jamie MacKenzie?" she asked in a soft French accent.

"Yes."

"Ah!" Her eyes closed slightly as she looked him over. "Well, Jamie MacKenzie, although Mrs Bolton doesn't know where Rae has gone, luckily for you, I do." She handed him a slip of paper. "Rae has talked about you. I believe you will be kind to her. She needs a friend now. I trust you will be that friend."

For a long moment, silence stretched between them, heavy with unspoken words. Then, with a deliberate nod that felt like a judgement, she closed the door.

"Is there someone else at the door?" Mrs Bolton called from the kitchen.

"No," Thérèse replied, her voice smooth, almost serene. A small smile touched her lips as she climbed the stairs to continue her packing. Lady Langton's acceptance letter lay on her bedside table, and Thérèse paused to read it once more, allowing herself a brief, private thrill of satisfaction. Tomorrow, her life would begin anew. The chauffeur was due to collect her and take her to Lady Langton's Mayfair residence.

Joe was at school. Rae was, at this moment, being driven to Mrs Kingsley's cousin's house somewhere in Essex. Tonight, when Thérèse joined Dr and Mrs Kingsley for dinner, Jack would be in bed. Then the fireworks would begin.

Of course, she ought to work her notice, but she suspected that after she told them about her new post at dinner that evening and then made her speech, Mrs Kingsley would be so furious, she'd be glad to see Thérèse go immediately.

She would miss Jack, who was a delightful boy, but now he was at school; she scarcely saw him, so there was no reason to stay with the Kingsleys. And the fact that Mrs Kingsley now expected her to do housework and other chores when Jack wasn't there was frankly unacceptable. She looked down at her perfect almond-shaped nails. These were not the hands of a woman accustomed to scrubbing floors or polishing silver. No, it was time to go.

In fact, if anything, she'd stayed too long. Until recently, she'd hesitated to leave because Jack had been so clingy – no wonder, with a mother like his. Mrs Kingsley had so many fine qualities; Thérèse didn't doubt she loved her children, but she couldn't understand why a woman so cultured and ambitious was entirely at a loss when it came to showing affection.

Joe appeared largely unaffected, somehow charming his way into his mother's good graces, but Rae and Jack? They needed so much more. Poor Rae. How the girl must be suffering, sent away to stay with a relative. As if she hadn't been through enough. But what did her mother know of that?

Nothing.

If Mrs Kingsley had prepared her daughter better, the incident with the dreadful girl, Bobby, could've been avoided. It was commendable for a woman to be ambitious. Indeed, Thérèse admired Mrs Kingsley immensely for pursuing her dream of becoming a doctor, but her children should have been her priority. There was no excuse.

Tonight, Thérèse thought with a flash of satisfaction, she would have her say. She would tell her employers precisely what she thought. The British had a phrase for it: 'home truths'. Thérèse flashed a smile of anticipation.

The following day, Lady Langton's chauffeur arrived and after carrying Thérèse's luggage downstairs, he loaded it into the boot of the car. Dr Kingsley had gone to work, Jack was at school and Mrs Kingsley remained in her bedroom nursing a headache, so only Mrs Bolton waited on the doorstep to wave her a half-hearted goodbye.

They'd never got on, although they'd established a truce.

So, that's it, thought Thérèse. Mrs Kingsley cannot even be bothered to say goodbye. Although to be fair, Thérèse had not spared her feelings the previous night and had been scathing of her employer's mothering skills to the extent that Mrs Kingsley had been reduced to shocked tears.

Good, thought Thérèse. Rae and Jack are too young and inexperienced to stand up for themselves. They need a champion.

Thérèse's *maman* and Lady Langton had been friends for many years, so a good reference hadn't been required, which was fortunate because Mrs Kingsley most definitely wouldn't have provided one.

The previous evening, after Thérèse had told her employers what she thought of them, Mrs Kingsley had accused the nanny of poking her nose in where it wasn't wanted.

"If you did more nose-poking into your children's lives, they would be happier people," Thérèse had said.

"That is no longer any of your business." Mrs Kingsley's voice had been cold and flat.

Dr Kingsley, ever the peacekeeper, had remained quiet, although he'd watched his wife with sad, resigned eyes.

Finally, he'd risen, signalling that dinner was over. "It just remains for us to thank you for looking after Jack and to wish you well." He'd hesitated before adding, "My wife has done her best. We both have. Despite what you may think."

He turned back to his wife after shaking hands with Thérèse.

She'd been dismissed. Well, she'd said her piece, although she suspected cold Mrs Kingsley hadn't taken any notice, and Dr Kingsley, as usual, had done his best to restore calm, while making it clear he was on his wife's side.

Thérèse sighed. There was nothing more she could do for the

Kingsley children. She was starting a new life.

As the chauffeur started the engine, Thérèse turned to look at the house one last time.

"So, I hear you're French," said the chauffeur, looking at her in the rearview mirror. "Where're you from?"

"Paris," said Thérèse, without making eye contact with the man. She raised her chin and stared out of the window.

It wouldn't do to encourage him. She had greater ambitions. The Kingsleys' country life had been a disappointing affair, far from the glamorous world she'd once envisioned. London would change everything. Soon, she would be back in the heart of it all, among people of influence, where her real opportunities lay far beyond the reach of this provincial dullness.

Chapter Eighteen

♥

When Rae had arrived home from Cranston's Point, her cheeks wind-flushed and her legs wobbly, she'd found her parents discussing how they were going to punish her and what she would do until the new school year.

"I simply can't cope with any more of your thoughtless impulsiveness," Mama had said, shaking her head at her daughter's dishevelled appearance. "So, I've arranged for you to stay with my cousin, Joanna, and her family."

If Rae hadn't been so shaken by her encounter with Jamie, she might have fought harder to stay at home, but she'd been numb. Her life felt like a kaleidoscope. As soon as she started to get used to a particular pattern and its colours, someone rotated the cylinder, sending all the shapes tumbling into new positions.

Without Bobby, school would be different. Now Mama was studying medicine, home was different. Even Jamie had changed. Perhaps it was a good thing she was being sent to Joanna's. But deep inside, it didn't feel like a good thing. It felt like punishment.

Early the following morning, a tight-lipped Mama drove her to Joanna's. The journey passed in silence. What was there to say? Rae was fighting back tears and Mama complained she had a nervous headache, which, although she didn't say, Rae felt sure was her fault.

Joanna and her four-year-old daughter, Faye, greeted them warmly at the door of Priory Hall, but after a cup of tea and an introduction to Mark, Joanna's baby son, Mama said she was sure she had a migraine coming and thought it best she return home as quickly as she could.

"Your poor mother," Joanna said to Rae as soon as Mama had gone. "Well, let's get you settled in, shall we? And then I'll show you around. Hopefully, Mark won't wake up for a while."

Joanna hinted she was aware of Rae's exclusion from school, but there was no condemnation and no questions. Calmly and patiently, Joanna set about making Rae feel at home.

Joanna's husband, Ben, was a solicitor who worked in the nearby town of Laindon, although he'd inherited Priory Hall and its farmland. But he, too, was also kind, and welcomed their new guest. It was obvious he adored Joanna and his children, and although Rae knew Papa loved Mama, she wondered why their house had never been as warm and loving as Priory Hall. Joanna and Mama were first cousins, but they couldn't have been more different.

At first, Rae assumed everyone was being polite because she was a guest. Soon they would forget their manners and what Rae understood as 'normal home life' would resume. But however much Mark cried, or Faye misbehaved, Joanna dealt calmly with each problem. No scowls, pursed lips or shaking of her head. There were no angry outbursts or arguments, just smiles and acceptance. It was unsettling, as if they were trying to lull Rae into a false sense of security. But for what? It didn't make sense. Could they truly be like that all the time? And if so, why were her parents so different?

As usual, everything was beyond her control, so she decided she'd be the perfect guest and, hopefully, no one would notice her and send her home. She wasn't sure exactly what her position was in the household, so she tried to help as best she could. One day while she was assisting the cook, she was sent out to see if there were any ripe peas. While she searched, she noticed the vegetable garden needed tidying, and set to, hoeing and weeding – a job that obviously hadn't been done for some time.

That night at dinner, Joanna told Rae how grateful she was for all she'd done in the garden. She'd seen Rae when she'd looked out of Mark's bedroom window that afternoon. He'd had colic for some time, slept fitfully, and needed a lot of attention, so she hadn't had time to spend gardening.

Rae glowed with pride at Joanna's praise. "I love working in the garden," she said. "Perhaps I could work out there tomorrow."

She preferred to be outdoors and when she'd finished in the vegetable garden, she sorted out the cottage garden, bringing that under control.

Days passed, and Rae realised she was dreading going home. She loved living with Joanna and Ben. But how long had Mama arranged for her to stay at Priory Hall? She dared not ask in case she reminded someone she was merely a guest and that, ultimately, she'd have to go home. Each morning, she awoke wondering if that would be the day Mama or Papa would arrive in the car ready to take her away.

One morning, a large envelope arrived, the handwriting unmistakably her mother's. Rae was tempted to stuff it in a drawer, unopened. But eventually, she'd steeled herself to slit it open, holding her breath and silently promising God, if he was listening, that she'd be good if only it wasn't a summons home.

There was a brief note from Mama, which Rae scanned, sighing with relief when she saw it mentioned nothing about returning to Barlstead. Also inside the envelope was a sealed letter from Switzerland, addressed in Bobby's handwriting.

Rae read it quickly, but there was no mention of a baby, and she wondered if there had been a pregnancy after all. Perhaps Bobby had been mistaken. Apparently, she was staying with friends of her parents in their chalet in the Alps, and she described the glorious mountain walks she'd taken, the delicious food and the promise of travel to Italy with the family the following year.

Thérèse had explained to Rae it was likely Bobby's parents would send her away from home to hide her pregnancy. Once the baby was born, they would find a family to adopt it and then bring their daughter home.

But what Bobby had written about was more like a holiday. Rae wondered if Thérèse had been wrong. However, she'd been right about everything else as far as Rae could see. Could Bobby have given birth and then handed her baby over to someone else? Surely not. But perhaps, Rae thought, it was better for a child to be somewhere it was happy than with a mother who didn't want it.

She stared at Bobby's letter for so long the words merged into each other. Why did Rae find it so disturbing? It didn't make sense. The letter was filled with the wonderful things Bobby had done and seen. Her plans for the future. Hints that she'd met a nice Swiss boy.

Finally, it came to Rae. The letter had been disturbing because of all the things it hadn't mentioned.

If Bobby hadn't been pregnant, she'd have said. So, obviously, there had been a baby. And yet, Bobby had described at length all the wonders of her new life. It was all for show. Just like a movie with the camera focusing on one tiny part of a scene and ignoring what was going on in the background.

Rae folded the letter and slipped it back into the envelope. She felt cold. Despite spending so much time with the girl she'd thought of as her best friend; doing as she wanted and trying to please her, Rae realised Bobby had been a stranger.

Two weeks later, at breakfast time, Joanna told Rae there was another letter for her on the hall table. Deliberately ignoring it, Rae slipped into the garden to start work. If it was another redirected letter from Bobby, asking why she hadn't replied, she'd simply feel guilty, although she had no intention of writing back. Bobby had a new life. She didn't need Rae, and Rae was keen to forget about Bobby's influence.

However, if the letter was from her mother telling her to pack her bags, she didn't want to know.

Rae attacked the weeds along the lines of vegetables with ferocity and by the time Joanna came out to bring her a glass of water, she was hot and sticky. Rae gratefully took the drink, noticing Joanna open her mouth as if to say something, then nibble her lower lip as if she'd changed her mind.

So, this was it. Joanna was going to tell Rae it was time to go home. Rae drank, feeling the cool liquid soothe her dry throat but do nothing for the tension knotted inside her.

She cradled the empty glass and braced herself.

Joanna finally began to speak, "So, Rae, dear, I was wondering..." She stopped and watched a robin hop along the hoed soil searching for insects. "If you might possibly consider another gardening job."

Probably her parents' garden in Barlstead, Rae thought.

Joanna took the empty glass from Rae and turned it round and round in her hands. "It's for my mother-in-law. She lives about a mile away, but she's..." Joanna paused and frowned. "Shall we say, slightly difficult? No, I'll be honest. She's very difficult, and I shouldn't blame you one bit for refusing. But you seem so at home in the garden, I thought perhaps..."

"Oh, yes," Rae said quickly, guiltily remembering the letter she hadn't opened that might insist on her return to her parents' home. But perhaps promising to work for Joanna would buy her time in Essex.

"If you find my mother-in-law a little... well, challenging, I shan't blame you for refusing to go there again," Joanna said. "She can be very..." She sighed. "Cantankerous. Very hard to please. But I should be so grateful. Ben has already engaged three men, and they've all walked out after one session."

"Well, I'll try," Rae said. She would put up with anything if it meant she didn't have to go home.

"Thank you, darling. I couldn't ask for more." Joanna smiled at her.

"When should I start?"

"Whenever you like. I'll give you the address when you're ready. Oh, and don't forget, there's a letter on the hall table for you."

"I'll finish this patch of weeding here and then I'll go to see your mother-in-law." Well, why not? If Mama wanted her home, she might be able to claim she'd started Mrs Richardson's garden and ask if she could at least finish it.

Judging by Joanna's awkwardness, it was obvious her mother-in-law was a difficult woman to deal with, but Rae told herself, if she could stand up to Mama, she could probably withstand Mrs Richardson's displeasure. After all, if the woman was too unreasonable, she could simply put her tools back in the shed and walk away.

Rae decided to set off immediately. Rather than change out of her muddy boots, she called at the kitchen door for the address. She wouldn't go through the house and therefore, there was no need to pass through the hall and see the letter she was trying to forget on the hall table.

Beneath Mrs Richardson's address, Joanna had drawn a map, showing how to find the house on Plotlands. It would be the first time Rae had ever been into the area, and she was looking forward to it. Once, when they'd been out in Ben's car, she'd glanced down one of the grassy avenues that was lined by simple cottages.

Now Rae was about to explore the area. She was determined to enjoy the sunshine and, hopefully, Mrs Richardson would ignore her and let her get on with the work.

Rae wheeled her bicycle down the drive, whistling and enjoying the sound of the tune in the clean summer air. Mama always told her off for whistling. From the front door, Joanna called out. "Rae, wait. I've packed lunch for you. I don't know if my mother-in-law will make you anything, and I don't want you starving all day – assuming, of course, you last longer than the others we've asked to sort out the garden." She walked down the drive to Rae and handed her the small parcel of food and the letter. "Here, darling, you keep forgetting your letter. I didn't know you knew anyone in Southend."

Rae looked at the postmark – Southend-on-Sea. The untidy handwriting definitely wasn't Mama's or Papa's. Sliding her finger under the flap, she opened the envelope and took out the letter.

"Is everything all right, darling?" Joanna asked.

"Yes, thank you." Rae stared at the name at the bottom of the letter. "It's from someone I once knew. A friend. Nothing interesting."

Joanna went back into the house and Rae continued to stare at the name at the bottom: Jamie MacKenzie.

Dear Rae,

I hope you are well. The day after I last saw you, I went to your house, but you'd already left with your mother. The nanny gave me your address. I hope you don't mind me writing to you.

I am now working at my uncle's boatyard in Leigh-on-Sea while he recovers from a fall.

I believe I upset you the last time we met, and I would like to apologise to you and, if possible, to become friends again.

I will be free this Wednesday afternoon and I will arrive at Laindon Station on the train shortly after noon. If you would be willing to see me so that I can apologise, perhaps we can meet outside Baxter's Tea Rooms. I will be there from one o'clock and I will wait until three o'clock.

I understand if you do not want to meet me,

Yours sincerely,

Jamie MacKenzie.

Rae's first instinct was to screw the letter up in a ball and hurl it into the bushes. He said he wanted to apologise, but what did he want to apologise for?

Was it for trying to pin her down with his arms in such a way that it reminded her of Andrew? Or was it because he'd shown his true feelings when she'd told him Andrew had kissed her? His expression revealing a mixture of revulsion, disappointment and self-righteousness.

She'd wanted him to tell her it hadn't mattered. That he understood she hadn't known what was going to happen. That it didn't change anything. To be fair, she'd wanted him to put something right that he had no control over. Nevertheless, she couldn't forget his face, frowning with condemnation.

If she saw him again, it would simply bring back the memories of their last meeting, of her shame, and worse, it would once again remind her of the night she'd been with Andrew – something she was desperate to forget.

How dare he? she thought as she cycled down the drive towards Mrs Richardson's house. She would tear it up when she got there and put it on the compost heap.

Chapter Nineteen

♥

Mrs Richardson's house was nestled in the middle of what was known as Dunton Plotlands. Ben had explained to Rae that, years before, farmland that had been hard to cultivate had been divided into plots and sold off. Over time, the new owners had put up an enormous variety of homes, ranging from buildings that were hardly more than large, wooden sheds to smarter brick-built, single-storey homes. While their houses were being built, they lived in tents, shacks and, in one instance, an old railway carriage.

He'd said that lots of people from the packed East End of London had bought plots so they could escape the smoke and grime for the weekend. Each Friday night, families carrying tools and other baggage they'd need for the short break packed the trains from Fenchurch Street Station. Arriving at Laindon, they made their way to their plots for two days of hard work and fresh air.

Joanna's story was interwoven with the Plotlands. She'd left London's crowded streets in search of a new life, met Ben – a man whose upbringing in wealth and privilege had placed him a world away – and together, they'd built a house of their own. How courageous Joanna had been to face the icy disapproval of Mrs Richardson. Rae could almost picture the young Joanna, her heart full of determination, standing in the shadow of Priory Hall, its grandeur cold and imposing, as Mrs Richardson sneered at the girl who dared to dream of belonging.

Once Ben's father had died, Mrs Richardson had realised she couldn't manage the estate on her own and had invited Ben and Joanna to live with her in Priory Hall. Apparently, it had been a horrible time for Joanna because Mrs Richardson had constantly found fault with her daughter-in-law. Finally, Ben had decided he'd take Joanna back to the house they'd built in the Plotlands.

However, after several falls, Mrs Richardson realised she couldn't live alone in such a large house. To her son's surprise, she'd insisted Ben and Joanna live in Priory Hall and as soon as she found a suitable house, she'd buy it. In the meantime, she'd live in the Plotland house. Inexplicably, Mrs Richardson had remained there, although she'd insisted on some enlargement to the building, and on having a cook and maid – something that impressed her neighbours who secretly called her Lady Richardson.

"Yes?" the young maid said when she opened the door and found Rae, hurriedly pulling her cap on.

"I've come to tidy up the garden," Rae said.

The girl's eyebrows shot upwards. "Good luck. You're going to need it."

"Who is it, Tilly?" came a sharp, imperious voice from within the house.

Tilly glanced nervously over her shoulder. "It's a boy come to do the garden, ma'am."

"I'm a girl!" said Rae. Although looking down at the overalls, she could see why the maid had been mistaken. She'd jammed the cap on her head before she'd knocked at the door, knowing that cycling through the lanes had blown her hair into disarray. In an attempt to forget Jamie and his invitation, she'd pedalled furiously, swerving on a patch of gravel at one point, and almost falling off.

"Show him around the back, please Tilly. And keep an eye on him. I shall hold you responsible if anything goes missing."

"Yes, Ma'am," Tilly called over her shoulder.

Tilly grinned cheekily as she led Rae to the tool shed in the back garden. "Don't worry, I'll let her know I was mistaken about you being a boy, but—" she hesitated, her gaze flicking towards the house. "Don't expect her to be happy."

"What d'you think she'd like me to do first?" Rae asked, her heart sinking as she took in the brambles clawing their way into flower beds and the choking weeds.

Tilly shrugged, "Beats me," she said, "but trust me, if you do something she don't like, she'll let you know. She's got eyes in the back of her head. She'll be watching us now from the window."

Tilly had been correct. As soon as Rae dug her spade into the hard, clay soil, there was a rapping on the window. Shortly after, it opened and Mrs Richardson leaned out and called, "You can start over there." Her voice cut through the air like a knife, and she pointed to the other side of the garden where brambles had begun to creep in from next door's overgrown garden.

A flustered Tilly came into the garden, an hour later. "What did you say your name was?" she asked. "Only Mrs Richardson wants to know."

"Rae Kingsley."

Tilly eyed her doubtfully. "You sure you're not a boy?"

"No, my real name's Hannah-Rae. My parents were going to call me Hannah if I was a girl and Raymond if I was a boy, after my Papa's parents. But in the end, they decided to put the names together."

Before Rae had finished clearing the brambles, Mrs Richardson emerged from the house and, tapping determinedly with her walking stick, she marched down the path. From her reputation, Rae had imagined she would be a large woman, so this small, frail-looking figure took her by surprise.

"You must be the gardener with whom Tilly is having difficulties."

"Difficulties?" asked Rae.

"First, she tells me you're a boy and then she changes her mind, although..." Mrs Richardson peered at Rae over the top of her glasses, "I can quite see her problem. I've never seen a girl attired in overalls before. And then, she tells me you have two names, one a boy's and one a girl's. So, perhaps you'd be good enough to tell me your real name before I assume you're up to no good."

Before Rae could answer, Mrs Richardson added, "But then you are related to my daughter-in-law, so it's only to be expected."

Realising Joanna and their family were being judged based on Rae's appearance and, by whatever response she made next, she swallowed and composed herself.

"Good afternoon, Mrs Richardson. First, please may I introduce myself; I am Hannah-Rae Kingsley, and I assure you, I am a girl. I expect the confusion has arisen because of my overalls, but I find they are much more practical than skirts, which tend to get tangled in brambles." She paused, hoping she hadn't overdone the politeness. It had been as much as she could bring herself to muster, reminding herself Joanna would be judged on her behaviour. But it appeared to have done the trick.

Mrs Richardson studied her through narrowed eyes. "I see, Hannah-Rae. Well, thank you for clearing that up. I suppose you, being a girl, explains why you haven't yet cleared that patch of brambles. If you don't do it today, I expect you to be back here bright and early tomorrow to finish the job."

Exactly how Rae managed to say, "Of course, Mrs Richardson," she didn't know, but she would not be beaten by this rude woman and risk making things worse for lovely, kind Joanna.

"And I hope you've dug up all the roots. I don't want them growing back. They shouldn't be growing there at all..." She glared at her neighbour's house. "But Miss Quinn seems incapable of containing her own garden. What a deplorable muddle! Now, when you've finished, don't forget to clean the tools before putting them away in their correct places." Mrs Richardson turned and tapped her way back up the path to the house.

Shortly after, Tilly appeared with a slice of cake and a glass of milk. "If you don't mind," she said apologetically, "please, can you take this over there where she can't see you from the window?" She pointed towards an enormous oak tree. "It's just that she told me to bring out water and a couple of biscuits, but you've been working so hard, I thought you might like something a bit nicer. Oh, and well done for keeping calm. Mrs Richardson can be a bit... well... nasty. Her son has sent over several gardeners, and none of them has lasted as long as you. D'you plan to come back tomorrow? I wouldn't blame you if you didn't."

"Yes," said Rae. "I certainly do. I'm not going to give her the satisfaction of making me give up."

As she put her gardening gloves back in the bicycle basket that evening, after tidying away the tools, she saw Jamie's letter and remembered she'd been going to put it on the compost heap. Well, it was too late now. She wasn't going back to the bottom of the garden just to get rid of it.

She took it out of the envelope and looked at it. The writing didn't flow; in fact, the letters were stiff and formal, as though each one had been painstakingly inscribed. She remembered how embarrassed

Jamie had been when he'd told her he was ashamed of his writing and wondered how long it'd taken him to write that single page.

She felt a stab of guilt that she had no intention of meeting him outside Baxter's Tea Rooms the following day. But then, she hadn't asked him to write, nor to come to Laindon. She screwed the letter up into a small ball and threw it into the basket.

On Wednesday morning, Rae arrived at Mrs Richardson's house, slipping quietly into the garden shed for the tools she would need. The morning air was crisp, with a promise of heat later. She wanted to finish the heavy digging before the sun climbed too high. More importantly, she wanted to make a good impression on Mrs Richardson – for Joanna's sake, if not her own.

At mid-morning, the familiar tap, tap, tap of Mrs Richardson's walking stick echoed down the path. Rae straightened, plastering on a bright smile. "Good morning, Mrs Richardson."

"Good morning, Hannah-Rae," Mrs Richardson replied, her voice carrying that imperious tone Rae had quickly come to expect. But then, surprisingly, her gaze softened. "I see you've already made a start. Splendid, splendid."

Rae braced herself, anticipating the sting of criticism. Instead, Mrs Richardson merely settled herself by the edge of the garden, silently watching as Rae worked to unearth the stubborn roots from the heavy clay soil.

"You really are a strange, young woman," Mrs Richardson said finally, her voice sharp but curious. "Are you sure you're related to my daughter-in-law?"

"Yes. Mama and Joanna are cousins," Rae replied evenly, digging her spade into the soil and pressing firmly with her foot.

"I see. And where do your parents live?"

"A little village in Sussex called Barlstead."

"And does your father work in the village?"

Rae hid a smile. It wasn't difficult to guess what assumptions Mrs Richardson had made about her family.

Rae looked up, feigning nonchalance. "My father is a top physician at the London Hospital in Whitechapel," she said lightly. "And my mama is training to be a doctor, too."

"Oh!" Mrs Richardson exclaimed, clearly caught off guard. Her eyebrows rose, and she sniffed as if trying to process the information. "The London Hospital, you say? I was treated there some years ago after I fell from a horse. Excellent medical care – first-class. And your mother, training to be a doctor? Well!" She huffed, the notion evidently challenging her opinions. "I don't hold with such nonsense myself. Women belong in the home. But... the world is changing. Perhaps I ought to revise my thinking."

She paused before adding, "And you, Hannah-Rae? Are you going to follow your parents into medicine?"

"No," Rae replied, shaking her head. "I like being outdoors. But I don't know what I want to do yet."

"Well, if you take my advice, you won't spend longer than you need in my daughter-in-law's company. She was a mere typist when she met and ensnared my son. She's nothing more than a scheming minx. I feel you can do better than that."

Rae's grip tightened on the spade. Anger flared hot in her chest, but she forced her voice to remain steady. "I think that's very unfair to Joanna."

"Nonsense, Hannah-Rae. You need to take more notice of your elders and betters. Now, I think you'd better carry on. You've missed a bit of root there. I can see it poking up. And make sure you clean the tools and put them away when you've finished. And arrange them tidily."

"Yes, Mrs Richardson," Rae said, biting back the retort that trembled on her lips. At least she'd stood up for Joanna.

Mrs Richardson turned and walked back up the path.

The rest of the morning passed in a haze of sweat and exertion. When Tilly brought out milk and cake, Rae gratefully retreated to the shade of the oak tree.

"Well, I see you're still here," Tilly said, her grin both conspiratorial and admiring. "Cook bet you'd be gone by midday."

"I'm not going to let her beat me," Rae replied, a defiant glint in her eyes. "But how do you and Cook put up with her?"

Tilly snorted. "Her son pays us double the usual rate to stay. I'm getting married in September and I'm making as much as I can now. But it's hard. She's a real bad-tempered old biddie. Dunton's such a friendly place – all the neighbours help each other out and there's a real community spirit, but she upsets everyone, and no one can stand her. Nobody visits, except her son, and he can't wait to get away. When he brings her grandchildren, the little girl cries. It's a shame. But if Lady Richardson can't control her temper and sharp tongue, she's going to have to put up with the loneliness.

"Tilly! Tilly! Where are you, you dratted girl?" It was Mrs Richardson, calling from the back door.

"No peace for the wicked," Tilly muttered, rolling her eyes before hurrying back to the house.

The brook at the bottom of the garden ensured the soil was damp and heavy to dig and by the time the sun was overhead, sweat trickled down Rae's back and face. She stopped and mopped her forehead with her sleeve. Tilly's words played over and over – *she's a real bad-tem-*

pered old biddie – she's going to have to put up with the loneliness. It reminded her of Pop's description of her own grandmother who lived in an East End street full of friendly neighbours, none of whom wanted anything to do with her. Even her husband and children had deserted her.

How sad.

Mama showed signs of becoming like her own mother. Rae tried to remember the last time her mama had cuddled her or spent any real time with her. There were plenty of memories of arguments – the last one being when she'd been sent home from school in disgrace.

That, Rae acknowledged, had been her own fault, but she had a feeling Joanna would have handled it with more understanding and kindness. She was so gentle with Faye and Mark.

So, what had turned Mama, Gran and Mrs Richardson into such angry, unreasonable women? Since she'd spoken to Pop and had first recognised, she must be wary of becoming like her mother and grandmother. She hadn't given it much thought. School and Bobby had been her world. She'd seen very little of Mama and had no reason to think about her gran. Life had revolved around Bobby and her moods, and Rae had tried to fit in with whatever her friend had wanted.

But now, there was nothing meaningful to shape her life – her future was uncertain. What did she want? Who did she want to be?

Definitely not an irritable, ill-tempered woman like Mrs Richardson.

Her mother's voice surged through her mind, "Hannah-Rae, sometimes, I simply don't know what gets into you."

Would it hurt her mother to simply ask what got into her? To find out and to talk it over. That's what Joanna would do.

But perhaps her mother had been right. Perhaps she knew Rae was destined to become an angry, unpleasant woman.

A ROSE IN PLOTLANDS

Did it run in families? Was it inescapable?

Rae stabbed at the earth with her spade. No, she couldn't believe that. She must have the final say on how she turned out.

She was nothing like her mama. Yes, from time to time, she lost her temper, but as she got older, she knew she'd grow out of it.

But the nagging voice of doubt asked if perhaps she might be growing *into* it.

I've kept my temper with Mrs Richardson, and she's really tiresome, she told the voice.

Because it suits you, the voice said.

Well, that was true. But she hadn't lost her temper recently – apart from when she received Jamie's letter.

Exactly, said the voice. *He made the effort to contact you so he could apologise, and you won't even see him.*

It was true. Rae's chin dropped to her chest in shame, and she groaned. She could have at least met Jamie and listened to his apology. But she hadn't considered him. She'd screwed his letter up in contempt and had planned to snub him.

Her shame at her poor behaviour and her insecurities weren't his fault, she reminded herself.

Rae checked her watch. It was twenty-five past two. Would he still be waiting for her outside Baxter's Tea Rooms? Knowing Jamie, he would be. But one thing was certain: by the time she cleaned the tools, tidied up and cycled to town, he'd be gone.

If only she hadn't been so hasty. It wouldn't have been hard to show him some courtesy. So why hadn't she? Rae's fingernails bit into her palms. She wanted to be different from her mother and grandmother. She would be different...

Piling the tools under the tree out of sight of Mrs Richardson, she closed the tool shed door. Later, she'd come back and clean them, but now she had to get to Laindon. Running to her bicycle, she seized it without a backward glance.

The avenues of Plotlands were unmade and rutted. It was impossible to cycle over them, so she wheeled her bicycle as fast as she could over the furrows and grassy tussocks until she reached the smoother streets nearer the High Road. Then she mounted and pedalled madly.

Steel bands around her chest squeezed the air from her and she was gasping for breath by the time she arrived at Baxter's Tea Rooms.

Ten past three.

No sign of him.

Breathe!

No time...

She ran along the front of the tea rooms, peering through each window. Hands on either side of her face. Nose against the glass.

No Jamie.

Well, of course not.

She bent double, her hands on her knees, sucking air into her lungs.

He'd gone.

But perhaps he hadn't left Laindon yet.

Hope flickered inside.

She picked up the bicycle she'd flung down and set off for the railway station. Legs pumping the pedals. Thigh muscles screaming. Throat and lungs burning. She pushed harder, the ache in her muscles nothing compared to the knot of regret tightening in her chest.

Perhaps he was still there.

She might catch him yet.

As she approached the station, a plume of smoke curled skyward and a train pulled away from the platform with a hiss of steam, slowly gathering speed.

He'd gone. She bit her quivering lower lip.

What must he think of her?

Nothing worse than she thought of herself, that was for certain.

Then, with relief, she realised the train was heading towards London, not Southend where Jamie would be going.

"Oi! Watch what you're doing!" a man shouted at her as she skidded to a stop and hurled the bicycle from beneath her onto the pavement outside the station. She rushed into the ticket office.

Thrusting her hand into her pocket, she fumbled for coins. Why hadn't she thought to bring money?

Would they let her through onto the platform without a ticket?

"Rae?"

It was Jamie. He was looking at the timetable on the wall.

She suddenly caught sight of herself in the reflection of the ticket office window and saw what a fright she looked in her dirty overalls and with her sweat-streaked face and unkempt hair.

"Oh, it's so good to see you," he said, stepping towards her. "I thought you weren't going to come." His face lit up with a smile. No distaste at her dishevelled appearance. Indeed, she might have strolled into the ticket office in a pretty summer frock the way his eyes glowed as he took her in.

"I can't stay long," she gasped, trying to catch her breath. "I've got to get back to work, but I didn't want you to think I hadn't bothered to come."

"Have you got time for a cup of tea?" He took a step towards her and then checked himself and paused.

"I can't go into Baxter's like this." Rae's cheeks flared as she looked down at the mud that was caked over her overalls and boots.

She noted Jamie had taken a great deal of care with his appearance. He looked so smart and handsome in his suit.

"Perhaps I can walk you back to work?" he asked. "I wouldn't want you to get into trouble because of me."

She nodded, feeling suddenly shy, and led him outside to where her bicycle lay discarded on the pavement.

As they strolled down the High Road, he told her about his dad's brother, Uncle Gordon, who'd fallen and hurt his back a few weeks before. Since Jamie's father had Alex and lots of men working for him, Jamie had offered to help in his uncle's boatyard in Leigh-on-Sea.

Rae glanced at him from the corner of her eye as he spoke. He'd changed. The boy she remembered seemed a lifetime away. He was taller and there was a quiet confidence in his voice. His arms, once as skinny as pipe cleaners, now showed the strength of someone accustomed to physical work. When he took his jacket off, she could see his muscles rippling beneath the rolled-up sleeves of his shirt. How hadn't she noticed the last time she'd been with him? Because, she admitted to herself, she'd only been thinking of herself.

She felt small beside him, in more ways than one.

As they reached the unpaved tracks of the Plotlands, the conversation eased into a lull. Finally, Jamie spoke again, his voice hesitant. "I suppose I might as well get it over." He stared at the ground and his words, which had been so assured before, now faltered. "When I last saw you, I upset you. I'd like to explain and put things right... if you'll let me."

He glanced at her quickly to judge her reaction. To see if she'd allow him to continue.

Rae nodded. She swallowed, wondering if this was the point when their friendship would change forever. For good or ill.

"That time you came with your friend Bobby," Jamie began, his words slow and deliberate, "I overheard her say I was childish—"

"Oh, Jamie," Rae interrupted, her voice breaking. "I didn't realise you'd heard. And I'm also sorry I didn't put Bobby in her place." How could she have been so thoughtless?

"No need to apologise. She was right." He paused. "But I wasn't sure what to do about it, so I listened to the lads in Dad's yard, and I picked up all sorts of things about how a man is supposed to behave. They were talking all sorts of nonsense, as it turns out. But I didn't know that then. And when you told me about that... that boy, I thought what you needed was for me to... well... hold you... like a man. But I got it all wrong." His cheeks were now scarlet, and Rae grabbed his arm and stopped him.

"Jamie! I had no idea what was going on in your head. I'm so sorry. I was ashamed and embarrassed by what I'd done, and I thought you found me revolting after I told you Andrew had kissed me... And I couldn't bear it."

Jamie's brow furrowed, his expression one of astonishment. "Rae, I could never find you revolting. I was shocked at what you told me and if I'm honest, I was jealous, but never, *ever* revolted."

Jealous? It hadn't crossed her mind he might be jealous. How strange. The whole incident had been nauseating. What was there to be jealous of?

"So, do you forgive me?" he asked, worry lines still etched into his face.

"There's nothing to forgive." This was so unexpected. It had been she who needed his forgiveness, and yet he was asking for hers. It was time to tell him how horrible she was and to apologise to him, however much it hurt. He was a decent person, and he deserved that.

"If anyone needs to ask for forgiveness, it's me. I'm a dreadful person and I don't know why you've ever bothered with me. The very first time I met you, I..." she couldn't bear to say it. Yes, she'd been little more than a child. But really, punching Jamie had been such a dreadful thing to do. "You were right when you likened me to a thistle, except there isn't much that's soft about me. I'm all prickles."

Jamie shook his head. "No, I was wrong. You're not like a thistle at all. You're more like an English rose. Beautiful. And, yes, you've got thorns, but they're just for protection. I know that. I've always known that."

She expected him to grin at her and punch her arm jokingly or perhaps grab her around the waist and swing her around as he would have done before Bobby had disrupted everything. She'd have squealed as they'd spun, and he'd have pretended to become dizzy and stumble. She'd have insisted he put her down and then when he did, she'd have punched him playfully and then run away, knowing he'd chase her and when he caught her, they'd collapse in a heap, laughing until their sides ached.

But now, he merely smiled and nodded politely, his hands clasped behind his back. No teasing. No chasing. Just an unspoken finality hanging between them.

She had thorns? Well, that was a fair comment. But where did that leave them? They'd both apologised. The slate had been wiped clean. Presumably, now they would both carry on with their lives. Separately.

"So," she said brightly, feeling the need to fill the silence. "I'd better get back to work. Mrs Richardson will be after me if I don't clean her tools and tidy away."

"Yes, of course."

"Her house is just up there." Rae pointed further up the avenue, watching his face for some sign he might linger, might say something more, might not leave.

He nodded, and disappointment washed over her. This was it, then. Perhaps she'd never see him again. He'd changed from the fun-loving boy whose company she'd enjoyed to a polite stranger. If only she'd had the courage to speak up when Bobby had sneered at him. Would things have been different between them? Almost certainly.

"Will you be able to find your way back to the station?" she asked, hoping he'd say no and that he'd wait for her. But she knew he had a good sense of direction. He'd be able to find Laindon Station if he was blindfolded. And really, why would he want to waste any more of his life waiting for her?

He nodded. "Well, goodbye, and thank you for meeting me." His words were so formal, so detached, that for a second, she wondered if he was going to put out his hand and shake hers.

She watched him go and hoped he'd turn around, grin and run back, saying, "Fooled you! Of course, I'm not leaving you here."

She held her breath. Hoping. Hoping.

But he kept walking.

With a sigh, she carried on to Mrs Richardson's garden, her feet heavy, her heart heavier still. Maybe, if she hurried and cleared the tools quickly, she might catch Jamie up. And she also might escape without encountering Mrs Richardson.

No such luck. The old woman was waiting for her by the tree, her walking stick tapping the ground impatiently. "I thought I'd made it clear the tools were to be cleaned and stored in the shed."

"Yes, Mrs Richardson, I'm going to do that now."

"Well, see that you do! I shall expect you bright and early tomorrow. You haven't progressed much at all today."

"Yes, Mrs Richardson."

Rae hurriedly drew some water from the well and cleaned the tools, then she dried them and placed them in the shed. When she finished tomorrow, she'd sharpen and oil them, but there was no time now. Jamie's smile, the polite nod, the way he'd walked away without looking back – it all replayed over in her mind.

She sighed, she'd never catch him before he left, but just to satisfy herself, she'd ride to the station. Perhaps he'd stopped to have tea in Baxter's before he caught the train. It was possible, although highly unlikely. He'd done what he'd set out to do.

She arrived at the ticket office as a Southend-bound train pulled in and stopped with a hiss of steam and a shudder. Doors opened and slammed and as Rae rushed to the barrier, passengers who'd just arrived pushed past her. But ahead, on the platform, just boarding the train, was Jamie.

"Ticket?" said the collector, barring the way with his arm. "Sorry, Miss, you can't proceed without a ticket."

"Please, I just need to talk to someone. Please! I'll come straight back. I promise."

Doors slammed, the whistle blew, clouds of steam escaped with a hiss and the train jerked forward. Jamie spotted her and lowered the window, then leaning out, he looked at her questioningly.

"Meet me again?" she called, but the noise of the train creeping forward drowned her words.

He cupped his hand to his ear and shook his head to show he hadn't heard.

"Meet her here tomorrow at two o'clock," the ticket collector bellowed, tapping his watch and holding up two fingers.

Jamie nodded and waved, then was obscured by a cloud of steam as the train picked up speed.

Rae looked at the ticket collector in disbelief. "Why did you do that? You don't know if I'm free tomorrow at two."

"Look, miss, that poor lad's been here for some time. I thought it strange he let two trains go without getting on either of them, and then I saw his face light up when he saw you and I knew what was what. Turn up or don't turn up. It's no skin off my nose. But it'll be on your conscience if you break his heart."

"You don't know what you're talking about." Rae stared at him incredulously.

The ticket collector tapped the side of his nose. "You get to see all sorts of things in this job, miss. Trust me, I knows what's what." He turned and walked away.

Rae stared after him. Jamie had let two trains go before he got on? If that was true, it certainly hadn't been anything to do with her. He must have had a perfectly normal reason. And yet, the ticket collector…

No, despite the man's claim to knowing what Jamie had been thinking, he was wrong. Jamie had his own life. The scene she'd tried so hard to forget replayed in her mind. Rae; standing at the gate of the boatyard and the men calling out to Jamie that Susannah was waiting for him.

Susannah. Not a name Jamie had ever mentioned before. Neither had he spoken about her that afternoon.

Susannah, a girl who was presumably part of Jamie's life. Unlike Rae, who had foolishly given up her place.

Susannah. The name slithered through her mind like a snake, each sound curling around her thoughts with a sneering hiss.

It served Rae right. She didn't deserve a friend like Jamie. He'd always been kind and she'd taken him for granted. How hadn't she seen the one thing in her life that had remained constant? Well, it was too late now.

Jamie stared through the railway carriage window at the blur of the Essex countryside. The passing fields and hedgerows were a smear of green and brown, but he saw none of it. His mind was filled with the image of Rae – hair windswept and tangled, a streak of mud across her forehead – yet still, to him, the most beautiful girl he'd ever seen.

He'd longed to cup her face in his hands and to tell her how much he'd missed her. How she filled his waking thoughts and his dreams.

But he hadn't. He'd acted like a man, or at least the version of a man he thought Rae wanted him to be.

And it had hurt.

But if that was the only way he could spend time with her, then it would have to be enough. Her voice still rang in his ears – 'I met a boy. And he kissed me, and it was horrible. And I never want to kiss anyone ever again. Ever!'

That had been very clear.

He clenched his fists at the thought of that boy – Andrew. The name burned into his memory.

Unbidden, another memory surfaced – Susannah. He frowned, the recollection unwelcome and unsettling. Grown-up eyes in a child's face, promising something he hadn't been searching for, hadn't understood, hadn't wanted. His first experience of a kiss had been a shock. Maybe that's how first kisses were, he thought. Maybe they didn't matter.

If only he and Rae had shared each other's first kiss… But it was too late. Other people had stolen those moments from them.

And yet, despite everything, Rae had followed Jamie to Laindon Station and had wanted to see him again.

A tiny ember of hope flickered in his chest. He tried to crush it. Hope was dangerous. Hope could break a man.

Chapter Twenty

Rae was awake before dawn, the first light of day creeping through her window. She dressed quickly in her overalls and padded downstairs to the kitchen, where she brewed a pot of tea in the quiet stillness.

If she started work early in the garden, she would feel justified in leaving promptly – and after all, what could Mrs Richardson do? She could ask her not to come back, but even she must realise that finding someone else to tackle the wilderness of her garden would take time, during which the weeds and brambles would reclaim their territory.

"You're up early, darling," a soft voice startled her. Rae turned to see Joanna standing in the doorway, her hair slightly tousled, a kind smile on her face.

"I wanted to meet a friend this afternoon, so I thought I'd make an early start at Mrs Richardson's, if that's all right with you."

"Of course it is. I can't tell you how grateful Ben and I are for everything you've done in the garden. But I hope my mother-in-law isn't taking advantage of you, Rae. Please don't take any nonsense from her." Joanna poured herself a cup of tea and sat at the table. "Although," she added with a knowing smile. "I think you're capable of giving as good as you get. We come from a family of strong women."

It was meant as a compliment, Rae knew, but it still made her feel uncomfortable. "You mean Pop's wife and my mother?"

Joanna nodded silently. "Well, yes, and if there are two, I suppose there are others in our family."

"But you're not like that. You're kind and gentle. Nothing like my mother."

Joanna chuckled softly. "Not always, darling. I have my moments. And as for being like your mother, well, we're not blood relatives, but perhaps more importantly, we both had very different childhoods. Your mama is driven to achieve things, while I have all I want here."

Overnight, Rae's mind had churned with memories and regrets. "Do you think I'm going to turn out like Mama and Grandma Ivy?"

"Since you've thought about it enough to ask the question, I'd say, no, you won't – if you don't want to."

"No, I don't want to!" Rae looked at Joanna in horror.

"Your mama isn't that bad, Rae. As for Grandma Ivy..." Joanna grimaced. "Well, that's a different matter. But, you know, there's a difference between being strong and being bad-tempered. The problem is deciding where the dividing line lies... Anyway, don't let me keep you if you plan to meet a friend. I didn't know you'd made any friends here."

"Oh, no, it's someone I've known for a while." Rae took her cup and saucer to the sink and washed them up.

"Who is it, in case your mama telephones and wants to know?"

Rae hesitated, but she didn't intend to lie to Joanna. "Jamie MacKenzie." Rae held her breath, waiting for Joanna to query her further, but she merely stood and, with her head cocked on one side, asked, "Can you hear Mark? He's so restless at the moment. I've been up and down all night."

The unmistakable wails of a child could just be heard, and Joanna turned to go. "Well, have an enjoyable time today with your friend and don't work too hard this morning."

Mama wouldn't have said something like that. She used to complain Rae spent too much time with the 'boatyard boy'. Not, Rae thought, because he was a boy but simply because he was from a different class – a lower class. Mama had urged her to make more suitable friends. But Bobby might once have appeared to be suitable and look how that had turned out. Clearly, Grandma Ivy and Mama were snobs. Was Rae a snob? Absolutely not! That was one difference. So, it wasn't inevitable she followed them.

She *could* be her own person.

She *would* be her own person.

Later, when Rae reached Mrs Richardson's gate, Tilly opened the front door and put her finger to her lips, then glancing nervously behind her, she hurried down the path to meet her.

"There's good news and there's bad news this morning," Tilly whispered, glancing over her shoulder again. "Although the bad news is bad for me, and the good news is good for you."

"What's happened?"

"Mrs Richardson has one of her headaches, so Cook and me are going to be in strife all day. That's the bad news."

"And the good news?"

"You've got the day off. She doesn't want you in the garden – as she put it, 'making all that racket'. But apparently, she wants you back tomorrow. I pointed out it was Saturday tomorrow, but she bit my head right off."

"Shall I sharpen the tools or do something quiet?" Rae offered, guilt pricking her.

"No, I wouldn't risk upsetting her."

"Then I'll just pick some flowers for her room before I go."

Rae crept around the garden, snipping off rosebuds from the overgrown bushes and finding blooms from plants that were being overtaken by weeds. She tucked a rosebud into the fastening of her overalls. Jamie had likened her to a rose. Not that she'd deserved such a compliment, and she couldn't help thinking it had been as much about the thorns as the beauty. Brambles might have been a more apt comparison, she thought wryly as she cut back a large, spiny shoot.

She sighed. There was still so much to do in the garden. As soon as she had the brambles under control, she'd start pruning the plants that were supposed to be there. Ben had plenty of gardening books in the library and she'd been reading about garden care.

Rae caught Cook's eye through the kitchen window and passed her the posy of flowers, then with a wave, she picked up her bicycle and started for home.

What luck she didn't have to work that day. Despite planning to leave early, she suspected Mrs Richardson might somehow detain her and make her late. Today, she wouldn't turn up to meet Jamie looking dirty and dishevelled. Today, she'd be smarter.

Once back at Priory Hall, she took off her dirty overalls and washed herself thoroughly, cringing as she remembered what she'd looked like the last time she'd seen Jamie.

But what should she wear? The sky was cloudless and the day already hot, so whatever she wore would have to be cool. She peered forlornly into her wardrobe for something suitable. Most of the clothes she'd worn the previous summer no longer fitted, but as she'd needed either warm clothes or her school uniform since then, Mama hadn't bought her anything new.

Of course, if she'd finished the summer term and gone home under normal conditions, her mother would have taken her shopping for a new wardrobe. While she'd been at Joanna's, she'd either worn overalls or a blouse and skirt which, although slightly small and rather dowdy, were still acceptable.

She had one dress which the previous year had been her favourite, but it made her look so young, with the bow at its Peter Pan collar, the short, puff sleeves and the full body with a matching belt. She hadn't planned on wearing it again. But now, she'd have to. It was slightly too short, but at least it wasn't as tight as the blouse across her chest. She pinned the rosebud to her collar.

Rae stared at her reflection in the mirror and cringed. She looked like an adult actress she'd once seen who was playing the part of a little girl. But it would have to do. It was either the dress or the plain skirt and blouse. And if she didn't hurry, she risked being late again, despite having all morning to herself to get ready.

By the time Rae arrived at the station, it was twenty to two. She looked out for the ticket collector so she could thank him, but he didn't appear to be on duty. She was embarrassed about not having been polite to him the previous day. If it hadn't been for him, she wouldn't be seeing Jamie today. So, thank goodness he'd butted in.

She studied the posters on the walls, advertising Southend-on-Sea and Westcliff-on-Sea while she waited in the ticket office for the next train from their direction.

Five minutes later, a train pulled in with a squeal of brakes and a hiss of steam. Doors opened and people passed through the ticket barrier. She scanned the faces, not expecting Jamie to be on the early train, but he was there behind a large woman who was blocking the way with two hatboxes.

He smiled when he saw her, lifting his hand in a wave. Rae's breath caught in her throat. He looked so handsome in his suit, his confident stride making her heart ache with a confusing mix of emotions.

She wondered what he must think of her in such a childish dress.

"Well," Jamie said when the large woman with the hatboxes finally found her ticket and moved out of the way. "That was a surprise yesterday. I didn't expect to see you again. What did you have in mind?"

"What did I have in mind?" she echoed, her voice faltering.

"Well, yes, you asked me to meet you today at two. Was there a reason?"

Before she'd thought it through, she'd blurted out, "Oh, no, that wasn't me. That was the ticket collector."

Jamie looked puzzled.

"I called out to ask you if we could meet again, but you didn't hear, so he took it upon himself to ask you to come today."

The smile slipped from Jamie's face. "Oh, I see. I'm so sorry, Rae, I had no idea you meant sometime in the future. Well, there'll be a train along shortly. I'll just go home."

She couldn't bear to see the disappointment on his face. How could she have been so foolish? Why hadn't she pretended it'd been her idea? She could've said she wondered if they could go to Baxter's for tea, but instead, she'd been honest and hurt him. "Oh no! Jamie, I did want to see you—"

"But perhaps next month. Or next year." He nodded politely and turned to leave.

She caught his sleeve. "No, I did want to see you! Really! It's just that the ticket collector got in before me." Even to Rae's ears, that explanation sounded ridiculous. She looked like a child. She sounded like a child, and now she felt like one too.

Desperate, she blurted out, "I wonder if we might go to Southend. I've been looking at the posters and it looks so nice... that is, if you don't mind?"

Jamie's face lit up, the gloom lifting in an instant. "Yes, you'll love it! There're loads of boats to look at. And there's the pier, of course."

Rae let out a breath she hadn't realised she was holding. Somehow, against all odds, she'd rescued the situation, and he was now full of enthusiasm – just like she remembered him.

She felt a knot of anxiety in her stomach as she glanced at him, her fingers fidgeting with the fabric of her dress. Memories of their carefree friendship flooded back, but they were tempered by the weight of time and change.

Too much had happened. They were both older now, but Jamie had matured in ways that made her feel small and uncertain. Could they find their way back to the easy bond they'd once shared?

Or had that door closed forever?

Chapter Twenty-One

♥

When the train arrived at Southend station, Rae was startled by the crowds. It reminded her of the times she'd visited London with Papa. Although by the seaside, the pace was more leisurely, presumably because many people were on holiday.

Jamie stepped forward into the swirling tide of holidaymakers, and Rae nearly lost sight of him in the throng before he offered her his arm. She tucked her hand beneath it with relief and held on tightly as he steered them towards the Esplanade.

It had only been a few years ago that she'd grabbed his arm as she'd pulled him under the surface while they were splashing in the water at Cranston's Point. Now, she couldn't encircle his biceps with her hand. His muscles were firm beneath her fingers as he steered her through the crowds and when they arrived at the water's edge, she was disappointed when he allowed her hand to fall.

He didn't offer her his arm again as they walked along the Esplanade, admiring the boats and remembering times they'd spent on the *Wild Spirit*. Thankfully, the conversation and laughter flowed easily as they recalled so many shared moments.

With a stab of panic, she wondered if there'd be anything left to say once they ran out of reminiscences. But they hadn't reached that point yet.

She'd worry about that later.

Had he ever been to Southend with the mysterious Susannah? If he had, Rae was sure he'd have held her arm. Would Jamie and Susannah have as much to laugh about and remember as he and Rae? Possibly not yet. But in time...

She wondered whether to ask him about the girl if the conversation dried up. But really, it was none of her business. And anyway, perhaps she was mistaken and Susannah meant nothing to Jamie, despite her self-doubt being determined to taunt her. Whatever the truth, Jamie had been kind and polite to Rae, and that was more than she deserved.

When they arrived at what Jamie told her was the longest pier in the world, he bought tickets for the tiny, electric train that ran from the shore, travelling about a mile to the pier head. Thankfully, during the journey, there was plenty to see to provoke conversation. Families ambling along the pier, laughing and shouting, solitary fishermen with their lines over the side, lovers; arm in arm with eyes for no one else.

Jamie showed interest in all Rae had been doing while she'd been staying with Joanna. Nevertheless, he sat rigidly, keeping distance between them as if they were strangers, and drawing away from her when the rattling train threw them together.

Once back on the Esplanade, Jamie bought them both ice creams. They ate while strolling on the beach, watching the tide recede to leave small boats lying on their sides, stranded on the glistening mud.

Rae noted the dresses and outfits worn by the women who walked with their arms tucked into their husband's or sweetheart's arms. Summery dresses and elegant hats, even parasols to match. She couldn't bear to look down at her dress – her little girl's frock. No wonder Jamie kept his distance from her. He was treating her like a younger sister. And that, she knew, was what they looked like – a dutiful brother taking his younger sister on an outing.

"Shall we go on the rollercoaster?" Jamie asked as they wandered through the Kursaal Amusement Park, looking at all the fairground attractions.

The ticket seller for the Caterpillar Ride must have noticed their indecision and called out, "Roll up, roll up! Come on, sir! Take yer sweetheart on the Caterpillar! You'll never 'ave a better excuse for a kiss an' a cuddle, if yer know what I mean!" He winked at Jamie, who blushed and, shaking his head, steered Rae away from the ride.

Her mind reeled, desperately searching for an escape from the humiliation. If she'd known how to get back to the station, she'd have run away to save Jamie from the embarrassment of being with her. Instead, she walked next to him, her head hanging in shame.

"I think, if you don't mind, Jamie, I'd like to go home, please. I'm suddenly rather tired," she said, trying to keep her voice level and hide how close she was to tears.

He nodded, "Yes, of course." He turned and pointed in the opposite direction. "The station's this way."

Was that relief she heard in his voice? She dared not look at him to check his expression for fear he'd see her brimming eyes.

Their progress was slow through the throng of families and couples who strolled and chattered excitedly, soaking up the holiday atmosphere. Although he made sure she was close, he didn't offer her his arm again.

They finally arrived at the station, and Rae took out her return ticket so she could disappear as quickly as possible through the barrier and make her way home. The sooner she was gone, the sooner Jamie would be rid of her, but when she turned to thank him, he'd gone.

Good, she told herself. The embarrassment was over, and she'd soon be home. The entire trip had been a mistake, but it was nearly finished.

Why did her stomach churn with disappointment?

Once, she'd been insensitive to Bobby's comments about how childish Jamie was. Now she understood how wounded he would have been. Not that Jamie had called her childish. He'd been a gentleman. In so many ways. But he'd left her behind. He was a man, and she was now the naïve one.

She had no right to be hurt. Jamie had been so keen to get rid of her; he hadn't even said goodbye – just delivered her to the station and then left.

She sat down on a bench on the platform and closed her eyes, tears pricking her lids. The faint tang of steam and soot lingered in the air, and the bustling sounds of the station seemed distant, muffled.

"Rae?"

Her eyes flew open to find Jamie crouching in front of her. "Are you crying?" he asked softly. His hand moved toward her cheek, hesitated, then dropped.

"No." She angrily wiped her face with the back of her hand. "Some dust blew into my eyes, that's all. What are you doing here?"

"I had to buy a ticket and when I looked around, you'd gone." He frowned, as if trying to read her expression.

"I thought you'd walk home. I know it's not far." She looked down, hiding the tears that still filled her eyes.

"But I'm not going home yet. I'm taking you back to Laindon."

"You don't need to do that," she said, the words tripping over themselves. That would mean yet more awkwardness, more chances to embarrass herself. She wanted to hide her disgrace, even if it meant she had to travel home alone. "I'm quite capable of getting off a train, thank you."

He winced at her words, and she wanted to sink into the earth. How rude she'd sounded. How like a spoilt child. But he could make this so much easier by just walking off and pretending he didn't know her.

However, he obviously didn't intend to leave her. "Rae? What's the matter? Please tell me."

Her eyes opened wide in amazement. Of course, he knew what the matter was. Surely, he didn't want her to actually say the words, 'You are embarrassed by me and I'm so ashamed. I want to go home to put us both out of this misery,' did he?

"Nothing," she said, her voice flat. "I just want to go home."

"Well, you'd better come with me then," he said lightly, a faint smile touching his lips.

How dare he laugh at her?

"Why don't you leave me alone? I'm quite capable of finding my own way home." Her voice trembled, dangerously close to tears.

Jamie sighed, running a hand through his hair. "I would leave you alone, but I'm not sure you *are* capable of finding your own way home. This is the wrong platform. If you get on the next train, you'll end up in Shoeburyness."

Rae groaned. Her humiliation was complete.

"Come on," Jamie said gently. "Let's cross to the other platform or we'll miss the next train. Now I'm going to take you as far as Laindon and then, if you prefer, I'll leave you there. I can see you've had enough of me."

He stood and turned towards the footbridge. She caught his arm as he was halfway up the stairs. "What d'you mean you can say I've had enough of you? I didn't say that!" she demanded, breathless. "Surely, it's the other way around?"

"Come on," he said, grabbing her hand as a whistle shrieked in the distance. "There's a train coming. Quick!"

They arrived on the correct platform just as the train pulled in, steam hissing. Jamie held the door open for Rae, then climbing into the carriage after her, he slammed the door. The day-trippers were still enjoying the delights of Southend, so Jamie and Rae were the only passengers to board the carriage of the London-bound train. The guard blew a piercing blast on his whistle and waved his flag as a puff of steam blew and the train lurched forward with a chug, chug of the pistons.

Jamie sat opposite Rae and leaned forward, his elbows on his knees. "It's clear I've upset you – again. And I tried so hard not to. But, since we're stuck on this train until Laindon, perhaps you'd be good enough to tell me what I've done." His voice was a monotone. Flat. As if he was beaten and had given up.

His words cut through her anger, leaving only confusion. She blinked at him, stunned. "But you haven't upset me," she whispered. "It's me who's upset you."

They stared at each other in bewilderment.

"I don't understand," he said with a puzzled frown.

Rae hesitated, her gaze dropping to her hands. She owed him an explanation, even if it stung to say the words aloud. If she spoke quickly, maybe he could get off at Leigh-on-Sea and leave her to face the rest of the journey alone.

"I...I could see how uncomfortable you were when that man on the Caterpillar Ride assumed we were sweethearts and... well, I couldn't blame you. So, I thought if I went home, it might save you more embarrassment."

Jamie's eyes widened. "Embarrassed?" he repeated, shaking his head. "I *was* embarrassed. It's true. But not for the reason you think.

I was trying to make it clear we were just friends because I thought that's what you wanted."

The train pulled into Chalkwell Station. The next stop would be Leigh-on-Sea. Rae and Jamie continued to stare at each other.

"This isn't making any sense," Rae murmured. It appeared Jamie needed things spelled out in more detail. "That man didn't upset me. It wouldn't have bothered me if he'd thought we were sweethearts. In fact, I'd have been quite proud but—"

"Proud he'd assumed we were together?" Jamie's jaw dropped open. "But I thought I acted too young for you. I was trying hard to be grown up—"

"So was I!" Rae interrupted, her voice rising. "But it's really difficult when I'm dressed like this!" she said, looking down at the frock and tugging the skirt angrily.

"Rae! You look fine. It doesn't matter what you wear, you always look beautiful to me." He gasped, his eyes opening wide in alarm as if he'd said too much.

She stared at him with an expression of incredulity. "But this dress is... hideous."

He looked at the dress as if it was the first time he'd seen it, frowning and shaking his head as he took it in. "What's wrong with it? It looks perfect to me."

"It's a little girl's dress. This year, it doesn't even fit. There were so many ladies at Southend out with their men and I felt ashamed you had to put up with me."

"Rae!" Jamie cut her off, his voice firm but incredulous. "I wasn't putting up with anything." He turned his hands palms up in disbelief. "Seriously, you're worried about a dress?" He paused, nibbling his lip as if unsure whether to continue. "I promised myself I wouldn't say anything like this but... but I loved having you with me."

"Then why did you make sure you were always several inches away from me?" Rae asked, her voice faltering. "You offered me your arm and then as soon as we got to the Esplanade, you almost pushed me away."

"That's a slight exaggeration, Rae. I did nothing of the sort. I simply thought you wouldn't want people to think you were with me – other than as a friend."

The train pulled into Leigh-on-Sea station.

Doors slammed. Whistles blew.

"Aren't you getting out?" Rae asked softly.

"Of course not. I'm taking you to Laindon. And anyway, I still don't understand what's going on. You seem to think I'm embarrassed to be seen with you, and that's simply not true. I was keeping my distance, so I didn't embarrass *you*. There's nothing I'd have liked more than to have walked along arm in arm with you."

He stood and, for a second, she thought he was going to get out of the carriage after all. But he sat next to her and took her hand. "I promised myself I wouldn't tell you this, but I may never have another chance, and I want you to know. The first time I set eyes on you, I fell for you, Rae. I know people would scoff and say I was too young, and perhaps they're right, but I know how I felt. You took my breath away."

Rae stared at him. If he hadn't looked so serious, she'd have assumed he was joking. How could he possibly have fallen for her all those years ago? And especially after what she'd done to him.

"Not that day I punched you?" Rae whispered, shame flaring in her cheeks.

Jamie smiled at her. "I thought you were the most beautiful thing I'd ever seen. You still are."

"Oh, Jamie, I'm so sorry. I thought you were staring because you found me ridiculous in that dreadful coat my mother made me wear." She wanted to bury her face in her hands. "I had no idea you felt like that. I'm such an idiot... I can't tell you how sorry I am."

He reached out to straighten the rosebud on her collar.

"Yes, you're definitely more of a rose than a thistle. Beautiful—"

"With vicious thorns..."

Jamie smiled ruefully. "Forget the thorns. You just need to be treated with more respect than other flowers."

"Respect?" Rae wailed. "Why couldn't I be normal? Like a daisy or a dandelion? Why do I have to be so prickly?" She shook her head angrily. "Well, there's no point asking you that, I suppose. But I am trying not to be so difficult. I really am."

"You're not always prickly, Rae. You're just spirited. And that's all part of what I..." he hesitated, "...like about you."

It had sounded like he was about to say *what I love about you*. But that couldn't be possible. How could someone so... well, wonderful... love her? That was just wishful thinking.

She stared out of the window; the green blur of hedgerows and fields was a backdrop to so many scenes from her past. Tiny pieces of a gigantic puzzle were clicking into place, forming a picture she hadn't dared to see before.

How could she not have known Jamie felt like that? Bobby had said he'd had puppy eyes for her, but Rae had simply told her to shut up. If she was honest, she had suspected he was sweet on her but hadn't allowed herself to believe it. She wasn't worthy of anyone's attention. There was something wrong with her, otherwise her parents would have made her feel loved. Bobby might have treated her as an equal. So, she'd dared not hope she was special to Jamie.

"I know you don't feel the same, Rae." His tone was soft, resigned.

"Oh, no! It's not that. Truly." she blurted. "I just don't know how

I feel. Bobby and I used to go to the cinema each Saturday afternoon, and we watched all sorts of Hollywood films and, after a while, I started to believe that's what life would be like when I grew up. I don't know why it didn't occur to me that wasn't real life. And then..." Her voice faltered as memories of Andrew crept in. "And then I went with Bobby to meet that boy. Things were so different. So unpleasant. I wasn't sure what to believe anymore, so I blocked it all out. But I do like you, Jamie. I've always enjoyed being with you."

He looked down, his disappointment clear.

Rae's stomach twisted. How could she explain? She didn't understand it herself, but she had to try. Once the train reached Laindon, it was doubtful she'd have another chance to speak to him.

Words tumbled out in a rush. "I don't know how I feel, but yesterday, when I realised I might not see you again, I couldn't bear it. I felt so empty inside. It's all so confusing. Can you wait until I've sorted things out in my mind?" She looked through the window, dreading reaching Laindon.

Jamie's gaze softened, and a small smile played at his lips. "I'll wait for you forever, Rae. But don't worry, I won't pressure you for anything – not spending time with me nor... well, anything."

"D'you mean things like kissing?" Rae asked and felt a hot blush. Since they were both being so open, she thought she might as well find out exactly what he meant.

Jamie nodded; his own cheeks tinged pink.

"That's good," said Rae, "because I'm not sure I'm going to like that part of things." She carried on, despite his disappointment. Surely, it was best now to be completely honest?

"Andrew had blubbery lips, and his eyes were cold when he kissed me. It's not something I want to remember... or repeat. It was like... like... well, kissing a haddock."

Jamie's laughter burst out, a warm, rich sound that chased away the tension in the carriage. "I don't think haddocks have blubbery lips."

"Well, that's what he reminded me of," Rae said, her own laughter bubbling up in response. Suddenly, hope surged through her, like a strong wind inflating a sail. It was a start, wasn't it? Laughing together. That was good, wasn't it?

They continued to giggle at the thought of puckered-up, blubbery, haddock lips until the train pulled into Laindon. At least for the first time, they were in accord. Just like old times.

From time to time, despite their aching sides, they still burst into giggles as Jamie walked Rae home to Priory Hall.

That night Rae lay in bed going over the strange events of the day. There was plenty to think about, but the one memory that stayed with her was when Jamie left her at the gate of Priory Hall. He'd kissed the tips of his fore and middle fingers, then placed them gently against Rae's cheek.

"See you next Saturday," he'd said, and then he'd walked away, but unlike the previous day, when he'd left her, he'd turned back and waved.

Rae touched her cheek, where the warmth of his fingers had lingered. A strange sensation stirred inside her – not confusion, not doubt, but something else entirely.

Something that felt a little like hope.

Chapter Twenty-Two

♥

The following Saturday afternoon, Rae and Jamie met as arranged at Hadleigh Castle. They'd decided to cycle to a point halfway between Leigh-on-Sea and Laindon but since neither of them was familiar with any of the villages, Jamie had suggested they meet near the unmistakable ruin of the castle that stood on a hill overlooking the Thames.

It meant a slightly longer ride for Rae than Jamie, but since he often had difficulty getting away from his uncle's boatyard early, it made more sense. It also meant that neither of their families knew about their meetings.

"Not that there's anything wrong with us spending time together," Jamie had said as they'd planned the meeting. "But if my uncle tells Dad, he won't be happy about me seeing you."

Rae understood. She could see why Mr MacKenzie might not like Jamie seeing her. She wondered what he thought about the still mysterious Susannah. He probably approved of her.

It took all Rae's courage to broach the subject that had been gnawing at her mind since she'd first heard the girl's name. "Who is Susannah?" she asked at last, her voice as casual as she could make it.

Jamie looked startled. "Who?"

"Susannah," Rae said, avoiding his eyes. "I overheard the men at the boatyard mentioning her."

Jamie frowned, a wary look flickering across his face. "Oh, her. She's just a girl." He glanced down, his tone guarded. "She had a crush on me, but I don't feel the same. She's nice enough, but... she's not for me."

Jealousy seared Rae's heart. It was absurd – Jamie had said he felt nothing for Susannah – but the thought of another girl holding even a fragment of his affection tore at her heart. She forced herself to focus on the present. Jamie was here, in Essex, and they were friends. That mattered far more than a girl from Sussex who belonged to Jamie's past.

Each Saturday afternoon after that was spent sitting on the hill in the sunshine, watching the boats and barges sail up and down the Thames. On the odd occasion when it rained, they explored Hadleigh and Benfleet and found a tea shop where they could shelter. Rae was sure Joanna wouldn't mind her seeing Jamie. After all, she'd told her about him after receiving his letter, and Joanna had appeared to give her blessing. Not that she ever talked about Jamie for fear of bringing it to the forefront of Joanna's mind. That might risk her mentioning it to Mama, who wouldn't be in favour of Rae spending time with him. It might even prompt her to demand her daughter return home. No, it was no one's business. They were simply friends, and they weren't hurting anyone.

Ben had asked one of his farmhands to take over the gardening duties at Priory Hall while Joanna was busy with Mark. This allowed Rae to spend more time at Mrs Richardson's, taming the garden and bringing it back under control. Miraculously, the old lady tolerated Rae and although she was often sharp, she treated Rae well.

"I think she recognises your strength of character, Rae," Joanna said with a smile. "You're the only person she isn't rude to. Well, not often, anyway," she added.

Uncle Gordon's back was gradually improving, and Jamie had more free time, so occasionally, if he finished work early, he cycled to Dunton, and when he arrived at Mrs Richardson's, he walked past the cottage, whistling the tune to *Only a Rose*.

It was their signal, and Rae would pretend to go to the tool shed for something and wave to let him know she'd heard. He'd carry on wheeling his bicycle to a small lake set in a wooded area not far from the house and wait for her to join him when she'd finished. Then he'd walk her home across the fields.

As the days passed, Rae grew more anxious. Although Mrs Richardson's garden was one of the largest on Plotlands, she'd worked so hard, that soon there wouldn't be enough to keep her there each day and she feared she'd lose her freedom.

Uncle Gordon was also spending more time in his boatyard and Jamie suspected that as soon as his uncle was back at work full-time, there would be no reason to stay on, and his father would ask him to return to Sussex.

And then, of course, September was fast approaching when Rae would be expected back at school.

"I don't think I can bear it," Rae said gloomily as they sat in the shade next to the lake.

"Well, I'll probably be back at Dad's by the time you come home for Christmas," Jamie said, clearly trying to think positively. "I'll see you then."

"It won't be the same though, will it?" Rae said gloomily. "We won't be able to get away on our own. And Christmas is months away."

The following day, Rae was at the bottom of the garden hammering a new fence post into the ground when her attention was caught by rustling from the garden next door. She wondered if the badger, or whatever had caused the damage to the fence, was trapped. But to Rae's surprise, it was a tall, willowy, grey-haired woman parting some of the overgrown vegetation in her garden to peer through at her.

"I'm so sorry to startle you, my dear, but I thought you might want to know your young gentleman friend is outside whistling his little heart out like a bird waiting for you."

Rae gasped. How did this woman know Jamie was whistling for her?

"It's all right, my dear. Your secret's safe with me. Now I suggest you hurry before he thinks you're not here and goes."

"Th... thank you," said Rae, clutching the hammer to her chest and running towards the tool shed. However, Jamie had gone. Rae hurried out to the front of the house and ran after him.

"I was beginning to think you'd left for the day," Jamie said when she finally caught up with him further along the avenue.

Rae told him about Miss Quinn, the lady next door.

"D'you think she'll tell Mrs Richardson?" Jamie asked.

"I don't think so. Mrs Richardson's often very unkind about her and she doesn't keep her voice down, so I wouldn't be surprised if Miss Quinn's heard. Anyway, she said our secret's safe with her. I suppose I'll have to trust her."

"I came to tell you some news. You know Uncle Gordon's going to be back at work full-time from next week and we thought I might have to go back home?"

Rae nodded, her stomach tightening at the thought.

"Well, one of my cousins is going to buy into the cockle-fishing business, so he won't be around to help Uncle. That means I'll be staying – at least for a while." He smiled triumphantly.

"Once I go back to school, it won't matter if you're here, home or in Scotland," she said bitterly. "I won't get to see you much."

Rae shivered. The wind was brisk and cold and although she'd been sweating while she worked, she suddenly felt chilly. She'd taken her pullover off earlier and left it at the bottom of the garden.

"I'd better get back. Will you wait for me by the lake?"

Jamie nodded.

Rae hurried up the path but was intercepted by Mrs Richardson. "Where have you been, Hannah-Rae? I looked out earlier to see why you'd stopped that infernal hammering and you weren't there. I pay you to work, not stand around idling. So, where were you?"

Before Rae could answer, a voice came from the other side of the hedge. "I'm so sorry, Mrs Richardson. I was speaking to your gardener. I take full blame."

"Well, I... that is..." Mrs Richardson blustered, then before she could regain her composure, Miss Quinn added, "I would like to speak to Hannah-Rae about the possibility of sorting out my garden. With your permission, of course."

"Certainly not!" Mrs Richardson snorted. "Hannah-Rae is much too busy working for me."

Miss Quinn nodded with understanding. "It's just that it would be a shame if all her hard work in your garden was undone by fly-away seeds from all the weeds in my garden." She held her hands up as if in surrender. "My arthritis is playing up, and it's not easy for me to do my own digging now."

Mrs Richardson's eyes dropped to the claw-like hands her neighbour displayed. For a moment, her lips pressed together, and a flicker of something unreadable crossed her face but she said nothing.

"I would pay her well, of course," Miss Quinn said. "And I wouldn't expect her on the days you wanted her, Mrs Richardson. Perhaps you'd both like to think it over. I shall be in tomorrow, Hannah-Rae, if you'd care to call and we can discuss arrangements. Good afternoon to you both." She nodded and walked back to her house.

"Well, the nerve of the woman! Should you accept her offer, I would definitely expect my garden to take precedence, Hannah-Rae." Mrs Richardson tapped her way back to her house.

Rae tidied away and ran back to where Jamie was waiting for her.

Relief flooded his face when he saw her. "You were a long time. I thought you weren't coming back. What is it? What's happened? You look thrilled."

"I think I have a plan, and it might be a way of staying at Priory Hall if Joanna will allow it."

Rae told him how Miss Quinn had stepped in to save her from having to explain to Mrs Richardson where she'd been and then about the proposal.

"The only thing is, I'm not sure if she meant it about me working in her garden. Suppose she only said that to throw Mrs Richardson off the scent?"

"I suppose you'll find out tomorrow. But anyway, it looks terribly overgrown. You're not going to get all those weeds under control before you go back to school."

"I know!" said Rae gleefully. "That's my plan! I'm not going back to school. I'm going to work."

"But won't your parents be disappointed? They might not let you leave."

"Well, there's only one way to find out. I'll have to ask them. I'm not clever enough to be anything like a doctor and I don't want to work anywhere indoors. I love it outside. It's perfect."

Would Rae be allowed to take control of her life? Surely her parents would be pleased she'd thought through a sensible course of action?

They didn't have as long as usual by the lake, but Rae was so excited, Jamie appeared to be carried along by her optimism.

That evening, as they said goodbye, she expected Jamie to kiss his two fingers as usual, and touch her cheek, but instead, after placing the kiss on his fingers, he brushed her lips with them, leaving his kiss there. Had it been an accident? Her breath caught in her throat as she saw the pleading look in his eyes, asking for her approval. She smiled at him, knowing he'd done it deliberately, and she shivered with pleasure.

Rae looked down at her muddy hands. She wanted to kiss her fingers and place them on his mouth too, but they were much too dirty. The next time they met, she would make sure her hands were clean. Had he got caught up in the excitement of her plans and forgotten himself? She hoped not. Desperately, she wanted him to 'finger-kiss' her lips again.

She'd touched his face before, during their horseplay; nose-pulling, pretend slaps – even that shameful punch on the nose, but as she imagined kissing her fingers and placing them on his lips, she quivered with a feeling she didn't understand; warmth radiating through her.

How strange that on the day she'd decided what she wanted to do with her life, her mind wasn't full of plans for the future. It was reflecting on what Jamie's lips would feel like beneath her fingertips.

The following morning, Rae knocked at Miss Quinn's door. The paint was peeling and the areas around the letterbox and keyhole were scratched and worn. In fact, the entire house was tired and shabby.

Rae hesitated, her knuckles brushing the weathered surface of the door. It appeared to be too good to be true. Why should a woman put herself out for a stranger in the way Miss Quinn had for Rae?

"Call me Ada," Miss Quinn said as she led Rae into her house. "I'm not one for standing on ceremony. Unless I'm talking to Mrs Richardson, of course. Something I usually try to avoid." Her eyes twinkled.

Judging by the unruly garden, Rae expected the house to be untidy too, so she was surprised to find it clean and neat. Almost bare, Rae thought, with few ornaments and photographs in frames or pictures on the walls. It was as if Ada had just moved in and not yet unpacked all the keepsakes that older ladies such as Mrs Richardson had collected during their lifetimes.

Ada shooed the black and white cat from the sofa and invited Rae to sit while she made tea.

"Titan! Leave Hannah-Rae alone," she said when she returned and found the cat sitting on Rae's lap.

"Please call me Rae. And I think I took his seat, so I'm quite happy to tickle his ears in return."

"Well, Rae, you've certainly won him over. He doesn't take to new people, so he must have seen something very special in you." She smiled knowingly. "Now, shall we get down to business? You've seen how overgrown the garden is. I'm afraid as I said yesterday, I suffer from arthritis, so I find it painful to use tools. Do you think you'd be able to help me out in the garden? I'd pay well and you could work when it suited you. I wouldn't even mind if you slipped off with your young man from time to time." Her eyes sparkled with amusement.

"Oh, he's not my young man. He's just a friend," Rae said quickly, her cheeks reddening.

Ada raised a sceptical eyebrow. "Not your young man? Well, you'd better hurry and claim him, Rae, before some other young lady beats you to it. Are you sure *he* doesn't think he's your young man? He seems to spend a lot of time standing outside whistling for you."

"Please don't tell Mrs Richardson. We really are just friends," Rae said in a lowered voice, leaning slightly forward. "She wouldn't approve, and I've managed to keep it from her so far."

"Your secret's safe with me," Ada said, and then added wistfully. "I'm very good at keeping secrets... Now, what do you think about my proposal? Do you think you could tidy up my garden?"

When Rae got home, she found Joanna in the kitchen and told her she didn't want to go back to school in September. "Could I stay on here at Priory Hall instead? I'll get more clients, and I can pay you. I'll work hard – I promise."

Joanna paused, a dishcloth in her hands, and studied Rae carefully. "Darling, I think it's wonderful you've got a plan, but are you sure people will employ a female gardener? Some people are so set in their ways."

"There are quite a few ladies on their own in the district, and Ada said she'd rather not have a strange man around the house. Perhaps others might feel more comfortable with me. I'd like to find out, anyway." She nibbled her lower lip. "How d'you think Mama will take the news?"

Joanna winced and reached out to pat Rae's hand. "Hmm, I suspect she won't be happy. I think it best if I invite your parents over at the weekend and you can discuss it with them then."

The weekend came all too quickly. Rae sat rigidly in the drawing room at Priory Hall, her hands clasped tightly in her lap, bracing herself for what she knew would be an uncomfortable conversation.

"It's absolutely out of the question, Hannah-Rae!" Mama said. "You're going back to St Helena's in September and that's the end to it."

"Amelia," Papa said calmly. "Perhaps we could at least discuss it."

"Discuss it? What's there to discuss? I fought tooth and nail for an opportunity to study. And our daughter wants to abandon her education to dig up weeds! She leaves school over my dead body." Mama crossed her arms and observed her daughter through narrowed eyes.

Rae held her breath. She'd warned herself so often in the days leading up to this meeting not to lose her temper. Act like an adult, or your mother won't treat you like one, she'd told herself. She'd almost convinced herself that by remaining calm, she'd win her mother over. Apparently, it was going to take more than that.

"But you were stopped from doing what you wanted to do when you were young, and you've always resented it, Amelia. Is it right we stop Rae from doing what she wants to do? Might she one day resent us?" Papa asked.

"Resent us?" Mama's voice rose an octave. "After everything we've done for her!"

Other than the clock ticking, there was silence in the drawing room in Priory Hall. Joanna and Ben exchanged anxious glances but remained silent, sipping tea. Joe looked out of the window, while Faye and Jack watched the adults in horrified fascination, their eyes huge and round. Mark began to cry, and Joanna rose to pick him up and comfort him.

"I think," Papa said, his voice steady but firm, "perhaps we ought to go for a walk, Amelia. This is the height of rudeness. We've been invited to Joanna and Ben's home. The least we can do is remain civil."

Mama looked startled, then chastened. "Yes, of course," she said, her tone softening. "I apologise, Joanna. It was a bit of a shock, that's all."

Joanna nodded, still rocking Mark in her arms. "Of course. I understand."

Mama and Papa went for a walk in the garden and through the window, Rae watched Mama gesticulating wildly and Papa making placatory motions with his hands.

"Well, you've done it this time, Rae old girl," said Joe, shaking his head.

It wasn't possible to guess the outcome from her parents' faces as they returned. Rae's heart sank at the sight of Mama's furious expression and Papa's grim determination.

"We think the best thing to do is to wait for a week and let everyone think this over carefully," said Papa. "We're hoping Rae may change her mind but I'm very impressed at how she's beginning to take responsibility for her life."

Presumably, Mama isn't impressed, thought Rae, but at least her parents hadn't both said no, and she had a week to convince them she knew what she was doing and could be trusted. She would do her utmost in that time to find some clients and then her parents would find it harder to send her back to school.

"And you're sure you're all right with Hannah-Rae staying with you, Joanna?" Mama asked.

"Of course! She's been a marvellous help to me, and I know my mother-in-law's extremely pleased with all her work." Joanna smiled. "And the lady next door must be impressed if she's asked Rae to do her garden. Rae's a lovely girl – a credit to you, Amelia. She's become part of the family. And she's made friends here too. Well, one friend, anyway, haven't you, Rae?"

Rae gulped. Now wasn't the time to bring up Jamie, surely? She nodded, hoping Joanna wouldn't say anything more.

"And is your friend still at school?" Mama asked.

Rae shook her head.

"So, what does..." Mama paused, waiting for someone to fill in the name.

"Janie," said Joanna.

"So, what does Janie do for a living?"

There had been no point lying. After her initial confusion, Rae explained Joanna's error in assuming she'd said 'Janie'. And worse, she'd explained the Jamie in question, was Jamie MacKenzie.

After that, there had been a lot of shouting.

Mama was furious with Rae for spending time with a boy unsupervised. "I'd have thought you'd have learned a lesson from that dreadful Bobby." And unfairly, she'd been angry with Joanna for not keeping an eye on Rae.

"It's not Joanna's fault," Rae said. "It was a misunderstanding. I thought she knew I was with Jamie. I didn't know she'd assumed I was with a girl. Anyway, Jamie and I are just friends, so there's nothing to worry about."

Joanna's face had gone white. "I'm so sorry, Amelia. I should have been more careful—"

"What's Jamie MacKenzie doing around here?" Papa asked. "I thought he was working for his father."

"He's helping his uncle in his boatyard in Leigh-on-Sea." Rae's mind raced. How had things unravelled so fast? She'd never have deliberately tricked Joanna. And now, with one mistake, Mama believed

Rae had been deceitful. That really hurt.

Papa was trying to keep Mama calm; presumably anxious she'd lose her temper. And that hurt too because if he'd thought about it, surely, he'd have known Rae wasn't a liar – for all her other faults. Memories of Bobby and her instructions to keep quiet about having accompanied her to meet Andrew and Philip flooded into her mind. She'd lied then. But she wasn't a liar…

Then, a silent Joanna, exchanging glances with an equally silent Ben. Gentle, loving people who'd looked after her and perhaps were now asking themselves if Rae had been dishonest about anything else.

One stupid mistake and everything had spun out of control.

"It doesn't matter who the boy is, Hannah-Rae, or whether you know him. You should still have been honest," Mama said finally.

What was the point of disagreeing? No one believed her. Anyway, the lump in her throat was so large, she doubted she could have pushed words past it – assuming she could have thought of anything useful to say. She blinked rapidly, forcing back the tears that prickled behind her eyes.

In the end, it was decided Rae would stay until it was time to go back to school. Mama and Papa were planning to sell their house in Barlstead. They'd bought a place in Chelsea to save the daily train journeys, and they were in the middle of packing up their belongings. Papa would return with Rae's school things and then take her directly to St Helena's at the beginning of term.

Until then, Rae would be allowed to work at Ada's and Mrs Richardson's, but was forbidden to see Jamie.

"If only you'd think before you act, Rae," Papa said to her quietly, as he left that evening.

"But Papa, please," Rae begged. "I truly didn't know Joanna thought I was meeting a girl. And you know Jamie. You like him.

You've always said so. He's kind."

"It's not about liking the boy or not liking him, Rae, it's the fact that you were deceitful."

"I didn't know Joanna had misunderstood," Rae whispered, her eyes filling with tears. "Please believe me."

Papa sighed, his shoulders sagging. "Rae, don't upset your mother further. Just do as you're told."

In one afternoon, Rae had lost the fight to leave school, lost everyone's trust and lost not one, but two homes – she wouldn't have a chance to say goodbye to the house at Barlstead and in two weeks, she'd leave Priory Hall, a place she'd come to think of as home.

Back in her room, she picked up the tiny wooden boat Jamie had given her that first Christmas. She placed it on her bedside table and stared at it through blurry eyes, the tears finally spilling over.

That night, Rae cried herself to sleep. But as the tears fell, she vowed to herself that one day, she'd leave with Jamie. Together, they'd travel the world, moving from place to place. If she was always on the move, it wouldn't matter that she didn't belong anywhere.

Chapter Twenty-Three

"I see. Well, it's kind of you to come and tell me, Hannah-Rae," Mrs Richardson said when she learned Rae would be returning to school in September.

"I shall be sad to see you go," she added, to Rae's amazement. "But I agree with your mother and father. School is important and you must do as your parents say. Perhaps when you return to Priory Hall, you'd be good enough to ask my son to arrange for another gardener? Not that much will grow over winter, but I've become accustomed to having it well-kept and I don't want to see it descend into chaos again. Perhaps when you see Miss Quinn, you'll suggest she find a gardener too, so the work you've done so far on her wilderness will not be undone."

Tilly and Cook expressed their sadness at Rae leaving, and Cook even baked a fruit cake, although she said it'd been without Mrs Richardson's knowledge, and it might be best if Rae ate her slice out of sight under the large oak tree. She also wrapped a large wedge of the cake in cloth and gave it to Rae to take home.

Rae had expected Mrs Richardson to be angry about the inconvenience of finding someone else to look after her garden, so she'd been quite touched the old lady seemed almost sad she wouldn't be back.

But it was Ada Quinn who Rae was dreading telling about her return to school. She'd grown fond of the quiet, dignified woman with the sad eyes.

Unlike Mrs Richardson, who'd never invited Rae into her house, Ada always made tea for them both before Rae started work in the garden. Titan curled up on Rae's lap while they sat together and talked about France.

Ada had been the only person Rae had confided in about her plans to travel with Jamie when they were both older. The only other people who might have understood were Joanna and Ben, but if they'd known, Rae suspected they would feel obliged to tell Mama. And although her parents wouldn't be able to stop her when she was old enough, she knew there'd be pressure from them to 'behave with more common sense'.

But Ada had spent long enough working in France to be fluent in the language and to have developed a love for the people and places she'd visited, although she was rather vague about why she'd gone to France in the first place. She preferred instead to talk about her jobs in different cafés and shops as she travelled from the north to the south.

For a time in Paris, she'd been a life model for an artist who'd begged her to pose for him because, he said, he admired her long legs. She'd spent many hours draped in silk, propped against a wooden post in his freezing attic studio, while he magically transformed her on his canvas into a Greek goddess leaning against a marble pillar.

He'd made no money, as far as she knew, and eventually, she'd left Paris and returned to England.

"Now my travelling days are over," she said wistfully. "I don't have the energy anymore. But you, Rae, you must follow your heart. There are so many wonderful places to see."

Rae sighed. The future was such a long way off. And before then, she had the prospect of school and that meant not seeing Jamie for months.

"And what will your young man be doing while you're at school?" Ada asked, as if she'd read Rae's thoughts.

"He'll be here, I suppose, helping his uncle. But I can't bear not seeing him. It's all so unfair. It's not like I lied about him. It was all a misunderstanding. But even though everyone knows it was a mistake, they still act as though I'd been deceitful and Mama, particularly, won't hear Jamie's name mentioned."

"I expect your mama doesn't realise how grown up you are." Ada's voice was gentle.

"It's strange," said Rae, "you're the second person who's said that to me. If you and Thérèse can see it, why doesn't Mama?"

Ada sighed. "Don't underestimate how hard it is to be a mother, Rae. I wish I'd realised that many years ago, then I wouldn't have judged my own mother so harshly. There were too many bitter words spoken and after a while, there was no taking them back."

Rae frowned, disappointed. She'd thought Ada might understand her frustrations, but now it seemed she was justifying Mama's actions too. It was as if all adults closed ranks, siding with one another. "So, you're saying I should do everything Mama tells me, like forgetting Jamie?" Rae asked.

To her surprise, Ada shook her head. "No, not at all. It's hard being a mother, and they often make mistakes. They may not mean to, but no one's perfect. It's up to each person to do what they believe is right, regardless of what other people say. Of course, children need guidance until they're old enough to know better, but after having spent time with you, Rae, I feel you've reached that time. Live by your conscience. And as for Jamie, if you feel the way you say you do, then don't let anyone ever persuade you otherwise. *Ever!*" she added with such vehemence, Titan looked up at his mistress, jumped off Rae's lap and squeezed behind the sofa.

"You never know how life's going to turn out," Ada continued. "Seize every chance of happiness, Rae, because that moment may be all you have."

Her voice, usually so calm, was now passionate, and her face had become haunted. She stood abruptly and walked to the sideboard, where she opened a drawer and took out an envelope.

"This," she said, taking a sepia photograph out, "was Walter, my fiancé. He died in the trenches in northern France during the last war."

She handed the picture to Rae. It had been taken in a French photographic studio and, at the top, was written, *To my dearest Ada, with love from your own Walter.*

"I'm so sorry, Ada. How dreadful," Rae murmured, unsure how to console her.

Ada bit her bottom lip and tears gathered in her eyes. "I know people say I should be over it by now. But the truth is, Rae, I never got over losing Walter. And I never will... If there's any chance you can find happiness with your young man, then you need to grab it. You never know how much time you have on this earth." She paused and ran a finger gently over the edge of the photograph. "I was the eldest daughter in a large family and each time my father came home from the sea, he added another one. My poor mother was exhausted, and she relied on me to care for the other children. So, when Walter asked me to marry him, she forbade it. She said he wasn't right for me and made up all sorts of excuses, but the truth was, she couldn't cope without me. I didn't realise that until much later."

She slipped the photograph back inside the envelope. "Only single men were conscripted early in the war, so if Walter and I had been married, he wouldn't have been called up so soon, and we might have had some time together. But I did as my mother asked and waited…"

"Ada, I'm so sorry," Rae said, not sure what to do.

Finally, Ada patted her hand and said, "You're a good girl, Rae. I know you'll do the right thing. Whatever that turns out to be."

Later, on her way home, Rae realised why Ada had gone to France – she'd wanted to be near Walter.

Finally, the time came to leave Priory Hall. Papa came to pick her up and Rae was pleased Mama hadn't accompanied him. If she'd been there, Rae suspected memories of the last visit would be rekindled, and Mama would be angry. Having discussed everything with Joanna, the mistake had been cleared up and forgotten. Mama would only have reminded everyone.

As a tearful Rae had left, Faye had sobbed, clutching at her coat. Even Joanna had wiped her eyes and Ben, with an arm around her shoulders, had looked sad. How Rae wished she could stay with Joanna and her family. But there was no choice. It was back to school where she had no friends and no wish to be.

In 1939, halfway through the summer term, Mama and Papa were called into school by the headmistress, Miss Frost. Rae was summoned from her lesson as soon as they arrived.

Miss Frost wasted no time. "I regret to tell you, Mr and Mrs Kingsley, that despite several warnings to you and Hannah-Rae, she has not applied herself to her studies this year. Other than geography and French, her marks have been consistently low, and her attitude is appalling. She doesn't misbehave, but she puts the minimum amount of effort into school life, and that's not the St Helena's way. I gave her a second chance after the Roberta Taylor-Gale incident, but despite warnings, her behaviour has not been acceptable. Frankly, Hannah-Rae is simply wasting her time here. I'm afraid I must request you withdraw her from St Helena's. She will not return for the next academic year. I will leave it up to you as to whether she remains until the end of Trinity term or whether you remove her now."

The drive back to Chelsea passed in silence. Unusually, Mama was too shocked to speak, but the shouting would start soon, Rae thought.

Well, I told them I didn't want to go back to school.

Nevertheless, it hurt to be rejected.

Her parents' house in Chelsea was a large Victorian building with lofty ceilings and spacious rooms. It was like staying in a hotel, Rae thought. Cold and impersonal.

But it had a post box at the corner of the street and the first thing she did on entering her bedroom was to write to Jamie, telling him about her dishonourable exit from school and warning him not to send any letters – either to school because it was unlikely Miss Frost would bother to pass them on, or to the house in Chelsea, in case it angered her parents.

As she dropped the letter in the post box, she knew she was now cut off from Jamie, even though she'd be able to write to him. She shivered. The sun was shining, but inside she was cold. Numb.

This only strengthened her resolve to get a job and earn enough so she and Jamie could go off on their travels.

How much, however, was enough? Rae didn't know how much it would cost to go abroad.

"And so, until your father and I have decided what to do with you, Hannah-Rae, you can earn your keep by cleaning the house and taking

Jack to school in the morning and picking him up in the afternoon until the end of term, and, since you seem to enjoy gardening, you can keep ours tidy. Let's hope you can manage to do that," Mama said at dinner that evening.

Her days blurred into one another, an endless repetition of small, meaningless tasks. There was no spark – just the suffocating knowledge that her life was drifting in the doldrums.

While she waited for something to happen, she began to collect snippets of information about other countries and stuck them in a scrap book. She carried on learning French from her schoolbooks and writing long letters to Jamie, although she knew she wouldn't hear from him. It wasn't much but it filled the tedious hours.

Mama passed her medical exams and was working at the Royal Free Hospital, where she was carrying on with her studies to be a surgeon. Joe was still boarding at Bishop's Hall Boys School, and Jack was keen to walk to and from school with his friends – and without Rae. The garden was scrupulously tidy and although Rae would have been happy to work in anyone else's garden, none of their neighbours thought a girl would be able to manage. Perhaps if Mama or Papa had put in a good word for her, but neither thought of it.

"It's time you did something meaningful, Hannah-Rae," Mama said, and for once, Rae agreed with her.

"I wondered if I could work in France as a nanny like Thérèse did when she came here," Rae said.

Mama appeared to be impressed Rae had suggested something sensible, but surprisingly, Papa wasn't in favour.

"Things are too unstable on the continent at the moment," he said.

"That aggressive little man, Hitler, seems to be doing his best to cause problems. I don't trust him. He's already invaded Czechoslovakia and got away with it. Now he's got his eye on Poland."

The previous September, Prime Minister Neville Chamberlain had returned from Munich waving a piece of paper signed by Hitler, and to the country's relief, he'd declared he'd ensured 'Peace for our Time'.

She reminded Papa of the Prime Minister's words.

Even so, he remained doubtful about her going abroad. "Train as a nanny and perhaps, by the time you've qualified, things will have settled down. The best place is the Norland Institute, so I should contact them, although your academic record isn't exactly impressive. But at least you can find out if it's worth applying."

"You should have put more effort into your lessons when you were at school, and then it wouldn't be an issue," said Mama, making it clear she doubted Rae would be accepted.

Rae sighed. She thought it unlikely she'd be accepted either, but then, it wasn't that she wanted to be a nanny. She simply wanted to work in France until Jamie could join her. Then, after a while, they'd move on, perhaps to Spain... or Italy. Each day, as well as practising French, she now pored over the newspapers, taking in everything about the situation in Europe and paying special attention to what was happening in Germany.

And then, Adolph Hitler invaded Poland.

"The man's a lunatic," said Papa. "It's going to mean war; you mark my words."

War? Could it be possible?

On Sunday, the third of September, at eleven-fifteen, the Kingsley family gathered around their wireless in the drawing room and waited for Mr Chamberlain to make an announcement.

"I am speaking to you from the cabinet room at 10 Downing Street.

A ROSE IN PLOTLANDS

This morning the British ambassador in Berlin handed the German government a final note stating that unless we heard from them by 11 o'clock that they were prepared at once to withdraw their troops from Poland; a state of war would exist between us..."

Rae inhaled sharply. This couldn't be happening. War? It wasn't possible.

Mr Chamberlain continued, "...I have to tell you now that no such undertaking has been received, and that consequently this country is at war with Germany."

No one spoke. Each lost in their own thoughts.

Within minutes of the declaration of war, the air raid sirens sliced through the air. Seconds of inactivity passed while the Kingsleys struggled to take in the enormity of the announcement, followed by the sudden shrill warning of danger.

Papa was used to emergencies and to reacting speedily. He instructed everyone to take their gas masks and follow him to the Anderson Shelter, which they, like many of their neighbours, had installed in the garden. As they hurried to the shelter, Rae looked up, expecting to see hordes of black German bombers, like a swarm of mosquitos above them ready to drop their deadly cargo, but the sky was clear and blue.

How can we be at war? Everything looks so normal.

It turned out to be a false alarm, but the scene was set for the battle of nerves which lasted for eight months and became known as the 'Phoney War', the time when, although Britain was at war, it was involved in very little military action.

But despite that, all precautions had to be taken, and it became second nature to ensure the blackout curtains prevented light from being seen from the street. Everyone carried a gas mask at all times and many children were evacuated to rural areas which were considered safer than London and the big cities and ports.

Rae was like a rudderless boat that was completely at the mercy of the winds, bobbing about in the middle of the ocean. Travel was out of the question and training to be a nanny was pointless until the war was over. She was simply drifting.

Rae had written Jamie lots of letters telling him all about Chelsea and, eventually, she said it would be all right for him to write to her because she no longer worried it would anger Mama and Papa. She checked the post deliveries before her parents each day, so it was unlikely they'd find out he'd written anyway.

She eagerly awaited the postman, but so far, she'd only received one picture postcard in an envelope from him explaining he was very busy working in his uncle's yard and helping his cousin, Duncan, in his cockle-fishing business.

The photograph on the card showed the grand entrance pavilion into the Kursaal Amusement Park in Southend. Jamie had drawn two snails and next to them a compass showing they were heading east. *Us,* he'd written over the snails with a large arrow, as if by making his intentions even clearer, they might come true sooner.

The Kursaal was a special place for them. The ticket seller on the Caterpillar Ride had been the catalyst to them discovering how they felt about each other. Rae often wondered what might have happened if Jamie had simply escorted her home believing she hadn't wanted to be with him and if she'd believed he hadn't wanted to be with her. But fate, in the form of the ticket seller, had intervened, just like the ticket collector at Laindon Station had helped to bring them together. One day, fate would help them again and when the war was over, like the snails, they'd both head east – together.

Chapter Twenty-Four

1940

By May, the news from Europe was bleak, dampening Rae's hopes further. Hitler had invaded Denmark and Norway and unleashed his *Blitzkrieg* – Lightning War – against Belgium and Holland. In London, Prime Minister Chamberlain had resigned and was replaced by Winston Churchill. The country held its breath, dreading what might come next.

By mid-May, the BBC had announced the Admiralty wanted all owners of self-propelled craft between thirty and one hundred feet to submit details of their boats within fourteen days, so they could be requisitioned.

"Well, the *Amelia's* escaped then," Papa said with a wry smile. "If she were four feet longer, she'd have qualified."

"That would've been a shame," Rae said, her brow furrowing. "We've only taken her out once ourselves. What d'you think the Admiralty wants the boats for? Surely the Navy has plenty of ships."

"I'm not entirely sure," Papa admitted, his voice lowering slightly. "But a friend of mine who's well-connected in Whitehall said things aren't looking good for our boys in France and Belgium. It's all hush-hush, but the Navy may need to fetch troops. I can't fathom why they'd call for small boats, though."

Shortly after Rae had been sent home from school, Jamie's father had informed Papa he was closing his boatyard at Chichester Harbour. Alex had joined the RAF and Jamie was needed in Leigh, so although he'd intended to leave the business to his sons, they were no longer there.

Of course, one, or indeed, both sons, might return to the boatyard one day, but Mr MacKenzie couldn't wait, and he closed up and retired. He suggested that since the Kingsley family were moving to London, it would be better to move *Wild Spirit* to Leigh, where his brother Gordon could look after it.

Papa had taken a few days' leave from the hospital, and he, Jack and Rae had sailed the small dinghy around the coast to Essex. When they'd arrived in Leigh, Gordon MacKenzie had proudly shown them his boatyard, but to Rae's deep disappointment, Jamie had been out cockle-fishing with his cousin. She'd masked her dismay, listening politely, though her gaze had drifted to the horizon, as if Jamie might appear at any moment.

During the visit, Papa had taken an interest in a sleek twenty-six-foot motor yacht under construction in the yard.

"As it happens, that one's for sale," Gordon said. "The man who ordered it died before taking ownership. I'd be happy to come to some arrangement."

Though Rae loved *Wild Spirit*, she could see the glint of longing in Papa's eyes. He'd always dreamed of something larger and not long after, they'd bought the boat and named it *Amelia*. Rae had sailed her only once; a trip to Whitstable in Kent that now felt like a memory from another world. With the war deepening, it looked like it would be a long time before they'd have the chance to sail her again.

Days after the BBC's announcement, Papa telephoned from the hospital.

"Hello, poppet. Listen, I've got to dash back to work, but I wondered if I could trust you with a job."

"Yes, Papa?"

"Gordon MacKenzie at Leigh has telephoned to say the Ministry of Shipping has contacted him about any small boats they have or may know about. He had to tell them about the *Amelia* and they're going to requisition it."

"But I thought they wanted boats of thirty feet or more?"

"They did, but now they're after smaller boats as well. So, d'you think you could go down to Leigh, unlock the cabin and get all our personal things off the boat before it's taken? I'd rather the lock wasn't broken, and I've got an old compass my grandad gave me in the drawer. I'd hate to lose it. It's not worth much, but it's the only thing I've got that belonged to him. D'you mind, poppet?"

Excitement rose in Rae's chest. Leigh-on-Sea. She might see Jamie. But would Papa suddenly remember and change his mind? It was best to be honest, however much she yearned to see Jamie.

"I don't mind going, Papa, but I think Mama might not like it." She kept her voice matter of fact; holding back the pleading to go and the resentment that her mother would stop her if she knew. And particularly hiding her longing to see Jamie.

"Leave her to me, poppet. I know you're referring to the possibility of running into Jamie MacKenzie, but you seem to be growing up since you've been home. I've never had a problem with Jamie, anyway – he's a likeable lad, and you're a grown woman now – a sensible one. Just don't tell your mother I said that. I thought perhaps Joanna wouldn't mind if you stayed there one night. I could ring and ask. I'm a bit worried about delays on the trains and you being out after blackout."

"I don't think Mama would like if it you arranged it without her knowing. Joanna's her cousin." No, if Mama found out Rae had gone to stay with Joanna without her knowledge, especially once she learned about the possibility of bumping into Jamie, she wouldn't be happy. Not with Papa, Rae or Joanna. Why risk that? She had an idea. "I could ask Ada Quinn. She said I could sleep there when I like and if you don't mind, I could stay for a week and do a bit of work on her garden while I'm there, to thank her for letting me stay."

"Shall I telephone her to ask?" Papa said.

"No, Papa, she doesn't have a telephone. But don't worry. She won't mind if I simply turn up."

For her journey to Leigh, Rae had dressed in warm clothes that were suitable for sailing. With any luck, she'd have a chance to take *Amelia* out with Jamie before it was requisitioned and if not, perhaps they'd be able to take out *Wild Spirit*. But more than anything, Rae hoped Jamie would be there.

At last, a chance to see him. She could scarcely breathe with excitement. In her mind's eye, she saw him kiss his fingertips and place them against her lips. She closed her eyes with longing and wondered why her insides melted at the memory.

When Rae reached Fenchurch Street Station, she stood inside the entrance for several minutes; disorientated by the press of humanity and the charged atmosphere. Uniformed men and women clung to each other. Children wailed as they picked up on the tension. Tears and last-minute exchanges. Snatches of conversation – entreaties to return, promises to write, pleas to take care, stay safe. And everywhere, people with hands outstretched to a loved one, as if they were being ripped apart.

Men were leaving on a scale Rae had never dreamed of.

Her mind leapt to Jamie. How would she feel if she was saying goodbye to him, knowing he was going to war? The breath caught in her throat, and she placed a hand against the wall to steady herself as her head spun. What would she do if the last time she ever set eyes on him was here in this cavernous concourse that echoed with grief and loss?

No. Jamie would be safe in Leigh-on-Sea. He was a boat-builder. A reserved occupation. He wouldn't be required to enlist.

But he could if he wanted to... a tiny voice said.

A wave of resolve swept through her. She had to find him. To make sure he was safe. She'd arrived at the station with time to spare, but the weight of what she'd just witnessed had stolen precious minutes. As she took in the enormity of the moment: the mass exodus of fathers, brothers, sons, she felt something deep within her shift.

Weaving a path through the crowds and kitbags, she made her way to the correct platform. The carriages were packed and there was standing room only, although people cheerfully made a place for her. Finally, the train chugged out of the station, enveloped in a haze of smoke and steam. Rae exhaled a shaky sigh of relief. She was on her way. In a small town like Leigh-on-Sea, she'd be sure to find Jamie. She must find him... After witnessing so many farewells, she felt as though she, too, had lost something.

"Just said goodbye to yer sweetheart, ducks?" a round-faced woman next to Rae asked. "You've got that haunted look."

"Oh, no, I..." Rae began, startled.

The woman adjusted the scarf over the curlers in her hair and carried on. It appeared she was more interested in telling Rae what she'd been doing. "I just said goodbye to my youngest son, Billy. He's joining the Navy." She shook her head and then patted the scarf again. "My other son's out in Belgium." She made the sign of the cross and shook her head.

"It don't look like it's going well. I'd expected him to be in Germany by now, giving them Jerries a good hiding. But..." she paused, and her lower jaw trembled. "He can't tell me where he is, but I'm afraid our boys are losing ground."

"You shouldn't spread such unpatriotic nonsense," an elderly man in a bowler hat said, frowning as he turned toward her. "It's disgraceful."

A sharp-faced woman across the aisle rounded on him. "She's right. My Alf's written from France. He and his men have been pushed back repeatedly. I haven't heard from him for a while. Goodness only knows where he is now."

The bowler-hatted man harrumphed and turned to stare out of the window, muttering, "I still think you shouldn't say such things in public."

"No point sticking yer head in the sand," the woman next to Rae muttered. "It ain't going well for our boys and there ain't no point saying otherwise."

"Anyway, the government has made it public," someone else added. "They're calling for small boats. Sounds like things are pretty desperate to me."

Dread seeped through Rae. She hadn't allowed herself to believe the war would last much longer, and then the world would once again be safe to travel. How could she have been so naïve?

Her parents were working tirelessly in their respective hospitals. Joe was away at university, and as usual, his letters were few and far between. Until now, the war had been so far away as to be irrelevant. Of course, they were all subject to the wartime precautions that had been imposed and she'd read reports in the newspapers, but everything had been so remote, as if she'd been reading the reviews of a Hollywood moving picture.

Today, she had seen it in the tear-filled eyes of mothers sending their sons away. She had heard it in their trembling voices and seen it etched in their grief-lined faces. It wasn't something she could read about and then push aside anymore. Today, the war had stepped into her world, and there was no escaping it.

Rae had been to Leigh-on-Sea several times with Jamie and remembered it as a sleepy, little fishing town. It hadn't occurred to her that anything would be different from those occasions, so she was astonished to see so many people get off at the station. She was stopped by a policeman at the ticket barrier wanting to see her identity card and to know what business she had in Leigh. Once again, she wondered at her naïveté. Leigh-on-Sea was on the coast – albeit only just. It was near the mouth of the River Thames, but still, if the Germans invaded, they would land on any piece of coast – even a tiny fishing town.

She showed her identity card and told the policeman she was volunteering her father's boat to the Admiralty. He let her pass, and she slipped through the bustling crowds of fishermen, naval officers and ratings, and headed down to the waterfront, anxiety gnawing at her like a tide wearing away the shore.

She flattened herself against a wall as a group of naval officers strode past, their conversation clipped and urgent. They didn't notice her at all, and why would they? What had she been thinking, imagining she might go sailing with Jamie today? Foolish fantasies of sunny outings slipped through her grasp, and with them came the weight of reality. How had she been so blind to the seriousness of it all?

"Rae?"

She jumped at the sound of her name. Jamie stepped out of the crowd and was next to her, shaking his head in disbelief. "Rae! It's you."

"Oh, Jamie!" Rae threw her arms around his neck and held him tightly. Relief flooded her. He was here. Solid. Safe. An anchor in a world that had gone mad.

He held her for a moment before pulling back to look at her. His eyes searched hers. "Rae, what are you doing here?"

Words tumbled out as she explained, and Jamie's expression softened. "Come on," he said, taking her hand and weaving through the crowd, his pace quickening. "We'd better check on the *Amelia*. They might already be aboard."

Jamie held her hand, plying her with questions as they hurried along the waterfront towards the *Amelia*.

Thankfully, nobody from the Admiralty had yet claimed her, and after unlocking the cabin, Rae took out all the personal items she could find, including her great-granddad's compass.

"I'll walk you back to the station," Jamie said, checking his watch. "I've got time before…" His voice trailed off, his words hanging in the air, unfinished. With a soft expression, he said, "It's so good to see you, Rae. I've missed you so much. The only thing that keeps me going is the belief that one day we'll be able to set off together. North, south, east or west, I don't care which way, so long as you're with me." He paused. "You do still want that, don't you?"

"Of course." Her heart beat faster hearing his impassioned words. He still wanted to be with her. "If only the war would end."

"I know." Jamie bit at his lower lip. "The news from France isn't good. The Germans have pushed our boys back to the coast."

"The Navy will rescue them, though, won't they?" Rae asked, remembering the words of the woman on the train.

Jamie hesitated, and the flicker of uncertainty in his eyes chilled her. "I don't know. Apparently, there're thousands of soldiers trapped on the coast. That's what all these Navy people are doing here."

Rae's mouth dropped open. "Thousands?" Her skin prickled at the thought of so many men waiting for rescue.

"Don't worry, Rae, we'll get them back. We're setting off shortly." He checked his watch again. "Your train will be in soon. Now, I'd better go. Duncan's taking his cockle boat."

Icy chills ran through Rae's veins. She grabbed his hand. "You said *we*. You're not going, are you?" She could scarcely breathe.

"Of course, I'm going. How could I do otherwise?" He gently slipped his hand from hers.

She grabbed him again. "No, Jamie! Isn't this a Navy operation?"

He shook his head and gently prised her fingers open, releasing his hand. "No, they need small boats with a shallow draft to go to the beaches to lift off our men, and they need volunteers to help sail those boats. I can help, Rae. I can do something to try to end this war. But I need to go now." He held her hand against his cheek. "Please Rae, take your father's things and go to Ada's. This is no place for you."

She wanted to cling to him, to hold him tightly and feel the reassurance of his body pressed close to hers.

Tears welled in her eyes. Ada had let Walter go... and she'd never seen him again.

No. Rae wouldn't allow that to happen to Jamie. But she couldn't stop him from going. That much was obvious.

She caught hold of his jacket, clenching it in her fists, and standing on tiptoes, looked him in the eyes. "If you're going, I'm going with you."

Jamie's eyes opened in alarm. "Rae, you can't! Duncan won't take you for a start. And if you don't let me go now, he'll leave without me."

"Then let's take the *Amelia*. At least that way I can be with you. I'm a better sailor than you any day."

"It's too dangerous, Rae. No. Go to Ada's. I'll come and find you when I get back. I promise. I'll let you know as soon as I'm safe."

Rae shook her head. "No. No. I couldn't bear it. I'm coming with you and if you won't let me, I'll go on my own."

He tried to prise her fingers off his jacket. "Rae, don't be ridiculous. You can't go alone."

"Then I'll volunteer to go on another boat." She took her knitted hat out of her bag and pulled it on, tucking her shoulder-length curls inside. She wouldn't be mistaken for a man, but she could pass as a boy. Having planned to sail with Jamie, Rae was wearing trousers, a thick jumper and jacket – all boyish clothes.

"If things are as desperate as you say, I'll get on a boat one way or another. I'm a fine sailor. I'll be useful. And if anyone finds out I'm a girl and objects to me being there, we'll be at sea. And if they turn back, well, I'll just have to put up with it. But I'm going to give it a go."

Chapter Twenty-Five

Perhaps Jamie had recognised her determination and so had agreed to go with her in the *Amelia*. Or more likely, he'd assumed she would be stopped before she could set sail. But in the end, it had been surprisingly easy. She'd signed on as 'Ray Kingsley' and if anyone suspected she wasn't a boy, they'd shown no interest.

The *Amelia's* engines were fuelled, and blankets and freshwater were loaded with impressive speed. Sidney Fuller, the young naval sub-lieutenant who'd been assigned to take charge of the *Amelia,* was calm and professional and if he was nervous about the trip, he hid it from Rae and Jamie.

Later, Rae would reflect on how no one had taken a closer look at her or made any serious effort to dissuade a young 'boy' from going. That should have rung alarm bells, but it didn't. Sidney referred to the operation as 'Dynamo', a name that was brimming with energy and purpose, but Rae could not have known how desperate it truly was.

The *Amelia* joined the stream of fishing and cockle vessels leaving Leigh, which in turn joined pleasure craft and tugs from London.

Rae felt a surge of excitement as the boats poured out of the Thames, heading south to Ramsgate, where they would refuel before making the long journey to Dunkirk. She gripped the rail tightly as their little boat slipped into the flowing procession, one tiny piece of a colossal, determined effort.

The scale of the ragtag armada took Rae's breath away. So many people had answered the call to take part in Operation Dynamo and to rescue their boys, that tears filled her eyes. She turned away, afraid Sidney would notice and wonder why the 'boy' in his crew was acting like a girl. Not that the officer could do anything about it now. It was too late to turn back.

"We'll follow the channels that have been swept," Sidney announced cheerfully as the boat cut smoothly through the calm waters. He was a sandy-haired man, a year or two older than Jamie, and appeared to take everything in his stride. "Swept of mines," he added with a wink, noticing Rae's puzzled expression.

The sea was calm, the conditions nearly perfect. "Like a millpond," Sidney said with satisfaction. "Don't suppose there's any chance of a cuppa, Ray?"

Rae nodded. Before she could head below, Jamie caught her eye and followed her into the galley, his expression unreadable.

Once inside, he placed a finger to his lips and whispered urgently, his voice trembling despite his efforts to stay composed. "Rae... I don't think you realise how dangerous this is." He faltered, swallowing hard. "But if... if we don't make it back..." His voice cracked, and he took a steadying breath. "I need you to know something. I love you, Rae. I always have. From the first moment I saw you. And if we get through this, I'll do whatever it takes to be with you... if you'll have me."

His eyes were wide, full of fear, not just of the unknown, but of rejection. For a moment, Rae forgot how to breathe. Her heart thudded painfully in her chest as she stared at him. Vulnerability, fear, and hope were all etched into his face, and without hesitation, she threw her arms around his neck and clung to him. "Of course I want you, Jamie," she whispered fiercely. "I love you too."

Jamie loved her. If only her excitement hadn't been tinged with sadness. The reasons for his declaration were the dangerous conditions into which they were sailing and his dread that one of them or both might not survive.

It was the first time either of them had mentioned love. No romantic Hollywood backdrop, no passionate swell of violins. Just the steady throb of *Amelia's* engine, the smell of bilges and fuel, and the slap of waves against the hull. But it made the moment more real, more powerful.

Jamie closed his eyes, and his shoulders sank in relief at the knowledge that she loved him back. Raising two fingers to his mouth, he kissed them and moved to place them on her lips, but she caught his hand, shaking her head.

"No," she whispered, "kiss me properly, Jamie." Her hands slid behind his head, and pulling his face towards hers, she closed her eyes.

For a moment, he hesitated, but then his breath was on her cheek, and she drew him closer. The kiss was soft at first, tentative, as though he was afraid he'd misunderstood her. But as she pressed closer, her heart hammering wildly, he kissed her more deeply, his arms tightening around her. She clung to him, her senses overwhelmed by the warmth of his touch and the profound sense of belonging.

"Rae?" he whispered as he broke away.

"Kiss me again," she murmured, and before he could respond, she covered his mouth with hers, pressing her body against his. How could she not have known that kissing Jamie would feel so right?

As she clung to him, feeling the warmth of his kiss and body against hers, tears trickled down her cheeks. Why had she waited until now, until they were both in danger, to show him how much she wanted him?

When he detected the saltiness of her tears, he drew back again. "Rae?" He cradled her face, his voice full of concern.

She knew he was afraid they were raising memories she wanted to forget. But for the first time, she realised that on that dreadful evening, although Andrew had placed his mouth against hers, it hadn't been a kiss. It hadn't been anything like she'd just shared with Jamie. What had happened with Andrew had been nothing. Less than nothing. She swallowed back the lump in her throat, regretting how something so meaningless had coloured her view of what could have been hers. Hers and Jamie's. How did she always get it so wrong?

"I love you, Jamie," she whispered. "And I wish I'd kissed you sooner."

He smiled at her with relief, and they stood, their foreheads together, holding each other as if the world outside couldn't touch them.

A thud on the door to the cabin made them both leap guiltily away from each other. "Ray, are you boiling the water over a match?" Sidney called. "I'm parched. Get a move on!"

Jamie grinned sheepishly, his hand brushing hers as she stepped towards the stove. Rae's fingers tingled where his had touched.

Even as she returned to her tasks, her heart thrummed with the memory of his kiss, anchoring her against the storm that awaited them.

Chapter Twenty-Six

♥

As they neared the French coast, the fleet grew, reaching as far as the eye could see in all directions. The boats surged on the same course, their bow waves frothing ahead while feathered trails of churned water fanned out behind.

In the distance, enormous naval ships – destroyers, gunboats and transport ships, loomed like giants, following the lanes Sydney had said the naval minesweepers had cleared for them. Every now and then, the sunlight glanced off their steel-grey flanks; a fleeting promise of safety amidst the unknown.

"This is unbelievable," Rae whispered. A shiver of pride and fear ran down her spine at the scale of Operation Dynamo, although she couldn't help wondering if the Admiralty had made a mistake. Someone must have underestimated how many people would respond to their call because such an enormous number of boats couldn't all be needed to rescue soldiers. Most would go back to England empty, Rae was sure.

Gradually, they sailed into a sea mist. At first, it was as delicate as a veil, but as they pressed on, it thickened until even the nearest boats appeared ghostly and unreal, shrouded by the fog.

The slap of the sea against the *Amelia's* hull and the clanking of halyards on neighbouring boats were strangely muted by the mist, making it hard to pinpoint the source of sounds. But they could scarcely get lost with so many boats heading in the same direction.

Sidney wasn't disturbed by the lack of visibility. "It makes it trickier for us, but much harder for the Germans. I've heard the Luftwaffe have been attacking Dunkirk with Stukas, although the pilots probably won't take off in this weather. If the fog lifts, we might have problems, though..." He trailed off, but the weight of his unspoken thought hung between them.

Stukas. Rae had read about the Junkers Stuka German dive-bombers. Apparently, they screamed as they swooped through the sky to drop their bombs or strafe the ground, but it hadn't occurred to her they might attack a fleet of civilian rescue ships. Sidney was exaggerating, she was certain.

Rae longed to hold Jamie's hand to take comfort from him, but she dared not let Sidney see. Instead, she simply stared through the mist at the grey waves, keeping watch for anything in their path. Sidney believed the minesweepers had already cleared their way but, in this fog, who could tell?

They glided past Royal Navy cruisers and destroyers anchored in place and continued to creep forward alongside the other ghostly small boats towards the shore.

As they slipped through the water, the fog became denser and darker until it was almost black. An acrid smell of burning oil filled their nostrils and Rae realised it was the smoke from fires mixing with the fog, smothering them in a heavy pall.

But fires from what?

The crack of gunfire and the hollow boom of exploding shells drifted across the water from the direction in which they were heading and, gradually, Rae made out a red glow bleeding into the smoke and tiny pinpricks of orange light, like sequins in the blackness.

"That's Dunkirk," said Sidney, his mouth set in a grim line. "The Germans have pretty much destroyed it."

Jamie glanced at Rae with a flicker of fear in his eyes, his voice tense. "Then how can we land there?"

"We can't. We've got a shallow draft, so our orders are to head for the beaches. We'll get as close as we can, load up with men, and ferry them to one of the larger ships. Then we do it again and again... until there are no more men left on the beach... or we die in the effort."

Sidney sounded relaxed as if he were proposing a day boating on a lake, but Rae could see the lines of tension around his mouth. His casual attitude didn't fool her, and she saw Jamie frown. He didn't believe the nonchalance either. The gravity of the situation hung heavily between them.

While Sidney was preoccupied with their course, Rae placed her hand next to Jamie's on the side of the boat. She wanted to touch him, to make contact, to feel his warmth. As if he'd read her thoughts, Jamie slid his hand over hers and squeezed, then just as quickly removed it when Sidney turned to look at them.

The fog began to lift as they approached the wide expanse of beach, and Rae stared in disbelief. Thousands of men stood in snaking queues. They stretched from the water's edge to the dunes at the back of the beach, as far as she could see in either direction. Like orderly lines of ants, the soldiers moved forward when a boat approached the shore. But as soon as the men were taken from the front, they were replaced by more, in what appeared to be a never-ending supply. The desperate remnants of an army, waiting for salvation. Now, she wondered if the vast fleet of small boats that had appeared to be so ludicrously large would actually be sufficient to rescue this living tide of desperation. How could so many men need to be rescued? Rae had known things hadn't gone well in Europe for the Allies, but this... It was beyond belief.

Jamie gently shook his head in dismay as he stared at the beach. "This is a nightmare," he whispered. He opened his mouth to say something else, but the words were swallowed by ear-splitting screams that sliced through the air as if a demon were swooping on them from above. Hairs stood up on the back of Rae's neck, and forgetting about Sidney, she grabbed Jamie's arm.

"Stukas." Sidney's composure was now gone. He stared upwards with an expression of dread as a Junkers 87 dive bomber plunged downwards, heading for the beaches. Air rushed through the wind-driven sirens with terrifying shrieks as the aeroplane swooped towards the long lines of men. At the sound of the dive bomber's intimidating screeching and the *rat-tat-tat* of its machine gunfire, the men in the queues dived for cover – if they could find any. Most lay flat on the beach, pressing themselves into the ground, helmets clutched tightly, as the rapid hail of bullets kicked up bursts of sand around their bodies.

The horror of what Rae had just witnessed drove the breath from her body. Grabbing the side of the boat, she stood rigidly. "Please, please, please," she muttered over and over, unaware if she was begging the Luftwaffe pilot to go or praying for the men on the beach to be safe. It hardly mattered; neither plea was granted as the plane came in for another attack.

So, this was war. Not the stories of honour or the heroism of the propaganda posters, but men senselessly and mercilessly killed. If she'd thought about it, she'd have known it was so, but to see it in action was truly shocking. Rae gripped the railing for support, afraid her knees might buckle as helplessness seeped through her.

"We'll rescue them. Well... as many as we can." Jamie's face mirrored her feelings. Dread. Horror. Disbelief at such human suffering.

The blood-curdling scream of the Stuka faded, and on the beach, men stood up, dusted themselves down and, once again, took up their places in the orderly, if meandering, queues. Here and there, figures still lay on the sand and small groups of men gathered around, either to attend to the wounded or to remove the dead.

Few panicked. But then, Rae thought, what choice did they have? There was no point running inland straight into the oncoming German Panzers. The only option was to wait to be rescued. To wait for a boat such as the *Amelia,* which was now sailing towards them. Hopefully, giving them comfort.

Sidney steered towards the beach, stopping a short distance from the shoreline.

"That's as close as we get. The seabed shelves from here, so they'll have to come out to us," he said and cupping his hands around his mouth, he shouted to the officer at the head of the closest queue to send out a dozen men without their weapons.

The officer pushed twelve soldiers into the water towards the boat, and those behind shuffled forward to fill their places, enviously watching the men wade out, first up to their knees, then their waists and finally their chests. Twelve grey, resolute faces fixed on the *Amelia,* trudging forward as if the small boat was the last fragment of hope in a broken world.

Rae and Jamie reached out to clasp eager and desperate hands, pulling soaking men aboard, pointing out where to sit, so their weight was distributed equally. The three weakest soldiers were taken below, while the others remained on the deck, many with their dripping legs dangling over the side of the boat while they held onto the stanchions.

Warily glancing up for more German aeroplanes, Sidney slowly reversed the boat. He cautiously eyed the sandy bank on which the waves were driving her, and after pulling away, he turned, ready to head out to sea towards one of the naval ships.

Rae crouched beside a young private, speaking soothingly to him; the soft down on his upper lip suggested he was even younger than her. He was shaking so violently; she heard his teeth rattle. His enormous eyes, glassy and pleading, stared from a pinched face. 'They'll hate us, won't they?' he whispered, his cracked lips quivering.

"Who?" Rae asked, wondering if he'd lost his mind.

"The people. Everyone at home. We're retreating. We should've beaten the Jerries. But we didn't. We lost... We're running. We're cowards..." He shivered.

"No!" Rae said firmly. "You didn't lose and you're not cowards. It's just a setback. No one will blame you. You'll see." She stopped speaking and smiled, aware her voice would break if she carried on. It was important he believed her and if she cried, the hope that had lit his eyes would immediately be extinguished.

The truth was, she wasn't sure what the response would be to so many soldiers returning after failing to stop the Germans' advance. But no one could blame these men. No one could possibly be anything other than desperately sad for them. Surely...

Frantic shouts from the beach echoed across the water. At the end of one line, men splashed in the shallows. Pushing, shoving and scrambling over each other.

Panic.

Flesh thudded into flesh as punches were thrown.

An officer, his face contorted with frustration, fired his pistol into the air, trying to prevent a stampede. However, before he'd herded the men back into order, several soldiers had rushed past him. While he took control of the majority, a group surged through the water towards the *Amelia*. With desperate hands like claws, they grabbed at the legs of the men on deck, trying to pull themselves up. At first, the men already on board tried to help them climb up until the boat tilted dangerously under their weight, listing sharply to one side. Others had already foreseen the danger and were pushing them away.

"Get them off or we'll capsize." Sidney's voice rang out, loud and urgent as he swung the boat around. Once the bow was heading towards the naval ships, he opened the throttle, and the engine roared to life. Most of the men lost their grip on the soldiers' legs and were swept away into the churning water. One soldier, however, clung on stubbornly, his knuckles white as he held fast. For several agonising moments, he hung there, his face twisted with sheer determination. But after about twenty yards, his strength gave out and he slipped silently into the sea, vanishing beneath the surface without a sound.

"We can't just leave him." Rae's voice trembled in horror as she watched the man's form bob briefly, before sinking beneath the waves once more. The image burned into her mind, haunting in its sudden brutality.

Sidney didn't look back. His jaw was set, eyes focused ahead. "He's gone. Most likely drowned."

Rae's heart pounded in her chest. How could they abandon him like that?

As if sensing her confusion, Sidney added. "Wars aren't won by disobeying orders, Ray. No discipline, no success. I'm sorry you had to witness that, but those men should have followed orders and waited. If they had, they'd probably be on a boat like this on their way to safety like these men." He nodded toward the huddled soldiers on deck, their faces pale and gaunt. Most stared blankly ahead, lost in their own thoughts, too weary to process what had just happened.

"We must think of these lads now," Sidney continued. "One of them told me he hasn't had clean water for days. Jamie, perhaps you and Ray would get them a drink and make them as comfortable as you can until we get them to safety."

After transferring the exhausted men to a naval ship, Sidney turned around and set out for the shore. "Well, that's the first dozen as safe as we can make them. Now, back for more. By my reckoning, we're going to be making quite a few more trips before we make a dent in that lot on the beach."

Rae nodded, but her mind was still on the man they'd left behind, his final struggle before vanishing beneath the oily waves. The image remained with her, replaying over and over. But as she glanced up at the gaunt faces of the men now safely aboard HMS *Sabre*, their expressions full of relief, as they waved goodbye, she reminded herself why they were there. Each life they saved mattered. Those men who'd died had put them all at risk. She clung to those thoughts.

They navigated back towards the beach to pick up more human cargo, moving alongside other small, mismatched boats, all heading in the same direction. As they passed vessels already filled with men, sailing towards larger ships to offload their own weary passengers, the silent exchange of hope and exhaustion was palpable across the water.

The day dragged on; the sun climbing higher in the sky, and the fog that had once cloaked their approach lifted completely. However, instead of offering clarity, the clear skies brought more terror – the return of the Stukas. They bombed the ships, strafed the lines of men on the beaches and caused utter panic with their devilish screams as they nose-dived out of the skies.

Sidney expertly swerved the *Amelia*, narrowly avoiding the path of falling bombs, throwing everyone on board off balance. Rae gripped the railing tightly, hands slipping on the metal, as she tried to offer comfort to the men around her. She'd lost count of how many soldiers they'd rescued – five or six groups now. Not a vast number, but, she reminded herself, each one mattered to someone back in Britain.

Each one matters, she repeated silently to herself through gritted teeth.

Sidney swerved again as a Stuka screamed downwards ahead of them. Rae held her breath as bombs dropped, scoring a direct hit on a nearby boat. Not a Navy ship. Just a ferry such as might transfer people during times of peace from one riverbank to the opposite. A civilian boat, like the *Amelia*.

Red and orange flashes on the deck flung debris high into the air. The boom of the explosion and the blow of the shockwaves followed a split second later. Rae groaned with impotence as black, oily smoke billowed upwards and screaming men jumped into the water. What was left of the ferry sank with astonishing speed. Rae wanted to tip her head back and roar at the skies for it all to stop. Instead, she sobbed, scrubbing at her eyes angrily – not caring if Sidney saw her. He couldn't fail to be moved too; she was certain. All those soldiers now treading water amongst the wreckage and burning oil patches had just been rescued from the beach by small craft such as the *Amelia*.

For what?

To believe they'd reached safety and then to have the ship blown out from under them was too cruel.

Ahead of them over the beach, a Stuka swept down, its bullets throwing up successive bursts of sand and then splashes in the sea as the pilot's sights followed the lines of men. A soldier who was wading out to the *Amelia*, jerked sideways like a puppet whose string had been tugged, as the deadly fusillade passed. He clutched his shoulder, and his knees appeared to give way as he sank beneath the waves. The sergeant, who was counting men aboard the *Amelia* grabbed him, dragging him out of the water. He lifted the wounded man onto his shoulders and carried him towards the boat. By the time he reached the

Amelia, he was up to his neck in water and his strength visibly failing.

"What are you doing?" Rae asked as Jamie swung one leg over the side of the boat.

"I'll help the wounded man in. You grab his arms, Rae," Jamie said as he dropped into the sea with a splash.

"Jamie! No!"

It was too late.

Jamie helped the sergeant push the injured man up towards Rae and another soldier who'd already boarded. Between them, they hauled him onto the deck, and then he was dragged below to a bunk. Meanwhile, other soldiers clambered aboard, and the sergeant turned to wade back to the shore.

Jamie was still shoulder-deep in the water and Rae leaned out as far as she dared to take his hand and help him aboard. However, the plane had turned and, with a blood-chilling scream, headed straight for them. Rapid machine-gun fire sent up a shower of spray as each bullet struck the water. The *Amelia* lurched as Sidney surged forward out of the line of gunfire, throwing two men from the deck into the water and knocking Rae off her feet.

She scrambled up as the boat swung around, the gunwale slippery under her grasp.

"Jamie!" she screamed over and over, her voice hoarse with desperation, as the boat speeded away from him.

Jamie's head was visible, and she saw him touch his fingers to his lips, raise them as a salute to her before he disappeared beneath the wash caused by the sudden acceleration of the *Amelia*.

"Get down!" Sidney bellowed, and a soldier reached up and pulled her to the deck. Caught off balance, she fell heavily, and he lay on top of her, pinning her down. The German pilot veered the Stuka, banking sharply for another run, guns blazing. Sidney turned hard on the wheel, wildly swinging the boat away from the salvo, as men grabbed onto anything within reach and desperately clung on.

With her cheek pressed to the deck, Rae felt the impact of the bullets tearing through wood and she pushed the soldier away and scrambled to her knees to see how much damage had been done. The Luftwaffe pilot carried on, perhaps more interested in larger targets or perhaps believing he'd done enough damage to sink the boat. He turned and flew back towards land.

Miraculously, the bullets had hit the deck but didn't appear to have damaged the hull and, as far as she could tell, the boat was still seaworthy.

"Turn around! We've got to fetch Jamie," Rae shouted above the fading scream of the Stuka and the noise of the bullets spraying several nearby boats. She staggered towards Sidney. He obviously hadn't heard her and didn't realise they'd left Jamie behind.

But Sidney didn't turn. His face was set, his eyes focused ahead. "No," he said firmly. "We need to get these men to safety first. They've already been through enough."

"But we have to go back! We can't just leave him!" Rae grabbed Sidney by the arm, and it was then she saw the blood on his jacket.

"You've been hit!" she gasped.

"Quiet!" he snapped, his voice tight with pain. "It's nothing. But we're not going back. Not until these men are safe." His expression was resolute.

"You can't leave Jamie there."

But his determined face told her he wouldn't turn back.

For a second, she considered jumping overboard and swimming back to Jamie, but how would that help him? His only hope was if they returned to pick him up in the *Amelia*.

Sidney set a course for a large naval vessel and Rae told herself that when they'd unloaded the men, they'd go back to the beach and find Jamie.

A roar filled the air, followed by a deafening explosion. The ship they were sailing towards had struck a mine. Rae flung herself down again, hands over her ears.

"Hold on!" Sidney shouted, steering the *Amelia* directly into the wave created by the blast, rather than taking the force sideways. Within minutes, the large ship had sunk beneath the bubbling surface, leaving men bobbing like corks in its wake.

The *Amelia* picked up speed through the churning waves and Rae expected the boat to turn back to them, but Sidney maintained his course.

"Why're you sailing away from them?" Rae shouted.

"Where would we put them?" Sidney asked, and she knew he was right. His face was grey as he clung to the wheel and Rae wondered if his wound was worse than he'd previously admitted.

"We're heading to Ramsgate," he announced, and the men cheered. Then he added quietly to Rae. "If anything should happen to me, you're in charge. Can you handle it, Ray?"

Rae nodded, though fear clenched at her heart.

"We need to make sure the men have confidence in us. Understood?" He glanced down at the blood on his jacket.

"Yes."

"So, not a word about my wound."

Rae nodded. "Is there anything I can do to help?"

"Make sure they've all had something to drink. And keep their spirits up. Oh, and Ray? I'm sorry about Jamie. But this is war..."

Rae forced back her tears and did as he'd asked, offering water to the men, trying to reassure them as best she could. But all the while, her thoughts were with Jamie, lost somewhere on the edge of chaos.

Sidney remained at the helm until Ramsgate was in sight.

"Over to you," he said to Rae and then he passed out, his jacket drenched in blood.

Rae took the wheel and steered into the harbour.

Home.

But it wasn't home without Jamie.

She shivered. Her body was chilled and her heart frozen.

Chapter Twenty-Seven

As the *Amelia* glided into the harbour, local townspeople who'd gathered to greet the boats cheered and waved, welcoming the rescued soldiers like heroes. Eager hands helped the men disembark, while doctors, nurses and volunteers who'd been on standby led them away, handing out blankets, food and hot drinks.

Sidney Fuller was removed on a stretcher to a field hospital, along with those who required medical care. Rae stood aside, watching the men climb off the boat; their faces pale and haunted, eyes hollow from what they'd seen and endured. The memory of the young lad who'd feared the soldiers would be blamed for retreating came back to her and she was grateful her reassurances had proved correct.

But nothing could truly penetrate the numbness that filled her. She intended to remain aboard while the *Amelia* was checked over for repairs, refuelled and re-provisioned. Then, she'd volunteer to return to Dunkirk, although she wouldn't tell anyone she intended to look for Jamie.

However, the officer who took command told her it was out of the question that she'd be allowed to return, and furthermore, he wanted to know who'd allowed her to go on the first trip. She'd tried to argue, but her body had betrayed her, legs weak, head spinning. She'd lost her hat somewhere along the way, and the officer quickly realised she was a girl.

"I need fit and able men to sail back to Dunkirk. Be reasonable, miss. You're nearly dead on your feet. Get some food and rest. You deserve it." He smiled grudgingly, then added, "And don't come back aboard. That's an order."

He nodded to a sailor to escort her from the boat and hand her over to volunteers. After that, she remembered little and wondered if she'd passed out with fatigue. Or perhaps her mind hadn't been able to cope with the loss of Jamie.

When Rae finally returned to London, she was exhausted and feverish. The hospitals had been busy with the huge number of soldiers who'd returned from Dunkirk, so while Papa had remained at work, Mama had nursed her back to health at home. Later, Rae discovered that Papa had explained to Mama that Rae had been staying with Ada because he'd asked her to fetch a few items from the *Amelia*. Mama simply assumed Rae had a flu-like illness and as soon as her daughter had recovered, she'd hastened back to London to work. If Rae had muttered anything about Dunkirk while she'd been delirious, Mama must have assumed they were just nightmares brought on by the newspapers and BBC reports.

Once Rae had recovered, the secret stayed buried. There was no point in telling her parents now. Nothing could change what had happened. It was all in the past, and there was nothing anyone could do about it. Not that she'd expected her parents to punish her if they'd learned of her role in the Dunkirk evacuation. But if they had, Rae was beyond caring. In truth, nothing could touch Rae anymore. She was numb – grief, guilt and pain had hollowed her out until she felt like a shell of the person she'd once been. Papa had once admired her wild spirit, but that spark had been extinguished.

There was no spirit left in her now. Just the ache of loss, lingering like a wound that would never heal.

The memorial service for the Leigh-on-Sea fishermen and cockle men who'd lost their lives at Dunkirk was held at St Clement's Church, at the heart of the town. Not only Jamie and his cousin, Duncan, had been lost, but one of the cockle boats, *Renown,* and its crew had been blown up by a mine.

Rae took the train from London to the coast on her own. Papa had wanted to join her but the influx of soldiers, airmen and sailors who'd been involved in Operation Dynamo was stretching the medical services and he and Mama were spending more and more time at work – even sleeping in their respective hospitals when they weren't on duty. Papa had learned about Jamie's disappearance from his uncle and assumed Rae had heard the dreadful news from him too.

St Clement's Church was packed. Almost everyone in Leigh was related to – or knew at least one victim – and the silence in the church and the collective grief bore down on Rae; a crushing weight settling in her stomach, leaving her feeling hollow.

As the vicar spoke, Rae's thoughts drifted. How could this sombre gathering mark the end of Jamie's life? She felt a sense of drifting, as if the person she used to be had been abandoned on those foreign beaches along with Jamie. If only she had been left there with him.

After the service, as she moved through the sea of mourners, Jamie's Uncle Gordon stopped her. He opened his mouth to speak, but for a moment, the words stuck in his throat. "I'm so sorry, lass..." His voice trembled, and Rae could see the tears threatening to spill. His grief felt raw, as fresh as her own.

She nodded; her throat too tight to respond. What was there to say? He'd not only lost a nephew but also his son, Duncan.

A voice cut through the crowd. "You!" Jamie's father, Mr MacKenzie, stormed towards them, his face contorted in a mixture of fury and anguish. "I always knew you were trouble." His words were laced with venom. "I might have known in the end you'd hurt my lad. But I had no idea you'd lead him into danger and get him killed."

"Robert!" Uncle Gordon stepped between them; his face tight with tension. "Stop! Jamie thought a great deal of the lass. Don't you think she's been through enough?"

But Mr MacKenzie's rage was like a storm; wild and uncontrollable. His fists clenched and unclenched at his sides. "Been through enough?" he seethed. "What does she know? She hasn't been through anything. She hasn't lost a son. My Jamie was just a toy she played with. Pick him up. Put him down when she tired of him. Don't give her sympathy, Gordon. She's nothing but a spoilt, rich brat."

Rae flinched at the harshness of his words, but she kept her head bowed. His anger was understandable – Jamie had been his son. But she couldn't let him believe she'd played with Jamie's feelings. Swallowing hard, she lifted her head and forced herself to meet his burning gaze. Her voice was shaky, but steady enough to get her words out. "I loved Jamie. And I'm sorry you feel that way about me, Mr MacKenzie. But I truly loved him, and I always will." She turned and walked away, tears streaming down her cheeks.

Behind her, she heard Uncle Gordon call her name. He caught up and gently patted her on the arm. "Don't take any notice, lass. He always was hot-headed. He doesn't mean it. But I want you to know you're always welcome in my house. Remember that."

Rae nodded, grateful but unable to speak. Uncle Gordon gave her a sad, knowing smile before heading back to his brother, who'd turned his back on Rae.

Thank goodness Papa hadn't come. Not only would he have witnessed Mr MacKenzie's outburst, but he would also have discovered his daughter had been on the *Amelia* with Jamie when it had sailed to Dunkirk – a detail that still, Rae had told no one except Jamie's Uncle Gordon. She knew she ought to have spoken to Mr Mackenzie, but hadn't been able to face him. Instead, she'd told Uncle Gordon everything, knowing he'd deliver the tragic news. As for her family, everyone assumed she'd been with Ada. As soon as Rae had recovered, she'd written to Ada and told her what had happened. While Rae didn't want Ada to lie for her, she hoped that when Mama's letter arrived, thanking Ada for allowing her to stay, she wouldn't query it.

After the memorial service, Rae should have gone home, but she was reluctant to leave the place where Jamie had once lived and worked. The second she boarded the train for London, she'd be leaving him behind. It was nonsense, of course. She was no closer to him in that town than anywhere else. Delaying her return, she wandered down to the water and stood watching the boats bobbing. She should have known it would remind her of her return to Ramsgate and merely brought home the loss.

Chapter Twenty-Eight

Saturday 07 September 1940

Unusually, the Kingsley family were at home together enjoying the late summer sunshine when the sharp wail of the air raid sirens shattered the calm. It was almost five o'clock. Wave after wave of Luftwaffe bombers had crossed the Channel, their sights set on London's docks in the east. The piercing screech of the sirens signalled the danger hurtling towards unsuspecting Londoners.

That night, the raging fires in the East London Docks guided more German bomber pilots who continued to attack the capital, destroying buildings and maiming and killing civilians.

The following evening, the Luftwaffe returned to continue their aerial attack.

"I'm going to ask Joanna if she wouldn't mind having Jack and Rae for a while," Mama said, "at least until they stop bombing London. I can't concentrate on work when I know they're home here. And spending all night in the Anderson Shelter's so uncomfortable. At least in Essex, they should be safe."

Papa nodded solemnly and he placed a consoling hand on her shoulder. He didn't speak but a silent agreement passed between them.

Rae didn't care where she was. Although she wondered how she'd feel once she got to Dunton – in a place where she and Jamie had often met and spent time together. A place haunted by memories.

Joe accompanied Rae and Jack on the train. He'd been invited to stay at Priory Hall for a few days until, as a new trainee pilot, he'd leave for nearby RAF Hornchurch, where he was stationed.

As the train pulled into Laindon Station, steam billowed and hissed from the engine, mingling with the crisp autumn air. The platform bustled with activity, but amidst the crowd, Rae spotted Joanna and Faye waiting just beyond the ticket barrier, waving enthusiastically. She smiled and waved back, her spirits lifting at the sight of their familiar faces.

Rae had expected Joanna to bring Faye along, and perhaps even Mark, but as they passed through the barrier, she was taken aback to see two unfamiliar girls standing with Joanna. The pair looked slightly hesitant, clutching bags, their expressions a mixture of relief and uncertainty.

Joanna welcomed Rae and her brothers with open arms, her warmth as reassuring as ever. But it didn't take long for her to notice their questioning expressions.

"I know this is a bit impetuous," Joanna began, her voice calm but earnest. "But once you hear Miriam and Rebekah's story, you'll understand why I simply couldn't walk away and leave them to fend for themselves. Their situation is... complicated. I expect they'll tell you their story in their own time, but I couldn't just abandon them. I wouldn't have been able to live with myself." She paused, searching their faces for understanding.

A ROSE IN PLOTLANDS

Rae, still surprised, smiled gently at the girls. If Joanna thought it was the right thing to do, then it definitely was.

War had a way of bringing people together in the most unexpected ways.

Over the coming weeks, Rae found herself learning more and more about the two sisters, Miriam and Rebekah. Joanna had been right; it was impossible to remain untouched by their sad story, nor to ignore the quiet dignity they carried, despite all they'd lost.

Miriam and Rebekah had escaped the Nazi regime on a Kindertransport train, their young lives shattered by a bomb blast that had taken their parents. Since then, they'd settled happily with an English couple until tragedy had once again overtaken them and, finally, they'd arrived in Laindon, believing they'd find a home there. However, their German accents had resulted in suspicion and rejection until Joanna had offered them a home at Priory Hall.

Rae and Miriam shared a bedroom and immediately took to each other despite being different temperamentally.

At first, Rae couldn't understand why she felt so drawn to Miriam. They were as different as night and day – Rae's love of the outdoors, her work with the Land Army girls, was a world apart from Miriam's quieter presence indoors, helping Joanna. And yet... there was something that bound them. One day, it dawned on Rae. Both girls were lost. Miriam had been forced to leave the only home she'd ever known, while Rae had left hers voluntarily, yet she, too, had never felt she was valued or had a place.

Despite their closeness, Rae kept the memory of Jamie locked away. The wound was still too fresh – too deep to expose. She wasn't ready to share that part of herself with Miriam. For now, it was enough to know that, like her, Miriam was carrying grief of her own. Rae could see it in the glistening sadness that sometimes clouded her friend's eyes. Miriam was also secretly grieving for something or someone.

One day, perhaps Miriam would trust Rae enough to tell her about the sadness she tried to hide. But until then, Rae wouldn't pry. If Miriam wanted to tell her, she would do so in her own time and Rae would be there to listen. Maybe she'd tell Miriam about Jamie and the last time she'd seen him.

But not yet.

Chapter Twenty-Nine

Jamie crouched low in the shadows of the cliffs, his breath ragged, waiting for the signal to advance into the foaming sea. The salt-laden air clung to his skin, the waves a constant murmur against the shore. Beside him, Jean-Jacques Pierlot scanned the darkness, his sharp gaze flicking between the water and the beach. The French fishing boat – Jamie's escape route – bobbed quietly offshore, its silhouette barely visible in the inky blackness. The crew worked silently, their shapes shifting as they prepared for the journey to England.

Jamie's heart raced, but it wasn't simply the danger of the next few hours that gripped him. The steady roll of the tide brought back memories of Dunkirk; the ocean's whisper an eerie echo of distant screams and gunfire.

It had been weeks since that dreadful day, but the memories were still raw. The bullet that had grazed his leg as he braced himself, chest-deep in water. Soldiers screaming, diving for cover. Stukas shrieking above, tearing the sky apart. He'd watched in disbelief as the *Amelia* had swerved repeatedly to avoid the bullets, with Rae standing on deck, reaching for him. He'd sent her a kiss before the explosion had swallowed them. A column of smoke and water. Then... nothing.

Had *Amelia* been caught in the blast? Collapsing into the cold sea, Jamie had been sure it was over for him until firm hands had hauled him out of the water. Even now, the memory brought a cold sweat to his brow. He wiped it with his sleeve, trying to focus on Jean-Jacques and the signal they awaited. He shifted his weight, testing his injured leg. It would have to hold. There was no turning back now. Every second on French soil put them both in danger. If Jamie was caught, no one would miss him. But Jean-Jacques was vital to building the Resistance network. His absence would be keenly felt.

Jamie turned his attention to the strip of beach between him and the sea, willing his muscles to respond when the time came. Fifteen paces, maybe twenty. He could manage that distance, surely. He fixed his eyes on the waves that advanced and receded with a loud hiss. He shivered as he recalled the last time he'd heard that sound.

Jean-Jacques Pierlot and his men had saved him that day, dragging him onto a small boat they'd already filled with French soldiers. They'd sailed along the coast to Normandy, where Jamie had spent weeks recovering in the Pierlot family farmhouse. Jean-Jacques' mother had nursed him back to health hidden in the cellar, while Jean-Jacques risked his life rebuilding the shattered Resistance.

Now, here Jamie was – on the edge of freedom once more. His thigh throbbed, a reminder of how close he'd come to losing everything.

A low whistle pierced the air, urgent and deliberate. The signal.

"Stay close," Jean-Jacques whispered. "We must move quickly."

Jamie nodded; his throat tight. The plan was straightforward: board the boat under cover of darkness and sail to England with the morning tide. Enemy patrols had increased in recent weeks, but Jean-Jacques was confident they would be safe. The fisherman, an old family friend, had been carrying arms from England to the Resistance for weeks. Tonight, Jamie was the outward-bound cargo.

They crept towards the waves, keeping in the shadow of the cliffs. As they approached the rowing boat, a fisherman motioned him forward.

"Go, mon ami. God keep you," Jean-Jacques murmured, his hand on Jamie's shoulder.

"Merci." Jamie's voice was thick with emotion. This man had risked everything for him.

Gritting his teeth, Jamie waded through the cold water, pain stabbing through his leg as he was dragged into the rowing boat.

Minutes later, eager hands hauled him into the fishing vessel. The captain offered a quick greeting, then immediately turned to prepare for departure. Jamie slumped against the wooden rail, breathing hard, glancing back at Jean-Jacques, who remained in the shadows with his arm raised in farewell.

"Go," Jamie whispered urgently, aware that every second endangered his friend.

The crack of a gunshot pierced the night, cutting through the relentless sigh of waves dragging at the shingle. Bent double, Jean-Jacques ducked and ran towards the cliffs as a searchlight slashed through the darkness. Jamie's heart felt as though it had stopped. A German patrol. Had Jean-Jacques been trapped on the beach?

"Boches," the captain spat, revving the engine.

The fishing boat lurched forward, sending Jamie sprawling, but he pulled himself upright in time to see Jean-Jacques melt into the shadows.

As the fishing boat speeded away from the coast, searchlights flickered across the water, chasing them, but they were already slipping into the moonless night. Jamie's breath came in ragged gasps as the coastline faded. They'd made it – barely.

Please, please, let Jean-Jacques escape.

The captain steered them into the open sea, the gentle rise and fall of the waves a welcome contrast to the chaos they'd left behind. For a moment, Jamie allowed himself to believe he was safe. But the tension in his muscles refused to ease. They wouldn't be safe until they'd reached England.

The cool night air filled his lungs as they sailed further from Normandy, but with relief came a new sensation: nausea. The boat's gentle roll and smell of fish churned his stomach, and Jamie groaned softly, clutching his side.

"England. Soon," the captain called over his shoulder in a thick accent, tapping his watch.

Jamie nodded, but bile rose in his throat. He turned away, steadying himself against the relentless movement. The thought of reaching home was the only thing keeping him focused.

While he'd been in France, thoughts of Rae had been a constant presence, a deep, steady throb through the darkest moments. But now, with every mile closer to England, those thoughts swelled, becoming more urgent and overwhelming. There had been nothing he could do to find out what had happened to her, but now, as they neared the English coast, his worries pressed in on him, sharper and more insistent with each passing minute.

Soon, he would find out what had happened to Rae.

Gripping the rail tightly, Jamie stared out over the dark sea. He was going home. But what would he find?

Chapter Thirty

Upon reaching Southampton, Jamie was taken directly to hospital. The strain of the journey had reopened the wound in his leg, and the long weeks of immobility in France had left him frail and exhausted.

His first thoughts, once he woke up in the hospital ward, were of finding out what had happened to Rae. If she was alive, he had to let her know he'd returned. His father needed to know, too. A surge of urgency pushed through his fatigue. Too weak to hold a pen, he dictated to the nurse on duty, and she carefully wrote his words, then promised to post the letters for him.

For days, he waited, clutching at the hope that news would come. But no replies arrived. His heart sank with each passing hour. He dictated a letter to his Uncle Gordon and tried again, yet still, there was silence. He began to wonder if the letters had reached anyone. Frustrated and desperate, Jamie persuaded the nurse to let him use the hospital telephone. His father didn't have a telephone in his cottage, so he repeatedly dialled Rae's parents in Chelsea and Uncle Gordon's office. Every call ended the same way – with a hollow ringing tone and no answer.

It was as though he'd returned to a world that no longer remembered him. The emptiness left him questioning whether there was any point in his struggle to recover if there was no one left to care.

Under the watchfulness of the doctors and nurses, the wound healed properly, and as soon as he could walk with a stick, he discharged himself, despite Matron's concern.

"I've been away from home too long," Jamie explained, leaning heavily on his walking stick. "I need to find out what's happened to everyone."

She sighed but didn't argue. They both knew Jamie's bed was needed by men who were in worse condition than him.

I'll be fine, he told himself, after all, the journey from Southampton to his father's cottage wouldn't take very long and if he was too tired, he'd stay overnight and regain his strength, but surely, travelling by train wouldn't be too taxing. After that, he'd go to London to search for Rae.

On arriving at his father's cottage, he saw the air of quiet abandonment, with large weeds in what had once been his mother's flowerbeds. Dad had always kept them tidy. Now, dust coated the windowsills, and with growing unease, Jamie stooped to find the key that was usually beneath the upturned flowerpot. It wasn't there. He straightened, his heart thudding. Had something happened to his father? He hadn't been a young man.

Jamie peered through the window, but it confirmed what he already knew. The cottage was deserted and the pile of letters lying on the mat suggested Dad hadn't been home for a while. Well, clearly, the cottage would not give up its secrets, so he knocked next door to ask.

"Jamie?" Mrs Milton gasped when she opened the door, peering at him over her glasses as though she couldn't believe her eyes. "Yes, it's young Jamie MacKenzie, isn't it? But... they said you were..." she trailed off, her hand fluttering to her chest. "Well, obviously they were wrong. Glory be. I never thought I'd lay eyes on you again, son. Come in. Come in. You'll be wanting to know what happened to your dad, I expect. Or perhaps you already know?"

It was difficult to get a word in because she wanted to find out where Jamie had been.

"'Twas such a blow when word came you were... well, unaccounted for," she said, her face brimming with curiosity.

"And Dad?" Jamie reminded her. "How is he?"

"Oh yes, your dad. Well, I haven't seen him since his wedding, but I think he's well."

"Wedding?" Jamie hadn't expected that.

"Oh yes. He's living with his new wife. Your stepmother, I suppose... although I think she was once your aunt..."

"Aunt Lily?"

"Yes, I believe that's her name. I met her just before the wedding. A lovely lady. She reminded me of your mum. But then, she would, wouldn't she, them being sisters... Now, I expect you want to know where they are?" She hunted through the drawers in her dresser and, after finding a tattered book, read out the address.

So, Dad had moved into Aunt Lily's house. He was safe and, hopefully, happy with his new wife, although he'd be grieving over the loss of his son. Jamie's letter was probably one of those gathering dust on the doormat in Dad's cottage and that would explain why Jamie hadn't heard from him while he'd been in hospital. He must get to them as soon as he could.

Had he not been feeling faint with exhaustion by the time he arrived at Aunt Lily's house, he might have thought of a gentler way of warning his dad about his arrival, but knocking at the door had been the only option. Aunt Lily's polite expression froze. Her hand flew to her throat, and she staggered backward with a strangled cry. "Jamie," she whispered, stepping back as tears welled in her eyes.

"Who is it?" his father called from inside.

Aunt Lily embraced Jamie fiercely, her voice breaking. "Oh, my dear! How wonderful to see you. Come in." She wrapped Jamie in her arms, then released him as Dad let out a long sigh from behind her.

"Son." Dad's voice broke, and he held out his hand to shake Jamie's, his face contorted with grief.

"Get on with you, Bob," Aunt Lily said, pushing his arm. "Your son is home alive. If you can't hug him now, when will you?"

Dad wrapped his arms around Jamie for an instant and then stood back. But it had been enough to let Jamie know how much he'd suffered.

Aunt Lily took charge. "Right, in you come, love. You'll be wanting something to eat and drink and then – if you want to – you can tell us all about it. You look exhausted. You'll be staying with us for a while?"

"We'd like you to think of this as your home too," Dad said, his eyes begging Jamie to stay.

It was so good to see his aunt's happiness and his dad's contentment, and now their relief that Jamie had returned was evident. He told them how he'd been lost at Dunkirk, avoiding mentioning Rae's involvement.

Dad's face was heavy with something unspoken. "I understand you were with the Kingsley lassie."

Surely even now, Dad wasn't angry that Jamie had been with Rae. And, anyway, how had he known?

"She told Gordon what had happened when she got back." Dad said, as if hearing Jamie's silent question. He paused and looked down, almost as if he was embarrassed. "And I saw her at the memorial service in Leigh."

"She's alive!" Jamie squeezed his eyes tightly closed, relief flooding through him in such a torrent, he felt dizzy. Rae had made it back. Thank goodness.

There was obviously something on his dad's mind, although Jamie couldn't see the irritated expression that usually appeared when Rae was mentioned.

Dad cleared his throat. "I expect you'll be off to find the lass as soon as you can. When you see her, please apologise to her for my rudeness at the memorial. I had no right to speak to her like that." He looked down, and Aunt Lily patted his shoulder. "I was wrong. It was the grief speaking. I've had time to think it over. She… you both… showed a lot of courage. I shouldn't have been so hard…"

So, Dad assumed Jamie would find Rae. And there was no anger – simply his discomfort at having been rude to Rae. Jamie dared not imagine what he'd said. But at least now he knew Rae was alive.

The following morning, Aunt Lily insisted on preparing a large breakfast before Jamie left. "We've got to put some meat back on those bones," she said, shaking her head sadly at his emaciated body.

She'd warned him that London had been badly hit by the Luftwaffe, but even so, he wasn't prepared for the devastation he found when he finally arrived. His earlier optimism on discovering Rae had returned now dissolved into fear as he wondered if she'd survived the hell at Dunkirk, only to be bombed in her own home.

But to his relief, the Kingsley's house in Chelsea was untouched.

An elderly woman opened the door when he knocked. "Yes?" she said, glancing over her shoulder.

"I wonder if I could see Miss Rae Kingsley, please?" he asked, gripping his stick for support.

"I'm afraid Miss Kingsley's not home." The woman started to close the door.

"Please!" Jamie stepped forward in alarm. "Can you tell me when she'll be back?"

"No idea. I'm sorry."

"Please! Do you know where she is?"

The woman shrugged. "No, sorry, I've only been working here for a week. All I know is her parents sent her away from the bombing."

"Do you know if she's gone to Priory Hall in Essex?" Jamie asked.

The woman shrugged. "Essex? I wouldn't have thought so. Dr and Dr Kingsley..." she stopped to giggle. "Sorry, that just sounds so silly to say that. Anyway, the two doctors never do things by halves, from what I've seen. I would've thought they'd sent her further afield than that. Sorry, I can't be more help. Now, if you'll excuse me..."

Now what? He decided to go to Leigh-on-Sea and stop off at Laindon on the way.

It took longer than Jamie had expected to cross London to Fenchurch Street Station and his head was spinning by the time he boarded a train that would stop at Laindon. On reflection, he ought to have rested more, but he couldn't bear the thought Rae believed he'd died. He must find her as soon as possible – then he'd rest.

However, suppose she wasn't at Priory Hall? Would Joanna tell him where she was? Rae had always spoken highly of Joanna, but he didn't know how she'd feel about him if he turned up on the doorstep.

He found a seat in the carriage, and as he settled back waiting for the train to pull out of the station, he realised his eyes were heavy, his heart was racing and his leg throbbed. It wouldn't hurt to sleep for a while, he told himself, so long as he woke up in time for Laindon Station.

Two women got on the train and sat near him, placing their baskets on the luggage rack.

"Honestly, Edna, I can't believe my Sadie and her kids have had it so 'ard, what with the Blitz and everything," the tall woman said.

"I know. They've 'ad more than their fair share of bad luck, that's for sure," the woman called Edna replied.

"Still, at least Herr Hitler seems to have given up bombing the living daylights out of them," the tall woman said. "Well, for the moment, anyway. Who knows what's going to 'appen in the future?"

"I know, Vi. But at least we can help a bit. With all the food we grow. Your Sadie was so grateful for that veg," said Edna.

"Mm. Me and Alf moving down to Dunton was the best thing we've ever done, and we've got so much land to grow things. It's nice to be able to treat the family to fresh veg and fruit. How's your daughter, by the way?"

"Fine thanks, Vi..."

The conversation continued and other than the rather piercing laugh of the tall woman who was called Vi, Jamie ignored them and dozed off again.

The shrill train whistle made him jump, and he glanced around the carriage as the train chugged away from the platform. Beads of sweat stood out on his brow. He was so tired, it was hard to think, and he considered standing in case he fell asleep and missed his stop, but he wasn't sure he had the energy to get up, and his leg was throbbing.

"How's your son now?" Edna asked.

"Not in a good way. You wouldn't believe it. That girl just up and left," said Vi.

"Left? What! You mean she left Priory Hall?"

"Yes. Poor Frank. He's such a sensitive bloke. I told 'im there was no point holding a torch for her. She'd never shown any interest in him, but it was too late. He was smitten."

Jamie sat up at the mention of Priory Hall and listened to the conversation. There was no need to stand up. He was wide awake now.

"But if she told Frank she wasn't interested…"

"Oh, you know men. They don't listen, do they? He still thought he had a chance. I don't know what's wrong with the girl. He's a pleasant-enough-looking chap. And he's doing well for 'imself. But she didn't want to know."

"Well, where did she go? Back to London? I hear that's where she was living before she moved in with the Richardsons."

"No! You won't believe it; she's gone to New York."

"No."

"Yes. It's true."

"Are you sure?"

"Yes, I heard it from Dorothy Moore. She went into *Maison Maréchal* in Laindon the other day and got it from that nice little French girl who works there."

"Well, I never!"

Jamie felt as though there was a weight on his chest, and he was struggling to breathe. The women couldn't possibly be talking about Joanna's daughter, Faye, because she was still a child. It could only be Rae who'd gone to New York. No, it couldn't be possible. But why not? She believed he was dead. She'd even attended the memorial service for him and the other men who'd died at Dunkirk. Why shouldn't she have gone to New York? She'd always wanted to travel, and her parents would have been able to afford to send her. They probably had contacts out there who she might stay with. The woman who'd opened the door to him had thought Rae's parents would send her further away than Essex.

"Are you all right, dear?" Vi said to Jamie. "Only it looks like you're finding it hard to breathe. And you've gone very white. Can I do anything to help?"

Jamie shook his head. "No, no, thank you. I'm fine. Only, I couldn't help overhearing your conversation. The girl you were talking about, her name wasn't Rae, was it?"

She frowned. "That doesn't ring any bells. But I really can't remember. Why?"

"Was her name Hannah?" Jamie persisted.

"Well, it was an ordinary name like that." She frowned and shrugged. "It might have been. I just can't remember."

As the train slowed down, the two women got their baskets down from the luggage rack.

Edna turned to Jamie. "You sure you're all right?"

He nodded. It couldn't be true. Rae had gone to New York? No, the woman had been talking about someone else. But who? He'd find out when he got to Priory Hall. Squeezing his eyes tightly closed, he tried to clear his vision. When he opened them, everything appeared dimmer than it had, and black spots danced before his eyes. He wondered if he'd have the strength to walk to Priory Hall.

"Are you getting out here, dear?" Edna asked him as Vi opened the door, letting in a gust of steam and smoke.

He shook his head.

If he'd known Rae would be at Priory Hall, he'd have crawled there if necessary. But now? It was best that he carry on to Leigh. He wasn't even sure he'd be able to get from the station to his uncle's, but he'd worry about that later. He'd phone Priory Hall from his uncle's office. Yes, that was the best plan. He closed his eyes and drifted off to sleep again.

Jamie somehow arrived at his uncle's boatyard and collapsed. The cleaner found him the following morning, and he was taken to the local hospital, where he joined his uncle in the same ward.

Chapter Thirty-One

♥

Rae stood at her bedroom window, gazing out at the sprawling lawns and gardens of Priory Hall. Beyond the formal hedges and flowerbeds, the farmland stretched towards the horizon, bathed in the afternoon sunshine. It was a view she'd often enjoyed with Miriam and her sister, Rebekah.

Rae missed the two German girls, but especially Miriam, with whom she'd felt a special bond. She recognised the emptiness in Miriam and, without confiding in each other, the two girls had somehow offered each other comfort. It wasn't until Rebekah tracked down Karl, the boy who'd fled from Germany with them, that Rae understood the weight of loss that Miriam had carried – the loneliness, the unspoken yearning for someone she feared she'd never see again.

The morning the sisters had left for New York, Rae had never seen Miriam so alive. Her face had shone whenever she'd looked at Karl, and Rae had been genuinely glad for her friend, but that morning had also deepened her own grief. Seeing Miriam with Karl had made Jamie's absence all the more unbearable.

Determined to remain in touch, Rae had decided to write a little every day about what was happening at Priory Hall, ready to send the letter as soon as she had Miriam's address in New York. Miriam had invited her to stay with them when they were settled, and a thrill ran through Rae as she thought of one day being in the bustle and excitement of New York. She pictured herself surrounded by skyscrapers and neon lights – a world so different from the one she knew. It felt like a lifeline, a chance to escape the memories that weighed her down.

Rae got out the box in which she kept all Jamie's postcards and letters as well as the small, carved boat, the snail shell and the handkerchief with the embroidered thistle. Her fingers brushed over each item, lingering as if they held traces of Jamie that she might cling on to. It was foolish; she knew, yet her throat tightened, and she bit her lip, willing back the tears. This was all she had to remind her of Jamie, and without a photograph, she struggled to keep every detail of his face clear in her mind; the exact shape of his smile and the light in his eyes when he laughed.

But with each passing day, those memories slipped further from her reach like sand through her fingers. Her chest ached with the weight of it; with the fear he might fade entirely from her mind. She couldn't bear that thought.

One by one, she read the postcards. When the war was over, they'd have gone to New York together. And after that, wherever the winds might have taken them. They'd have kept going to Tokyo, Peking, Cairo, Hong Kong –– all the places they'd vowed to visit. The world had been so full of possibility then, so open until the war had stolen those plans.

And now?

One day, she would take off on her own. It wouldn't be the same without Jamie, of course. But nothing was the same now and nothing was keeping her here. It wasn't like she'd miss home. She didn't feel she belonged anywhere, so she might as well simply keep moving.

But how much longer would the war carry on? A year? Two years?

Ten?

Rae ran her finger over the embroidered thistle on the handkerchief. She pressed it to her cheek and closed her eyes, remembering Jamie's smile as he'd handed it to her after his holiday in Scotland. "All soft and fluffy but underneath as prickly as... well, a thistle."

It suddenly occurred to her she'd never been to Scotland, and she ached to see all the places Jamie had visited when he was a boy.

Obviously, she couldn't ask Jamie's dad. Maybe his Uncle Gordon could help. He'd once told her she'd always be welcome in his home, though Rae had learned he was now recovering in hospital from a heart attack. As soon as she could, she'd visit him and find out where in Scotland the family had originated. She knew Jamie's dad and uncle had both come south together and had settled in Leigh-on-Sea, where they'd bought a boatyard, but when Jamie's dad had married, the couple had moved to the south coast where Jamie and his brother, Alex, had been born.

In fact, there were many places she'd never visited in England and Wales – places on her own doorstep. Perhaps now was the time to think about travelling. Not going on holiday, of course, but if she joined the Land Army, she might be stationed anywhere. And then, when the war was over, she'd simply keep going.

And joining the Land Army would ensure her a wage. She knew from the girls who worked on Ben's farm they earned twenty-eight shillings a week, although they had to pay for food and accommodation out of that, but if she was careful, she could save a little for her future.

There was also *Wild Spirit*. Jack wasn't keen on sailing and now Joe was in the RAF, he had no time, so Papa had given the boat to Rae. The *Amelia* was still at Ramsgate where it'd been repaired and was awaiting collection, but Papa had been too busy, and Rae never wanted to see the boat again.

She wasn't sure she wanted to see the *Wild Spirit* again either, but at least the thought of it didn't bring back the chaos of the beach at Dunkirk and the image that was seared in her memory, of Jamie standing shoulder-deep in water with his arm raised, a kiss on the tips of his fingers.

If she sold the *Wild Spirit*, it would raise money to help finance her travels. Although she doubted anyone would be interested in buying her while the war was raging.

But first, she would have to clean her thoroughly, then, when she visited Jamie's uncle in hospital, she would ask if he knew anyone who would be likely to want her. Perhaps he'd buy her from Rae and sell her for a better price after the war was over.

She added her new plans to Miriam's letter, folded it and placed it back in her drawer, ready to write more tomorrow.

Having made up her mind about selling the *Wild Spirit*, Rae decided to cycle to Leigh.

Why not make a start on cleaning her up as soon as possible? She put a pail over the handlebars and filled it with brushes, cloths and a bottle of vinegar.

Had Joanna been home, she would undoubtedly have given Rae some of the precious rationed soap, but she was away with Ben and the children for a few days. Rae wouldn't take advantage of her, so vinegar would have to do, and if she scrubbed hard enough, she should make a good job of it.

Rae hadn't cycled through Hadleigh since the last time she'd met Jamie near the castle, and the sight of the ruins silhouetted against the sky brought memories flooding back. She stopped to wipe her tears and once her vision had cleared, she kept her eyes on the road. The sooner she joined the Land Army and moved to another part of the country, the better it would be, she told herself, fighting back the tears.

Rae was having second thoughts about selling *Wild Spirit*.

Cycling through Hadleigh, seeing the stark remains of the castle where she and Jamie had spent so many afternoons, walking through the narrow streets of Leigh where they'd once strolled and now looking at the boat on which they'd sailed together, her resolve wavered.

There were too many memories, and they were flooding into her mind until it was brimming with mental images – and pain.

How many times had she turned, thinking she'd seen Jamie in a crowd, only for her heart to sink when it wasn't him? The fleeting joy turned to a sharp, unyielding ache, reminding her he was gone. And now, standing on the jetty, she wondered if she could bear to part with the one place where they'd been happiest together.

She'd known *Wild Spirit* would set her remembering – that alone was a good reason to sell it. Once it was gone, at least it wouldn't be a constant reminder. But when she reached the jetty and saw it rocking gently back and forth in the water, she began to wonder if she'd be strong enough to sell.

There's no point clinging to the past, she reminded herself, hearing the words as if spoken by Jamie. *If you're going to move forward, Rae, you'll have to let go.*

She climbed aboard and, leaning over the side, dipped her hand into the water and closed her eyes, imagining what it would be like to sell the one thing that brought Jamie back to her more than any other.

Rae sighed. If she wanted to travel, she would need money, and the easiest way for her to do that was to sell the boat.

I will sell it, she thought… But perhaps not yet.

She didn't have the heart to start cleaning. What was the point? It would be a while before she was ready to part with the *Wild Spirit* and by that time, it would need to be done again.

She stared at the water swirling around her fingertips, watching the ripples and wavelets, the shadows and highlights. It was mesmerising. Almost as if the water was alive. A living thing that had taken the one person in the world whom she'd loved with her entire being.

Rae stood up and wiped her hand dry on her sweater. There was no point lingering in Leigh, if she was going to be miserable, she might as well go back to Priory Hall, to her bedroom, or even better, go to find the Land Girls and do something physical that would exhaust her and take her mind off her grief. She picked up the pail, ready to clamber out of the boat.

Ahead of her, where the jetty met the road, three young men stood talking. Rae wondered if any of them had known Jamie. Perhaps they'd sailed to Dunkirk – and returned. The sun was shining in her eyes, and they were simply dark figures against the brightness.

They shook hands and two of them walked away, leaving the third at the end of the jetty.

Her eyes were playing tricks on her again, trying to convince her the silhouetted man was Jamie. He was similar in height, and he tilted his head like Jamie used to, but this man was thinner – much thinner, and his stance was different – he was leaning to one side. And when he took a step, he limped. Rae looked away from him, not wanting to give in to fanciful dreams and believe it was Jamie, only to experience the agonising loss once again.

"Rae? Rae, is it you?"

Her breath caught in her throat because he even sounded like Jamie and as the sun disappeared behind a cloud and she was no longer dazzled, she saw him clearly. "Jamie!" The blood drained from her face, and she dropped the pail onto the deck.

Even as she ran, she couldn't believe he was there. Would she get closer only to find he was a stranger?

No. No. This was Jamie. Her Jamie. Questions tripped over themselves on her tongue, "How…? Where…? What happened…?" But that could wait. For now, it was enough to cling to him, to breathe in the smell of him – salty air and sea lavender, filling her nostrils like a coastal breeze. She realised he was thinner, and she drew back to look at his face. It was pinched, with dark shadows beneath hollow eyes.

"What happened after…?" She couldn't bring herself to say the words aloud. It still felt like a betrayal, even though she'd been powerless to turn the boat to rescue him.

But he obviously had questions he needed to be answered. Pulling her close, he murmured into her hair. "I thought I'd missed you. I thought you'd gone to New York."

"New York? No, not yet. Not until the war's over. What made you think that?" She had told no one about her plans. How had he known?

He breathed a shaky sigh of relief. "I overheard a conversation on the train about someone leaving Priory Hall for New York and I thought it was you."

"Oh no. That was Miriam, Rebekah and Karl. They've been staying with Joanna."

His eyes were haunted as he looked at her with longing. "But not you. You're not going?"

"No, I'm not going anywhere. I'll explain who Miriam is later. But first, I want to know where you've been for so long."

"Why didn't anyone at Priory Hall answer the telephone? I called several times."

"Ben has taken Joanna and the children away for a few days, so the house has been empty, and I've been working with the Land Girls.

Now, please! Tell me where you've been."

He exhaled deeply, as if filled with relief. Immediately, his expression grew serious as he took her hand, his eyes full of uncertainty. "Come to my uncle's house and I'll tell you everything. We won't be disturbed. Uncle Gordon's in hospital. I've just come back from visiting him." He winced as he turned and lowered his gaze, as if unable to look into her eyes. "I'm sorry, Rae, I'm not the same as I was. The wound..." He tailed off.

Rae gently took his arm, swallowing hard to keep the tears back as he limped along the road, each step visibly causing him pain.

As they went, Jamie explained what had happened after the *Amelia* had left him in the sea and by the time he'd found the key under the mat and opened the door to his uncle's house, he'd given her the main details.

As soon as they were inside, Jamie disengaged his arm. "I just want you to know that now everything has changed. I don't expect you to... that is, please don't feel obliged... because I'd understand... I know you said you loved me but that was before..."

She frowned at him. "If you're saying my feelings might have changed because you've been wounded, Jamie MacKenzie, you don't know me at all!"

"Rae, I'm trying to be reasonable. I'll always walk with a limp. And as for my leg... it's not healed well. It's unsightly. No..." His shoulders slumped. "No, it's worse than unsightly. It's repulsive, and I'd rather you didn't see it."

She kissed her fore and middle fingers and placed them on his lips. "Don't say anymore. Nothing matters to me other than that you're here. I loved you then, and I love you now – just as you are."

"Rae, are you sure?" His eyes were now full of hope.

Putting her arms around his neck, she stood on tiptoe and kissed his lips, gently at first and then hungrily. She was shocked at how bony his shoulders felt beneath her hands. Well, she would spend the rest of her life looking after him and in time, he'd regain his strength, but for now, he needed to know she loved him and that she accepted everything about him.

Rae opened the top button of his shirt, but as she moved down to the next one, he caught her hand. "Rae! What are you doing?"

"I think it's pretty obvious, Jamie MacKenzie," she whispered, removing his hand from hers and undoing the next button. She kissed the skin she'd revealed, then opened the next button, placing a kiss further down.

"Are you sure this is what you want?" he asked, his breath coming in short gasps.

In answer, she slipped his shirt off and caressed his chest.

"I've never been more certain of anything in my life," she said. "You will never, ever get away from me again."

He unbuttoned her blouse and, as he held her close, she shivered with pleasure as his skin pressed against hers.

"I want to feel every inch of you against every inch of me," she whispered, "and I want to feel—"

Jamie placed two fingers against her lips to silence her. "Then come with me," he said and led her to his bedroom.

Later, Rae awoke in bed, still wrapped in Jamie's arms.

"Well, that was unexpected," he said, stroking her cheek, "but then you always were a wild spirit, Rae Kingsley. You've always taken me by surprise."

"It looks like you've tamed me now." She smiled and wriggled closer to him. "You've removed all my thorns."

He whistled a few bars of *Only a Rose* and after they finished laughing, he held her tighter. "I'll never let you go, Rae."

She sighed with contentment. For so long, she'd yearned to find a place where she felt at home and now, at last, in Jamie's arms, she knew she belonged.

Chapter Thirty-Two

♥

"Can't we run away and get married?" There was an edge of desperation in Rae's words. She knew exactly how Jamie would respond, but hope flickered in her eyes anyway, in case this time he'd surprise her.

Soon, Uncle Gordon would return from hospital and although he'd told her she was welcome in his home, she suspected he wouldn't be happy to find her living with his nephew. Joanna and her family would be back at Priory Hall in two days. It would be obvious Rae hadn't been there. Questions would be asked, explanations demanded.

She stared out of Jamie's bedroom window at the grey sea. As it churned, so did her resolve. One thing of which she was certain, they would marry as soon as they could, and nothing, and no one, would stop them from being together.

Jamie shook his head in mock exasperation. "You know we can't run away, darling. That would make it look as though we had something to hide, and I want everyone to know how much I love you and how lucky I am you love me."

Rae sighed and turned away from the window. "But your dad and my parents aren't going to be happy. I think Joanna and Ben might be on our side, but we couldn't tell them without telling my parents because that puts them in a difficult position. Joanna knows I didn't deliberately mislead her but she's still embarrassed at mistaking you for a girl and not checking with Mama in case she wasn't happy. And who knows what Mama thinks of Joanna?" She frowned. "I suspect the only people who'll be pleased for us are Uncle Gordon, and possibly my granddad. Although even he might take Mama's side... Oh, and Ada Quinn. I know she'll be pleased."

Jamie took her hand, his grip reassuring. "If we want people to respect us and our decisions, we need to show them we know what we're doing. We won't do that by running away. They need to see we're ready for this – together."

Rae sighed. Could she think of a compelling reason why they ought to simply run away? "I know. But suppose no one comes to the wedding?"

Jamie smiled. "Rae, no one will come if we run away... We just need to tell them all. Then, it's up to them what they do. They'll come if they care enough."

Rae frowned. "That's what I'm worried about." She nibbled her lower lip. "So, who do we tell first?"

He thought for a moment. "Maybe start with Joanna. She's close to your parents so she'll understand how best to approach them, and it won't put her in a difficult position if she knows you plan to tell them soon, anyway. She might even have some advice. And your granddad is her uncle, so she knows him well; she can give us a sense of what to expect from him." Jamie paused, his gaze steady. "Then we'll tackle my dad. I don't think he'll be as much of a problem as you fear. He's changed since I last saw him, and I'm certain Aunt Lily will be on our side."

Rae nodded in resignation. "The sooner we start, the better. When

Joanna's home, we'll go and see her. It's time I introduced you and after that, we can beg for her help."

Thankfully, both Joanna and Ben welcomed Jamie warmly, although when Rae mentioned the marriage plans, a flicker of doubt crossed Joanna's face, so brief it might have gone unnoticed if Rae hadn't been watching her so closely.

"Ah, I thought I detected a sparkle in your eyes, Rae. Well, congratulations to you both. I hope you'll be very happy." Joanna hugged them warmly, her voice light, but Rae could feel hesitation beneath the words.

"But?" Rae's heart pounded. She braced herself, half-expecting Joanna to say she couldn't risk jeopardising her own relationship with Rae's mother by taking sides in a family argument.

"But I expect you'll meet opposition from your parents." Joanna glanced questioningly at Ben, who, after a sigh, nodded in silent agreement.

After a moment's thought, she added, "However, if you'd like to invite them here and break the news somewhere neutral, you'd be very welcome. I'll make it an occasion. We can invite your granddad too. It's about time we all got together, don't you think?"

Rae smiled, though a shadow of doubt lingered. Joanna hadn't voiced it, but Rae couldn't help wondering if she was thinking, 'Because, after this news, it may be the last time we're all in one room together.'

However, if that had been in Joanna's mind, she gave no sign. She rose. "Well, there's no point delaying. I'll telephone Amelia now and invite her over on Saturday afternoon and I'll write to your granddad.

I won't say why I'm inviting them."

Joanna smiled mischievously. "I'll leave that to you."

On Saturday, Pop arrived first and looked knowingly at Rae when she introduced Jamie. However, Mama and Papa knocked at the door immediately after, and thankfully, Pop turned his attention to his daughter and son-in-law. Papa halted mid-step as he took in Jamie's presence, and Mama, nearly colliding with him, craned her neck around to see what had stopped him. Her eyes widened as they landed on Jamie.

Papa stepped forward and held out his hand. "Jamie MacKenzie! I... well, I never thought I'd see you again." He glanced at Rae, his expression a blend of curiosity and concern.

Joanna smoothly ushered them into the drawing room. "How lovely to all be together to catch up with everyone's news. Now, make yourselves at home, and Ben and I will be back with tea." Her tone was overly bright, and Rae sensed Joanna was giving them space to adjust to the unexpected sight of Jamie beside her.

"So, Jamie, you must have a story to tell?" Papa said. Mama's eyes traced back and forth between Rae and Jamie, who sat next to each other on the sofa – far enough apart to be respectable, but still together.

Jamie launched into the story of Dunkirk – how he'd made his way there, what he'd endured. Papa listened intently, nodding along until Jamie mentioned the *Amelia*. Papa's brows knitted together. "You said *Amelia*. I thought you'd gone with one of the cockle boats?"

Jamie shot Rae an uneasy glance, realising his slip. It would have been simpler if her parents had never discovered her part in the

Dunkirk evacuation, but on reflection, it was best they knew the truth. From now on, there would be no more lies.

"Jamie sailed on the *Amelia* to look after me." Rae kept her voice steady.

Her parents and Pop stared at her.

"You sailed to Dunkirk, Hannah-Rae?" Mama's voice rose.

Rae lifted her chin, meeting her mother's gaze. "I did. And Jamie came aboard to look after me."

Mama's face turned white, and she shook her head in disbelief. "Honestly, sometimes I don't know what gets into you, Hannah-Rae. How could you have taken such a risk?"

"Like mother, like daughter," Pop said kindly. "She's brave and determined. She did her country proud." He shot Mama a look of quiet pride, though she responded with a glare that told her father she didn't share the sentiment.

"Rae was extremely brave," Jamie said. "She's extraordinary. And having survived the entire thing, we've realised…" He turned to look at her, his eyes pleading to know if it was the right time. She gave a slight nod. Mama wasn't shouting; she appeared to be too stunned for that, and this might be the best opportunity they'd get.

Jamie stood and faced Papa directly. "We've realised that we love each other and that we want to be together, so Dr Kingsley, I'd like to ask your permission for Rae's hand in marriage."

The air in the room appeared to freeze. Eyes darted from one person to another, each family member taking in Jamie's words. Papa gazed fixedly at Mama. Pop looked back and forth between Mama and Rae, while Mama's eyes kept returning to Jamie, a mixture of shock and disbelief in her expression.

Rae rose and clasped Jamie's hand, aware he was the only one standing, and wanting to support him.

Finally, Papa found his voice, although it sounded strained. "I... I see. Well, I certainly hadn't expected this." He cleared his throat, the old authority of a father now softened by uncertainty. "How, um, how do you plan to provide for my daughter?" His gaze flickered to Jamie's leg. "I noticed... your limp. Are you able to work?"

Jamie gave Rae's hand a reassuring squeeze. Had he come to the same conclusion as her? That Papa was taking them seriously. They were on safe ground now, if that was so.

"I am, sir. My father recently sold his boatyard and gave a portion to my brother and me. I've invested mine in my uncle's business, where I'm now a partner. Over time, I'll take on full responsibility. My uncle's moved to a smaller cottage, and if you give your blessing, Rae and I will move into his house."

"I see. Well, that sounds satisfactory." Papa turned to look at Mama.

"And what will you do with your life, Rae?" Mama asked.

In years past, Rae would have expected her mother's question to feel like a challenge, but today, there was genuine curiosity in her voice. Rae swallowed, gathering her thoughts.

"I'll work in the boatyard office. Jamie's uncle is going to show me what to do. That way, the business stays within the family. I'm certain I can learn, and I believe I'll do well." She glanced at her mother, searching for a sign – approval, disapproval – but Mama's face was calm, although her expression had softened. At least she wasn't frowning or shouting.

Now what? Rae held her breath in the silence. "Papa?" she whispered. It was enough to break the spell.

"Well, I..." Papa looked at Mama, who shrugged slightly, her face still dazed. He continued, "I suppose that's all in order, then. You have my permission."

Rae felt her knees go weak with relief. At the same time as Pop leapt up and shook Jamie's hand, then turned to kiss Rae, Ben opened the doors and he and Joanna entered with tea, as if they'd been listening for exactly the right moment to enter.

The flurry of movement and Pop's welcome into the family broke the awkwardness, and even Mama managed a faint smile.

Ben hurried away to bring a bottle of champagne and glasses to toast the engaged couple, and thankfully, Mama and Papa didn't appear to notice it was already chilled.

Pop tapped his glass, calling for everyone's attention. "A toast to my daughter and my granddaughter. You are both remarkable women – strong, determined, and unafraid to follow your hearts. I am proud to be a part of your lives."

A warm shiver of emotion swept over Rae as she raised her glass. She looked at Mama, surprised to find her nodding with a soft smile. Could it be that her mother approved? Was it possible?

Mama rose and, raising her glass, turned to Rae. "Suddenly, today, I'm seeing my daughter through fresh eyes. I don't know how I didn't see it before, Rae, but you've grown up." She smiled and nodded at her daughter; her eyes brimming.

That was enough for Rae, who was fighting back her own tears. For the first time, she felt as though she had earned her mother's approval.

This was unfamiliar territory for both Rae and Mama, and she certainly didn't expect any mother-and-daughter discussions about weddings, but it far exceeded her hopes.

Pop caught her eye and smiled at her as he shot a look towards Mama. She knew he was telling her she'd done well, and that he approved, and even better than that, a possible family rift had been averted.

Later, it was agreed the wedding would be in Joanna's parish church with the reception at Priory Hall. Neither Rae nor Jamie had wanted the ceremony in St Clement's Church in Leigh, where she'd attended his memorial service, and where Jamie's father had been so hostile. Whether Mr MacKenzie would be as accepting remained uncertain, but for now, Rae felt she'd won a precious victory.

Having gained Rae's parents' consent, Jamie was keen to tell his father and aunt, so they set off the following day to visit. Aunt Lily opened the door and when she saw Jamie, her face lit up and she enveloped him in a hug. "And this must be Rae," she said, opening her arms wide. "Oh, my dear, how lovely to meet you." Aunt Lily wrapped Rae in a warm embrace, the scent of flour and lavender in a cloud around her.

Inside the cottage, Mr MacKenzie stood stiffly, though he softened when he saw Jamie. He extended a hand, grasping Jamie's firmly before turning to Rae with a faint, tentative smile. "I owe you an apology, lass. I was... well, harsh the last time we met. Unfair. It was the grief speaking." His voice was rough, yet there was a sincerity in his eyes that Rae hadn't seen before. She inclined her head, accepting his words gratefully.

"We have some news for you," Jamie said, glancing at Rae with a reassuring smile.

Rae bit her bottom lip as she watched his father's face, fearing an outburst. Yet, instead of the rigid look of disdain she'd half-expected, he surprised her with a gentle chuckle. His eyes crinkled, and a mischievous glint appeared. "It's obvious what you're about to tell us, son. Congratulations."

Even Jamie was taken aback by his words.

"It was as evident as the nose on your face," Mr MacKenzie said with a smile. "I can see the twinkle in your eyes. You've been besotted with the lassie for years. It was only a matter of time. You both have my blessing, for what it's worth."

Aunt Lily clapped her hands together. "Oh, how marvellous! A wedding. That's just what we need. A bit of happiness in this war-torn world. Welcome to the family, my dear." She hugged Rae again.

As they shared the news over tea, Rae felt an unexpected swell of belonging.

On Monday morning, Rae arrived at the boatyard office, her heart lighter than it had been in months. The train had been delayed from Laindon, and as she hurried inside, she found Jamie already there, waiting.

He leapt up at the sight of her, his eyes brightening. Sweeping her into his arms, he kissed her tenderly. "I missed holding you last night," he murmured, his voice soft against her ear.

"I missed you too, but it's best I stay with Joanna until the wedding. I can't believe things went so smoothly with our parents over the weekend. Let's not tempt fate now. And once we're married," she added, a playful glint in her eye, "we can do as we please."

Jamie's face lit up with a boyish excitement. "Speaking of which, I wasn't going to show you this until after the wedding, but there's no point waiting. I need to know if you like it."

He unfurled a large sheet of paper on the desk, smoothing it out with both hands. Rae leaned over, and her breath caught in her throat as she took in the delicate, intricate lines of a boat design.

Rae gasped with delight. "Oh, Jamie, it's beautiful. Who are you building it for?"

Jamie smiled gleefully. "For us, of course."

"But we can't afford that!"

"I'll build it in my spare time," he assured her. "Piece by piece, with no rush. It might take years, but when the war is over..." His voice softened, and his gaze met hers, full of promise. "We'll sail away on this, Rae. We'll see all the places we dreamed about."

She could barely speak, overcome with the thought of a future together on the open sea. Her heart raced, and the hairs on the back of her neck rose at the vision that stretched before her: sailing away, seeing the world, and sharing all her days and nights with Jamie.

He shifted his hand to reveal the bow of the boat in the drawing where a name was written in careful script. "I've drawn a name on there, but it's just a suggestion. We can call the boat anything you like." He looked at her, his eyes full of love, desperate for her approval.

She leaned closer, blinking back tears as she read the name he'd written there: *My Lady Rose*.

"It's perfect," she whispered, her voice thick with emotion.

Jamie's thumb moved slightly, revealing two small, hand-drawn snails on the side, one following the other. Rae choked on a laugh, a tear slipping down her cheek.

"It's more than perfect," she said, her voice barely above a whisper.

In that small office, surrounded by the scent of timber and sea, Rae saw their future as clearly as the lines on the paper before them – a future she had never dared to believe in before Jamie. And as he wrapped his arms around her once more, she knew that no matter what lay ahead, they would face it together.

END

Dawn would be thrilled if you would consider leaving a review for this book on Amazon and Goodreads, thank you.

If you'd like to know more about her books, you can find out more from her newsletter on her website: dawnknox.com

About the Author

Dawn spent much of her childhood making up stories filled with romance, drama and excitement. She loved fairy tales, although if she cast herself as a character, she'd more likely have played the part of the Court Jester than the Princess. She didn't recognise it at the time, but she was searching for the emotional depth in the stories she read. It wasn't enough to be told the Prince loved the Princess, she wanted to know how he felt and to see him declare his love. She wanted to see the wedding. And so, she'd furnish her stories with those details. Nowadays, she hopes to write books that will engage readers' passions.

From poignant stories set during the First World War to the zany antics of the inhabitants of the fictitious town of Basilwade; and from historical romances, to the fantasy adventures of a group of anthropomorphic animals led by a chicken with delusions of grandeur, she explores the richness and depth of human emotion.

A book by Dawn will offer laughter or tears – or anything in between, but if she touches your soul, she'll consider her job well done.

If you'd like to keep in touch, please sign up to her newsletter on her blog and receive a welcome gift, containing an exclusive prequel to The Duchess of Sydney, three short humorous stories and two photo-stories from the Great War.

Following Dawn:

Blog: https;//dawnknox.com

Amazon Author Central: Dawn Knox https://mybook.to/DawnKnox

Facebook: https://www.facebook.com/DawnKnoxWriter

Instagram: https://www.instagram.com/sunrisecalls/

YouTube: https://tinyurl.com/mtcpdyms

BlueSky : https://bsky.app/profile/dawnknox.bsky.social

Also by Dawn Knox

A Cottage in Plotlands

The Heart of Plotlands Saga – Book One

London's East End to the Essex countryside - will a Plotlands cottage bring Joanna happiness or heartache?

1930 – Eighteen-year-old Joanna Marshall arrives in Dunton Plotlands friendless and alone. When her dream to live independently is cruelly shattered, her neighbours step in. Plotlanders look after their own. But they can't help Joanna when she falls in love with Ben Richardson – a man who is her social superior… and her boss. Can Joanna and Ben find a place where rigid social rules will allow them to love?

Order from Amazon: https://mybook.to/ACottageInPlotlands

Paperback: ISBN: 9798378843756 eBook: ASIN: B0C4Y9VZY9

Also A Folly in Plotlands, **A Canary Girl in Plotlands, A Reunion in Plotlands** and **A Rose in Plotlands.**

Coming soon – A Wooden Heart in Plotlands

The Duchess of Sydney

The Lady Amelia Saga – Book One

Betrayed by her family and convicted of a crime she did not commit, Georgiana is sent halfway around the world to the penal colony of Sydney, New South Wales. Aboard the transport ship, the Lady Amelia, Lieutenant Francis Brooks, the ship's agent becomes her protector, taking her as his "sea-wife" – not because he has any interest in her but because he has been tasked with the duty.

Despite their mutual distrust, the attraction between them grows. But life has not played fair with Georgiana. She is bound by family secrets and lies. Will she ever be free again – free to be herself and free to love?

Order from Amazon: https://mybook.to/TheDuchessOfSydney
Paperback: ISBN: 9798814373588 eBook: ASIN: B09Z8LN4G9
Audiobook: ASIN: B0C86LG3Y4

Also, **The Finding of Eden, The Other Place, The Dolphin's Kiss, The Pearl of Aphrodite** and **The Wooden Tokens**

Printed in Dunstable, United Kingdom